The
Sentinel's
Map

WILLIAM HENSHAW

The
Sentinel's
Map

ISBN 978-0-473-52176-9

A catalogue record for this book is available from the National Library of New Zealand.

www.williamhenshaw.com

For family and friends who encouraged me to write.
Without you all, this story may not have seen the light of day.

'Caedite eos. Novit enim Dominus qui sunt eius.'

Kill them all, for the Lord knoweth them that are His.

Papal Legate Arnaud Amaury, Béziers, 1209

Prologue

"Tell me, old man!"

The stricken man sat in his leather captain's chair, one of three antique chairs in the timber-panelled room.

It was warm; a small fire burned in the Victorian cast-iron fireplace. A black iron poker protruded from the red coals at an awkward angle, as if thrust drunkenly into the grate. Ash had spilled onto the flagstone hearth. A crystal tumbler of whisky sat on the leather-inset oak desk, a half-empty bottle resting just behind it.

The older man picked up the glass and drew a good measure of the liquor across his dry lips. His assailant, wearing a black robe over trousers and socks, towered over him; his shoes were presumably outside the house, a precaution that had enabled him to reach the room without being heard. He was dressed totally in black, including his strange and ominous headwear – a medieval executioner's mask.

The mask covered the man's head as far as his nose, where it split, allowing it to protrude. His mouth and chin were visible beneath. He had a broad nose and thick lips, and his neck was muscular. His face seemed to be expressionless, impassive. He was clean-shaven and spoke calmly, with an unexpected pitch of voice reminiscent of Peter Lorre. The older man reflected momentarily that this giant would be a generation too young to have heard of Peter Lorre.

The assailant suddenly struck out, knocking the tumbler and its contents across the room. It flew past the open safe and smashed against the wall.

"Tell me where it is," he repeated.

The man held the interloper's gaze unsteadily but remained silent as he attempted to place the accent. Eastern Europe, he decided.

He knew what he had to do. No matter his fear of what his attacker was about to do, he would not forget the words he'd repeated to himself over the years.

He had some idea what to expect from his assailant. Immediately after the man entered the room, he had silently picked up the poker and thrust it into the fire, then lifted him out of his chair by the throat and softly demanded that he open the safe. After some remonstration, he had agreed to comply.

The safe was set into the wall to the right of the desk, and the intruder had stepped politely out of the way to allow the man to reach it. Only when he pulled the door open did the intruder quickly approach to ensure there was no concealed weapon. He had slowly withdrawn a small bundle of banknotes and some papers and carefully placed them on the desk.

"Take whatever you want." He slumped back into his chair, his breathing shallow.

"I don't need this." He struck the man across the face, a brutally crunching blow with the back of his closed fist. "You know what I want," he went on quietly. "Tell me where it is and this will stop."

The man in the chair wished he still had his whisky. He knew this was not going to stop. Blood dripped from his nose onto his crisp white shirt.

"We've been hunting your kind for centuries. We know you have it." The aggressor leaned in close, and the older man could smell mint on his breath. It seemed incongruent. "Tell me now."

"I don't know what you're talking about," the man replied, with a tremor in his voice. "Take the money. It's all I have."

"I don't want money." The huge figure in black loomed over the chair, the upper part of his robe parting slightly to expose a tattoo of the crucifixion on his chest. He crossed himself and struck the older man hard under the chin. As his victim slumped groggily, he quickly retrieved the poker from the fire. He crossed himself again, and with his left hand, he gripped the man's throat with breathtaking force, driving his head into the back of the captain's chair. At the same time, he placed his left knee across the man's legs to further restrain him.

The older man could not move. Aside from the attacker's strength and weight, he was frozen with an unexpected mixture of impotent fear and a resolute determination. The intruder's impassive expression did not change as the glowing poker pressed into the old man's left eye. He screamed as he struggled desperately to turn his head away. He could barely breathe, but as he did, he could smell the burnt flesh of his eyelid. The pain seared through his body, and although his eyes were screwed shut, he was sure he glimpsed a wisp of smoke rising from his left eye socket.

He briefly lost consciousness, a blessing soon curtailed as the big man threw whisky in his face straight from the bottle.

"Tell me where it is and this will stop."

He could not speak. The pain in his left eye was excruciating. An awful smell of burnt flesh and liquor, tinged with the coppery scent of blood, filled his nostrils. Whisky was in his eyes, and each time he blinked he wanted to scream again.

The big man's face was just inches from his. He mustered all the strength he had left. "I don't know what you're talking about." His voice was weak and fearful; ethereal and unworldly. Nothing like the strong and confident voice he had trained and perfected throughout his life.

"Dei gratia," said the big man softly. He crossed himself again and pressed the poker into the man's chest. There was a sizzling sound as the poker burned the whisky, blood and skin. He kept pushing. *He seems to have boundless strength*, thought the older man, by now unable to move, his good eye blinded by the pain. The poker seared the flesh as it slowly penetrated his rib cage, finding its way through the pulmonary artery and right ventricle, ultimately coming to rest in the plush padding of the chair's ageing leather upholstery.

I

Lucas Shaw woke to the sound of a distant alarm. For a moment he didn't know where he was. *This is not my bed. This is not a bed at all.* He looked around in the gloomy morning light that pierced the gap between the curtains, and slowly his kitchen diner came into focus. His head hurt, and his mouth was so dry he couldn't swallow. He'd slept on his sofa, still wearing the clothes he'd been out in last night. He gingerly sat up, holding his head, and mustered the strength to stand. He sat there a moment as his stomach settled. Taking a single step, his foot found something soft and wet.

"Kebab," he muttered hoarsely to himself. "Fuck." He peeled off his socks, the left now wet with half-digested kebab mixed with his last pint of lager. *At least I missed the carpet.*

He steadied himself on the coffee table, itself not much sturdier than Lucas currently felt. He looked at his hand on the table, fingers outstretched next to rings in the cheap varnish from where numerous glasses had tattooed their imprint. The hand was steady; that was a good thing. The other was shaking. *Wednesday. Fuck. Late for work again.*

He took a quick shower, drank more water, dressed, ran his fingers through his dark brown hair. *I need a haircut.* The longer his hair grew, the curlier it became. In the tiny kitchen he found some paper towels in a drawer. As he cleaned the floor, Lucas vaguely recalled leaving the pub and parting ways with his friends – the people he'd been drinking with for a few years now – and stopping at the kebab shop on the walk back to his flat. It wasn't that he was out drinking his fill *every* night, but lately, particularly since his father's letter, he had hit it harder. The letter had arrived over six weeks ago, and he was still angry. *Uncaring, self-centred, emotionless, cold bastard.* Ever since his mother died fifteen years ago, his father had been even more distant. His work was the only thing he cared about.

The shower helped Lucas look sufficiently less dishevelled to go to work. He'd also shaved. He sometimes didn't bother, but today he just looked like shit, so he thought he'd better at least make some effort. His red eyes betrayed how he felt, but that would improve as the day went on. He pulled the door of his flat closed, ran down the stairs still feeling a little queasy and made the stop just before the bus arrived. He would be about half an hour late for work. Again. He hoped the partners wouldn't notice, although, if he was honest with himself, he didn't much care. He was a nobody at the small law firm. The IT guy. One of the few people there who did not actually practice law in some way or other. It was the source of a lot of head shaking and sardonic looks from his father. 'You're a disappointment', his father's expression said. Not that he'd seen much of his father in the past decade. Geoffrey Shaw never seemed to have had time for his son, and Lucas told himself he didn't care.

He was first out of the bus at the stop near work, and the woman waiting to board stepped back out of his way, alarmed. Lucas was slightly surprised, until he realised he was angry and must have looked that way. He was angry most of the time. It had been building for a long time, probably years. The drinking took the edge off it. Sometimes he wondered whether he'd been angry since he was a child, when his father announced that the family would be moving across the world, from New Zealand to the United Kingdom. Seven-year-old Lucas had been forced to leave his whole world behind. He still remembered how upset and angry he had felt.

He walked half a block to the firm's office, passing his usual café and its warm smell of fried food and coffee. A toasted bacon sandwich would be a perfect breakfast, he decided – after he'd made a show of doing some work, of course. For now, he ordered a takeaway coffee. He hoped that would overshadow the lingering smell of alcohol on his breath.

"Hey, Luke." A friendly face greeted him as he entered the office.

"Joe." He nodded towards the young man. Joseph was the other dogsbody at the firm. He took care of a lot of admin and paperwork for the partners, although he at least had a good excuse for his nothing job; he was an intern, still another year of his law degree to complete, working part time to pay his rent.

"Big night?" Joseph asked. Genuine and non-judgemental.

Joseph will probably not make partner unless he becomes more of an arrogant prick like my father.

"I guess."

"Luke! Where have you been?" One of the partners stood in front of Lucas, looking a little redder than usual. "Email isn't working again. I need to get a document out immediately!"

"All right, I'll fix it now," Lucas said, thinking solicitors should be intelligent. *Why can't these stupid fuckers turn a router off and back on again?* He opened the server cupboard and pretended to make the reset look complicated. He wished he knew why he'd chosen to work here. He hated lawyers. *Self-important, arrogant, entitled bunch of ...* Well, maybe that was because of his father. And maybe his attitude was the reason he hadn't contacted his father's solicitors. It must have been at least a month since he'd received their letter, asking him to call them 'as soon as practicable, in order to finalise the matter of your late father's estate'.

Bastard. Even in death, his father had to make Lucas work. And there was his father's letter, too. Apparently held by his solicitor's office and sent immediately after his death on a standing instruction. How many other people had found out, by way of a business-like posthumous letter from a dead parent, that they were adopted?

Lucas had been shocked and hadn't believed it at first. Then he got angry. *Angrier.* That night at the pub his friends weren't in so he drank alone, occasionally cursing nobody in particular. Occasionally he cursed his father. He wished he could talk to his mother. He recalled snippets of odd comments his mother made before she'd been diagnosed. Now they started to make more sense. He wondered if that was why his father was such a prick to him. *Geoffrey Shaw was not my father at all.*

As these thoughts swirled around in his mind, fuelled and addled by the alcohol he drank, he started to wonder who his *real* father was. And who his *real* mother was. The woman who had raised him and loved him as her own, his *adoptive* mother, couldn't help him; she'd been killed by breast cancer just weeks before her fortieth birthday.

With each additional drink, the landlord became increasingly concerned as Lucas sat alone, shaking his head and muttering to himself. He was clearly a troubled young man. He drank until the landlord refused to serve him another one. Then he trudged back to his flat through a light but persistent rain, reaching his front door cold and soaked to the skin.

That night he stood in his kitchen, still brooding over the thoughts of his estranged father, and punched a hole in the wall. Then he cried like a child. Like he hadn't done for years. But release did not come.

The blow hurt his hand badly enough that he had trouble writing for the next few days. It took him more than a week to fully accept that it was true; that neither his mother nor his father were his *real* parents. That Lucas was not who he thought he was.

The next day he had searched out the New Zealand children's services organisation and made contact. He had filled in a complicated form, written a covering email and sent it off into the ether hoping to get some answers. But that was almost six weeks ago and he'd so far heard nothing at all.

"Win noticed you were late. She was asking where you were." Joseph had returned to find Lucas at his PC checking his personal emails. He seemed a little concerned.

"Thanks, Joe. You're a good lad," Lucas said. "Fuck, now I even sound like the old bastard," he muttered. Joseph now looked confused.

"My father. My dead father. Miserable old ... Well, I'm going to get something to eat. Do you want anything?"

"No thanks, I've brought a sandwich in," Joseph replied.

Lucas headed back to the café down the street towards that bacon sandwich.

2

Lucas's pocket buzzed. He wiped his greasy hands on the paper bag holding the remaining half of his toasted sandwich and pulled his phone out. "Hello."

"Lucas Shaw?" an older male voice enquired.

"That's me."

"I'm sorry to trouble you, Mr Shaw. My name is Trilby. I wrote to you some weeks ago," said the hesitant voice. Lucas waited for him to continue. "I'm a partner in your father's law firm, and, as you know, we are seeking to settle his estate, according to his wishes." Lucas bit back the angry feeling that had started to knot in the pit of his stomach. It was not Trilby's fault that his father was a prick. And perhaps it was time now to get the old man's affairs out of the way.

"I've been busy. Sorry." He wondered if Trilby could tell he wasn't sorry at all. "What do you need from me?"

"Well, Mr Shaw, I'd be grateful if you could please call in to the office, or arrange a time for us to meet elsewhere if you wish." Trilby spoke slowly and respectfully; there seemed to be no trace of the high-handedness Lucas expected from Geoffrey Shaw. "There are papers to finalise, at the earliest opportunity. And other matters of your father's estate and collection to deal with."

"He wasn't my father."

"Ah, yes, well, he always considered himself your father," Trilby said gently. *Bullshit*, Lucas thought irritably. *Definitely time to get this done and leave the old bastard behind.* "Okay. How about this afternoon?" The firm wouldn't miss him if he left a little early.

Trilby was clearly surprised, and there was a brief pause. "Oh, yes, that would be fine," the solicitor said, collecting himself. "Shall we say four o'clock? I'm afraid I must also ask you to bring identification."

"Sure. See you then," Lucas replied, and Trilby confirmed he had the firm's address, offering directions. "Don't worry," Lucas interrupted, "I'll find you."

Lucas slid the phone back into his pocket and took another bite of the now-cold bacon sandwich. He pondered whether to tell the office manager he felt unwell and needed to go home, or just quietly leave and say nothing.

Identification? What's that all about?

After he'd finished the sandwich, he went back into his building and the decision was made for him.

The office manager saw him come through the door. "Where have you been?" she asked. Win was a reasonable and calm woman, able to rise above the egos and occasional irritation of the firm's partners, although lately Lucas had become aware that her attitude towards him had hardened.

"I'm sorry, Win, I've been feeling unwell, and I hoped a bit of air would help," he ventured. Win studied his face, and her look softened as she apparently decided he did look unwell. "I'm afraid it didn't," he added, seeing the opportunity.

"Lucas, you're almost out of paid sick leave. Perhaps the pharmacy down the road can help?"

"I've already taken something, and it made no difference." Did a bacon sandwich count as 'something'? "I'd hate to throw up here," he said, hoping she would buy it.

"All right. I'll check again, but you may lose a half-day's pay."

So what, the firm pay me as little as they can anyway.

An hour and a half later, Lucas boarded the train to Leeds from Bradford Forster Square station. He'd been back to his flat to pick up the solicitor's letter, along with his father's. He reread Geoffrey Shaw's matter-of-fact letter and felt the resentment rise again. He slipped the papers into his jacket pocket, locked the door, jogged down the stairs and out onto Manningham Lane. The walk to the railway station had done little to appease his irritation.

The train was due in Leeds in about half an hour, from where he would change for Harrogate. Looking at his watch, Lucas realised he'd be more than an hour early for his meeting. The motion of the train and mostly empty carriage eventually helped him to relax. He wondered whether Win would dock his pay. He took his phone out to check the map for the solicitor's office, to discover that it was not in the centre of town as he'd expected. It was nearly a kilometre to the west, near Valley Gardens. It was quite close to Geoffrey Shaw's house, and he remembered seeing the gardens briefly on an unhappy visit many years ago. After changing trains, he decided that if the weather was clear in Harrogate, he would stop at the gardens on the way.

Just after two o'clock, Lucas reached the Cornwall Street gate of Valley Gardens and found a visitors' map sign. He was tempted to turn around and look for a pub instead, but something he hadn't expected caught his eye on the garden map. Just a few hundred metres away was the New Zealand Garden. Something from Lucas's home and possibly worth a look. He strolled through the gardens to find Māori wood carvings of objects and fauna from the land of his birth. Some things he could only just recall from his early school years in Wellington's Hutt Valley. Some of the words he read had a familiar ring; at least in his mind. As he walked around the garden, it brought back some fond memories of those early years and also reminded him that he should chase up the New Zealand authorities for a response to his request of six weeks ago.

Would he be able to find his birth mother? Would she want to know him? He'd always considered himself to be resilient, but learning that he was adopted, that he'd been abandoned by his own mother, had shaken him more than he cared to admit. It was still shocking to him, and he knew in his heart that he'd been drinking more because the alcohol dulled the range of emotions that had rooted themselves into part of his brain. What if he couldn't find her? What if she was dead, too? Then he would be left knowing simply that he'd been abandoned but never being able to find out why.

Why didn't the unfeeling old bastard ever tell me? Why didn't Mum tell me?

Lucas tried to push his glum feelings aside as he sat on a bench near a large tree to take in his surroundings. The bench had a curved carving at one end, and a spiral, a koru, carved near the other. A sign explained that it was a symbol of new life. He looked around at the vaguely familiar New Zealand flora and the Māori carvings, and felt a calmness he hadn't felt for months. Maybe not for years. Was it just the symbolism? The spirituality of the Māori culture and their connection with nature? Or was it something else?

A pigeon, testing whether Lucas had any food, landed on the grass nearby and broke his reverie. "Fuck off," he whispered to it, and it came closer.

Three thirty. Time to go to the solicitor's office.

As he left the New Zealand Garden, a light drizzle started, perfectly timed to remind him that he was in Yorkshire, and not the Land of the Long White Cloud.

He walked out the main gate and made his way back to Crescent Road, quickly finding the address he was looking for. The building was more modest than he'd expected; it didn't seem to suit Geoffrey Shaw's arrogance. He wasn't quite sure what he'd expected but would not have been surprised to see marble, gilt-edged furnishings and polished brass. Instead, it seemed much more down-to-earth. Even the small firm he worked for in Bradford had more opulent premises.

Inside, he shook off the damp and informed the young man at the reception desk that he had an appointment with Arthur Trilby. The receptionist stood and said he'd fetch *Mr* Trilby for him, inviting him to take a seat. While he waited, it dawned upon Lucas that what he'd been feeling was *anticipation*. It was a feeling that had been absent from his life for a long time. He had slowly slipped into an existence driven by habit. His work, his relationships – the few that he had – were all essentially habits, probably having simply evolved over a period of *years*. His life had become dull and apathetic, and now something new had interposed. Was it possible that the death of his father, his *estranged adoptive father*, was going to be a turning point? A new beginning, like the koru promised. It seemed a strange idea to Lucas, but as he felt a resuscitated enthusiasm slowly seep into his mind, he remembered something the solicitor had said on the phone earlier: 'Other matters of your father's estate and collection to deal with'. What did *that* mean? And what *collection*?

3

Raymond de Péreille, Lord of Montségur, had been watching the Crusader army, supported by French Royalist forces, growing ever stronger each day since the early summer of the previous year. It was now spring, and Raymond knew the enemy numbers had swelled by many thousands.

"The enemy grows too strong, my brother. They will soon break through." Raymond spoke the words that his young brother feared, though already knew in his heart.

Bernard knew they had been fortunate to defend the château for these nine months. The enemy was fierce and unrelenting. Their antagonists believed they had God on their side. But their god was not the same Christian God the Cathars embraced. Their God required blind allegiance to men like Pope Innocent III and the Papal Legate Arnaud Amaury, who had ordered the murder of almost 20,000 men, women and children at Béziers a generation earlier.

Reports from that terrible summer day in 1209 had quickly reached other Cathar cities and villages. The Crusaders, having seized control, had not been able to determine the Catholics from the Cathars. 'What shall we do, for we cannot distinguish between the faithful and the heretics?' Amaury had been asked. 'Kill them all, for the Lord knoweth them that are His,' the Papal Legate had replied. Theirs was a God unconcerned with the slaughter of thousands of innocent men, women and children. Their God demanded obedience to the new Pope, Gregory IX, who, following in Innocent's footsteps and with the aid of the Order of St Dominic, had devised a new means for eliminating those who did not accede to their view. It was called the Inquisition. Bands of visiting inquisitors, and their torturers and executioners, spread through France and Catalonia and beyond, to enforce the will of the Church.

"It is time, brother." Raymond de Péreille, Lord of Montségur, clapped his hand across his brother's broad shoulders.

Bernard nodded his head and walked with his brother to the small, unadorned chapel to give thanks to the Cathars' God.

Bernard summoned the men he had selected for the task ahead, while Raymond and another man went to the four corners of the citadel to fetch the sacred objects. Bernard knew it was not permitted for any man to touch all four talismans at one time. It was said this would surely kill a man.

Bernard's three men arrived just as Raymond and the other returned holding the sacred objects, closing the large timber doors to ensure their privacy. Each man was given one talisman, assigned by name, and each immediately secreted his sacred object within a hidden pocket inside his heavy brown cloak. Raymond ensured that no man ever touched more than two of the objects. Bernard was given the last talisman, also securing it inside his clothing.

"My brothers," Raymond said in a powerful voice, "you have in your keep the four pillars of the Gnostics. These are our most sacred relics. These hallowed ancient objects have existed for many centuries. We have been their guardians for ten generations, but they are as old as time itself. And now they will go with you to their new resting places. Places far apart so as to ensure that the ill wind now desecrating our lands cannot wield these pillars against humanity.

"Yours is a fated journey, and you must not fail. It is better to die than to fail. You must send these talismans to the four winds, precisely as my beloved brother Bernard will direct you. You will leave two hours after nightfall. Tonight, there will be no moon, and your path around the horde outside these walls is already secured. May God speed and protect your journey."

Raymond closed his eyes and prayed for the men. They stood silently and waited for him to open his eyes.

"We will meet at the agreed place on the northern wall," Bernard de Péreille said quietly to them as they started to disperse. Each man was ready and willing to give his life, were it needed. They scattered to eat their last meal inside the fortress, a hearty meal to sustain them, for they could take precious few supplies with them. The men with wives and children also went to say their goodbyes to their loved ones. Bernard himself was such a man. He went back to the small room in which he had lived with his wife and young son for the past nine months. It was now almost dark.

Bernard's young son was barely weaned from the breast and did not understand what his father was saying. Nor did he understand why his mother was crying. He just looked at his father's loving face and saw the tears forming in his eyes. Large tears grew in the boy's eyes, too, and slowly ran down his soft cheeks. He didn't know what any of it meant, he was confused and frightened. His mother understood what Bernard must do; she had known of his destiny for some months now, as the siege had intensified.

Tonight, her husband would leave the temporary sanctuary of the castle. He must leave them to their fate, knowing his cause was a higher calling. Tears streamed down her face also. Not for herself, not for Bernard, but for the little boy and the ominous foreboding that had filled the pit of her stomach for weeks. She told herself God would protect him, but she knew there was little evidence that God cared for them at all.

Bernard faced the three men standing before him at the north wall of the Montségur castle fortress. There were ropes already in place over the wall, and Bernard knew that this face of the rock upon which the fortress stood was treacherous and steep, and led to the thickest part of the forest surrounding them. Their informants from the nearby villages, the very people who had helped them keep the supply lines open during the siege, had advised Raymond that the invaders had no troops in the forest here. The terrain was so difficult the Royalists did not see any advantage in stationing troops; there were merely a handful of watchers and guards.

"We climb the wall and rappel down the rock face, each man alone. A villager will meet us and guide us north-west through a hidden forest pass. You have your daggers?" Bernard looked on as each man rechecked his sheath and nodded.

Bernard checked that he also carried the four scrolls that would guide them. He, and only he, had knowledge of where every man would be travelling. Raymond had helped prepare the map, but Bernard had determined the final location himself and inscribed it afterwards.

"The enemy will not be expecting us, but if we meet him, we must kill him quickly and silently." Again the men nodded solemnly. They all knew the enemy would not hesitate to kill them all. Each man secured to his belt his small pouch containing an allotment of gold coins and shouldered his leather satchel and goatskin flask.

Raymond walked towards the men and embraced his younger brother. "Godspeed, brother," he said. "Godspeed all of you."

The first man mounted the wall, quickly climbed the ridge and rappelled down the outside. Bernard held the end of the rope and when the first man gave three sturdy tugs, he sent the next man over, followed soon after by the third.

Bernard put his hands on his brother's shoulders and kissed each cheek. "God watch over you. All of you." Bernard had tears in his eyes as he said the words. He did not expect any mercy from the invading forces when they finally broke the castle's defences. He quickly climbed the ridge and disappeared from his brother's view.

A few minutes later Raymond felt the three tugs on the rope and hauled it back over the ridge. With heavy heart, he carefully rolled the rope and carried it to the largest of the cooking hearths. The lightly oiled rope burned magnificently, yielding thick, black smoke which disappeared into the oppressive black night sky.

At the base of the old stone wall, Bernard and his three men found their guide. He was a small old man with a long grey beard who, although quite sprightly, walked with a slight stoop. He had waited, concealed in the trees, watching all four men make their way down the wall, until he was satisfied this was not a trick of some kind. The men all embraced, and Bernard spoke with the guide in hushed tones. He handed the old man a consideration for his trouble – some gold coins that would likely feed his family for a month.

With no moon, the men were in far less danger than even a week ago, but moving through the forest quietly was more difficult. The guide instructed each of them to hold the cloak of the man in front and try to walk in his footsteps. Progress was slow, but they encountered nobody for almost the first hour.

"Sst," the old man uttered, almost imperceptibly, holding a pale hand in the air.

The men stopped silently and listened. Voices. Then rough laughter. They heard a man spit vigorously. The sound came from somewhere to the right. The old man led them slowly to another overgrown path to their left, where progress became more difficult. Bernard was following directly behind him and, at half a foot taller, every so often his head brushed the limb of a tree. He could feel drops of blood on his face, sporadically soothed by the soft kiss of damp leaves.

Two hours later their guide stopped them, feeling more confident to speak without being overheard by Royalist forces. The men took a small drink from their goatskins. The terrain since leaving the château had been mountainous and increasingly serpentine, though the old man was confident of his bearings. Bernard spoke with the guide briefly in his native Occitan, the language common to these parts of the Languedoc and Catalonia to the south. He then addressed his brethren.

"Soon we will pass the Château de Roquefixade, but we will not stop. It is rumoured there are Royalist spies amongst our own men. The terrain will be easier, but we will be in the midst of farmland. We must maintain our discipline." Bernard took another drink before slinging his goatskin over his shoulder.

"We will reach Foix before dawn, and from there we will take our despatches our separate ways. The fate of all lands and all men will ride with us."

4

An hour before dawn, as the early light just began to touch the overcast grey sky, Bernard saw the outline of the square towers of the Château de Foix, a castle on a rocky hill overlooking the town of Foix and the Ariège River. The château was the home of Roger IV, Comte de Foix, himself a Cathar supporter, as was his father. Roger-Bernard II the Great had died just three years earlier and was known to have supported the Cathars in their resistance to the French kings, Louis VIII and Louis IX. Roger-Bernard II had been excommunicated by the Pope on two occasions for his beliefs.

Bernard de Péreille felt they were entering a sanctuary. He touched the old man's shoulder, and the men stopped. Although they would have a brief respite, Bernard had started to feel the weight of the task that lay ahead. It would be a long journey for each of them. He thought of his wife and child; his young son's sad, trusting face, and his gentle wife who held no antipathy for any man, or any religion. Bernard fell to his knees to pray for the welfare of his family and for his community, who were likely to soon be at the mercy of the savages amassed outside their peaceful home. Tears streamed down his lacerated face.

He collected and calmed himself, and took a long drink. With all the strength he could summon, he stood to address the men. "We will reach the castle by dawn, and there I will give each of you your destination. There will be time to pack additional supplies and take another meal."

The men did not ask further questions; they knew they would be assigned their task in due time, and they would obey, or die in the attempt.

The old man spoke softly to Bernard in his native tongue, nodding towards the outline of the château and the river to their right. Bernard embraced him and thanked him again. They all shook hands and their guide quietly wished them all Godspeed, in French, before turning and heading back the way they had come.

The old man retraced his steps until he was difficult to see in the distance. Bernard watched him as he was silently swallowed by the shadowy forest at the edge of their path. He turned and followed his men towards the dark silhouette of the château. The men had quickened their pace as they walked along the bank of L'Ariège, the sound of the river masking their footsteps. Starlight was still their guide, although the early dawn sky was no longer black. Interspersed with the cockerels, there were occasional sounds of humanity as the village of Foix greeted the day.

As they neared the château, a hint of smoke in his nostrils affirmed for Bernard that they were indeed back in civilisation. He had decided that he would enter the château alone, leaving his satchel in the care of the men as a precaution, in the event that the Comte de Foix had been deposed by the Royalists or the Church. As they approached the lower gate in the outer fortifications, the dawn light was sufficient to make them visible from above. Bernard stopped the men and instructed them to stay well back in the trees, taking his satchel with them.

Bernard strode purposefully towards the gate, giving his best impression of a traveller and emissary, here to pass on a message from his master, for only the comte's ears. He spoke to the sole sentry in Occitan. He knew that if the man did not understand and spoke only French then it was likely the comte had been removed or murdered. The sentry spoke Occitan but appeared to Bernard to be nervous. Nonetheless, he asked Bernard for his name, and Bernard replied with the agreed name of his 'master'. The sentry stepped back from the gate and went up to the next gate to speak with its watchman. Presently he returned and the two men waited, as the dawn's light continued to paint the charcoal sky. A short while later a man came to the gate to report that the comte would see Bernard.

Roger IV, Comte de Foix, addressed Bernard in hushed tones. Bernard had an impression that Roger felt an immense weight from the king and his Royalist forces. It was written on the faces of Roger's men. It was certain that the events at Béziers, Carcassonne and Toulouse were known to Roger, and the more recent concentration of forces around Montségur had the whole Languedoc region braced for catastrophe. Bernard wondered how long it might be before Roger buckled under the weight of it all and gave his support to the Royalists.

For the present, however, Bernard became satisfied that Roger would aid his men and see them safely on their way, as long as they left quickly and quietly. He went back to the banks of L'Ariège with one of Roger's men and escorted his party into the château. The four men ate a small meal and, as Bernard took his portion, he retrieved the scrolls from his satchel. A small one for each man, and a larger one – the key map itself – for Bernard's own travels. He allocated them, instructing each man that no other person should look upon their map, and when their quest was completed, the parchment must be burned. Each man quietly studied his scroll, each one a copied portion of the larger one that Bernard held.

"Our host's hospitality extends to providing further supplies and horses for your journeys. We will depart as the bells ring terce."

The men stood, slung their satchels and goatskins over their shoulders and walked to the château stores. A visit to the stables followed soon thereafter. As the carillon sounded mid-morning, Bernard farewelled his men, repeating the edict of secrecy and the import of their task. He watched as each man guided his horse in a different direction.

Bernard had thanked Roger for his kindness but had told him nothing of their journey. He felt confident they would soon be forgotten as four travellers passing through, whose way had been cleared by one master providing a simple message to another. Nothing more. As he mounted his horse and guided the animal in the remaining cardinal direction – the four winds – he wondered how long it might be before Foix also fell.

5

A slim man in his late fifties emerged from the hallway into the reception area. His grey hair was neatly combed back and he had a thin moustache. A perfunctory smile creased his face slightly as he saw Lucas.

"Mr Shaw. Thank you very much for coming in today." Arthur Trilby extended his hand and introduced himself.

"No problem. And it's Luke."

"Very well. Please follow me." Trilby led Luke down the hall to a small room with a dark-timber bookshelf filling one wall and an old desk with a single box file upon it. The solicitor invited Luke to take a seat and he opened the box, withdrawing a small stack of papers and a thick, yellowed envelope. He asked Luke for his identification, and Luke supplied his passport. Trilby noted down the details and handed Luke a letter from the top of the pile, explaining that it was the solicitor's official letter describing the nature of Luke's inheritance.

He did not have any expectations regarding his father's will. The old man owed him nothing, just as Luke felt he owed Geoffrey Shaw nothing. He knew little of his father's financial affairs and half expected to be left with debts or other problems that matched any windfall he might receive.

As he read, Trilby explained that he'd known Geoffrey Shaw for more than a decade, and he, as with others at the firm, were shocked and deeply saddened to learn of his sudden death. One small mercy, perhaps, the solicitor said, may be that Geoffrey was well prepared. He had given Trilby instructions a decade ago, very soon after joining the firm, in case of an early demise. 'One can never know one's fate until it looks him in the eye,' Geoffrey had told his business partner.

"It's strange, you know," Trilby said. "At the time, he seemed so serious about it I wondered if there was something he wasn't telling me. I remember feeling as though Geoffrey expected something other than old age to take him. Sadly, how right he was." Mr Trilby paused to thumb through the papers, noticing Luke's expression. "In any event, I'm sure he confided in you, so perhaps I should take no more of your time than I need." Luke raised his eyebrows but did not correct him.

To his mild surprise, he learned that his father owned the Harrogate house unencumbered. The rest of the estate consisted of a modest share portfolio, a bank account with nearly £20,000 and a superannuation fund that made monthly payments into the bank account. "We will need to notify the fund of a change of bank account following probate, of course," Trilby advised. "Alternatively you could withdraw all the funds in a lump sum if you wish. It's all in my letter."

Luke's mind was wandering. He started to wonder why this needed a personal visit; surely papers could have been sent by courier? And then he remembered what the solicitor had said on the phone. "You mentioned a 'collection'. What is that?"

"Ah, yes," said Trilby, pulling out the yellowed envelope. Luke could see it had an old-fashioned wax seal. "This has been in our safe with your father's papers for the better part of a decade, and I recall it looked old when we received it." The solicitor turned the envelope over, and Luke could see his father's neat handwriting in black ink: 'Lucas Geoffrey Shaw. Confidential.'

"When he lodged this with me, he gave strict instructions that it was to be personally handed to you and no one else. It was all very serious, rather more so than I'd expected. I had instructions to verify your identity before releasing it. During the course of our working relationship, he made a point of reiterating those instructions several times." Trilby certainly knew how to build up a story. Luke willed the man to stop talking and hand it over.

"This is what he always referred to as the 'collection'. I'm afraid I don't know what he meant by that. I've never seen its contents." Trilby put his hand on the envelope. "I must also ask you one more thing. Geoffrey's instructions are that you should open this in the presence of no other person."

"I don't mind," Luke said, reaching for it.

Trilby held it tightly. "His instructions were very clear, and he was my friend ..." Luke could see a hint of sadness in the solicitor's eyes, "... so I'll leave it with you if you wish to open it now." He reached into the desk drawer and fished out a brass letter opener, handing it to Luke with the envelope. He stood and quickly left the room, announcing that he would wait outside. Luke could feel something solid inside; it wasn't just old papers. Curiosity gripped him, and he inserted the knife into the slit to break the old wax seal.

Inside he found some papers, and, tipping it slightly towards him, out slid a tarnished brass key. *Hmm. Now what could this be for?* A small blank slip of thick paper slid out with the key. He turned it over to find three numbers written in the same black ink. 43-27-70. *A code? A safe combination?* He slipped the key and the piece of paper into his pocket.

The sheet of neatly folded cream-coloured paper was addressed to Luke, written in his father's typically pompous prose. He started to read.

Dear Lucas,

You will be reading this letter after my death. If we have not spoken of these matters before now, perhaps my death was untimely. In any event, I am sorry. I am sorry for adding to your burden. At the time of writing, you are barely a man, just eighteen years, and I must hope that the task I will pass on is one that you can accept and embrace. It is a task that has been with the Shaw family for many generations –

"Oh get to the point, old man," Luke muttered.

– with the Shaw family for many generations. The Collection has existed since the mid-thirteenth century, and it is our role to keep it safe. We are its guardians. With this key you will find it.

As I write, I think of you in our younger days, and I am reminded of a happier time, gazing at the stars together, wondering what the future might hold. I have high hopes for you, my son, and now I am relying on your honour and judgement.

Affectionately,

Geoffrey Shaw

"For fuck's sake," Luke said. "*Really?*" It was odd, out of place. Geoffrey Shaw was not a sentimental man in any way. 'Reminded of a happier time'? *Fuck off.* He put the letter back into the envelope and stuffed it into the pocket of his jacket. Just outside the small room, he found Arthur Trilby patiently waiting in the hallway.

"Is everything all right?" the solicitor asked politely.

"Yeah. Just a shock, I suppose. I didn't expect all this." There was something about his father's letter that persuaded him to keep the contents to himself. At least for now. Perhaps it was just so out of character that Luke thought there must be something else to it. Something his father wanted him alone to find.

"I have some papers ready for your signature, if I may trouble you further."

"Sure, whatever," Luke said dismissively. "Whatever you need," he quickly added. There was no need to be rude to this man.

They both went back into the small office, and Luke signed the forms to enable the next step in the probate process. He was, at least, broadly familiar with it. The firm he worked for occasionally used him for low-level clerical work, no doubt charging it out at higher rates. Luke thanked Trilby and started towards the door.

"Thank you, Mr Shaw. Luke. It's been a pleasure meeting you today. Will you go to the house now?" The question caught Luke by surprise. He hadn't thought about it. Trilby evidently read the look on his face. "It's been empty a while now; there will be mail piling up and bills to pay, I'm sure."

"Hmm, that's a good idea." He would surely have time for a quick look around before catching a train back to Bradford.

"Do you have a key?" Trilby opened a desk drawer, and as Luke shook his head, he pulled out a small bundle of keys and handed them over. "The police left them with me, as his legal representative."

Luke thanked Trilby again, shook his hand and left. Five thirty. Maybe time for a pint and an early dinner. He walked down Crescent Road, back towards Valley Gardens, and found a bar.

6

Luke's meal arrived with his second pint. He'd been deep in thought, turning over the three numbers in his mind, and hadn't quite finished the first beer. He drained the glass and handed it to the waiter, nodding his thanks. One made immediate sense; his birthday was 27 April. The middle number. But what were the other two? Just random choices maybe, but Geoffrey was organised and well ordered. Luke had no doubt there must be some significance to them. *Well, as long as they open the safe.* He tried to recall a safe in his father's house but couldn't. It did seem to be the sort of thing Geoffrey Shaw would have, though.

After his meal, he stepped outside into Crescent Road to make his way up to York Road, to his father's house. His house. The area was a far cry from Manningham Lane. He saw no depressing blocks of flats, and there was grass. And trees. Most of the houses he passed looked grand to Luke, and they had well-maintained gardens. Some of the cars parked behind the iron gates probably cost several years of Luke's meagre salary. He felt a sense of anticipation as he walked along the leafy streets. And he felt safer here than he would wandering around his local streets alone at night. But he also felt like a fish out of water.

He found the house without too much trouble, remembering it from his last visit, a long time ago, back in his university days. It was the only house in the vicinity without any lights on. He went up the manicured gravel pathway to the timber- and glass-panelled front door, pulling out the set of keys Trilby had provided. As he tried a key in the lock, he wondered briefly if the house was alarmed. Trilby didn't mention it, so he hoped for the best. The door opened, and a lonely silence greeted him.

He stepped into the entrance hall, his footsteps giving a forlorn echo as he fumbled for light switches. *Click.* Nothing happened. The power must be off. *Dammit, didn't think of that.* He switched on his phone light and closed the front door. The house was cold and smelt of smoke; the smell of the spent coals of an open fire. There was something else in the air, too, something he couldn't quite put his finger on. Maybe it was just the cold. He shivered as he strode down the hall to the large sitting room. A neat stack of firewood sat on the side of the hearth. He could set a fire. Or he could find a jersey or coat upstairs instead, *if* he needed it. He chose the latter, not expecting to stay too long.

Faint moonlight shone through the open curtains, and he could see the piano keys reflecting back the pale light. The piano brought back a memory of his mother holding his hand as a young boy, placing his thumb on middle C and gently helping him to place his third finger two keys along and his little finger two keys up again. 'That's a C chord,' she'd said, smiling. Then she'd moved his hand one key to the right and he pressed again. She'd made a sad face and said, 'That's D minor. It has a sad sound.' He tried to find middle C and play the chord, but the piano was badly out of tune. He wondered why his father had kept it. He must have moved it up from Leeds when he'd relocated to Harrogate three years after Luke's mother's death.

By the light of his phone, he could see that the room had been disturbed. Ornaments were pushed to one end of the mantelpiece and books piled roughly on the shelves. He remembered the house as always being neat. His father did not like mess and clutter. The police had said it was a burglary. Perhaps the burglar searched the whole house for valuables, not just the usual electronics, jewellery, cash and the like. Across the hall, the dining room was the same. The whisky cabinet at the back stood open, but its contents seemed untouched. Was that unusual for a burglary? Leaving the expensive whisky behind? Luke didn't know. He went down the hall towards the kitchen, floorboards creaking loudly and echoing through the house. The kitchen was a bigger mess. Drawers had been pulled out and upended; their contents spilled out across the bench. *What were they looking for?*

He sprinted up the carpeted stairs and into his father's study – originally a large front bedroom. It looked like the epicentre of a disaster. Papers all over the desk, filing cabinet contents strewn across the floor, and some coals had spilled out of the fireplace to burn the floorboards adjacent to the stone hearth. The wall safe was open. *Did he keep valuables in the safe?* Luke didn't think so, but would he have known?

"I guess I won't need this then," he said, pulling the safe combination out of his pocket. He was about to throw it in the wastebasket when he realised something wasn't right. He looked again at the steel door of the safe. It was much more modern than the old key suggested, and there was no aperture. It did not require a key. *So what's the key for?*

He shone his phone around the room and noticed there was a discolouration in the flooring. It made a large square slightly lighter in colour than the perimeter. The carpet! It had been removed. *Now why would that be?* Why on earth would a burglar take carpet? Or had the police taken it away? And there was no chair at the desk either. *What happened here?*

The hallway floorboards creaked downstairs, and Luke jumped. Was someone else in the house? "Hello," he called, instantly wishing he hadn't. Could the burglar who killed his father have returned? He listened carefully; there was no sound. He went quietly back out into the carpeted hallway towards the stairs.

"Hello," he called again, taking the stairs slowly, relying on the feeble moonlight. His heart was beating faster as he reached the landing, half expecting to meet his father's killer coming up the stairs. He warily turned on the landing and continued down. To his relief, there was nobody. The front door was closed, just as he'd left it. Maybe it was nothing after all.

Perhaps the old floorboards had just creaked back into place after he'd disturbed them earlier. He breathed a sigh of relief and headed to the kitchen to pour himself a glass of water. "Settle down, man," he muttered to himself, walking through the kitchen doorway. He took his phone out of his pocket to search for a glass, and in the gloomy moonlight caught a brief glimpse of a huge, dark figure just inside the door. He had no time to run or cry out before he felt a vicious blow to the side of his head. His phone dropped to the floor as he lost consciousness, its light shining upward to reveal a giant of a man dressed from head to toe in black, looking down expressionlessly upon the prone young man face down on the flagstone floor.

7

The days were becoming warmer, although the nights were still cool. Bernard stopped by a river to water the horse and refill his goatskin. His journey was to be long and arduous, northward through much of France to Cherbourg, then across the sea to the lands of Henry III, ruler of the Kingdom of England.

Bernard had travelled through Toulouse, perhaps a dangerous undertaking with the Royalist forces amassed nearby, but he had sympathetic acquaintances in the town from whom he sought advice. While he rested for a few days, an emissary sent by one of his brother monks caught up with him, bringing news of troubles south of Catalonia that had led to an important decision. Bernard carefully penned a parchment recording the conversation, resolving to make an appropriate mark on his map after he had reached his destination, when it was safer.

Soon after Toulouse, he had turned to the west and entered the Duchy of Aquitaine, one of the lands ruled by the House of Plantagenet. Henry III's land. By Bernard's calculation, he was now close to halfway to the Duchy of Normandy, from where he would sail to the Kingdom of England. After making landfall, he would reach his destination within a few weeks, if the grace of God remained with him. It was now late spring, and the warmth of the sun had started to redden and dry his skin. With the sun high overhead, he was pleased his faith did not require the tonsure of the more devout and devoted Catholics.

Loneliness did not trouble Bernard. His holy task kept him going, and when he encountered strangers, he conversed minimally, often replying in Occitan so they would not understand him. He had made peace with God for his occasional pretence at being Catholic. It was a lie and a sin, but he made a promise to God that he would seek atonement after he had completed his despatch. The people of Aquitaine had been kind, offering food and shelter in many villages, treating him as a simple traveller, often communicating in gestures.

The trail climbed a low hill, and as he reached the top, Bernard could see the distant churches and smoking chimneys of the town of Poitiers. He would arrive before nightfall. The Cathar friends in Toulouse had warned him that the Comte de Poitou was allied to the Roman Church, though he was comforted that his guise of a simple traveller was proving most effective. Here he would speak French, as his native Occitan revealed his Languedoc origins, potentially hinting at Catharism to the suspicious minds of the Inquisition. He took a long drink from his goatskin and spurred the horse forward.

Poitiers was a bustling market town. Eleanor of Aquitaine, wife of Henry II, had famously resided in the town during the previous century, and its location was coveted by the local rulers for its defensive advantages. Bernard crossed the River Clain and followed the cobbled streets to the market square, a veritable treasure-trove. Supplies were abundant, though he chose prudently to preserve his remaining funds.

With horse fed and watered, he walked through the town, past the churches – vast, opulent edifices, each a monument to the excesses of the Catholics. Bernard's faith renounced these things. It renounced the fighting, the enforcement of man's will upon others. It renounced the greedy materialism of the Pope's Church. It renounced *all* materialism as the work of the devil. His faith, Bernard believed, was the true Christian faith, notwithstanding the fact that the Catholic Church, for many decades, had accused the Cathars of heresy and unrelentingly persecuted them.

Bernard found refuge at a modest farm on the northern edge of Poitiers. A gentle, decent couple, with a sickly child, growing vegetables on their plot of land. They fed Bernard a simple vegetable broth with a small amount of oily goat's meat and shared a rough red wine with him. They spoke of the *chevauchée*, a tactic being employed by Royalist forces to terrorise rural towns and keep the masses under control. Quick cavalry raids to destroy crops, burn houses, take livestock and show the people the might of the king.

There had not been a *chevauchée* since early winter, but with tears in their eyes, the couple told Bernard of their daughter, just a few years older than the boy. In previous attacks, the mother had been quick to hide the girl away inside the farmhouse, but on this terrible occasion she had been too slow. The marauders had taken the girl from the field; one of the men had seen her and grabbed her arm as he rode by, dragging her up onto his horse. The other men had soon followed him into the hills. The couple had searched for hours, anguished and distraught, until the boy had found her, bleeding, whimpering and left for dead. She'd had the strength to protect her innocent modesty and cover herself with her torn clothing, but she had been defiled so violently that she had lost a great deal of blood. They carried her back to the house and for some hours did their best to care for her. It was to no avail, though, and she slipped away soon after dark. The boy had not recovered from what he had seen.

Bernard was deeply touched by their story, and when he took his leave to sleep in the relative warmth of the stable, he silently prayed for the boy, and for his parents. As he lay awake in the straw bed he had fashioned for himself, he wondered if the ill wind plaguing his homeland would ever truly pass by.

8

With his head pounding painfully, Luke cautiously opened one eye. He could see the glint of moonlight shining off the stone floor. He wasn't sure he could move, but with some effort managed to lift his face a few centimetres off the cold stone. Then, slowly and with considerable determination, he pushed himself up onto his knees to scan the kitchen. His attacker was nowhere in sight. He gingerly touched the lump on the side of his head and looked at his hand. *No blood. I guess that's good.* He felt dizzy and steadied himself, sitting on the flagstones for a moment, recalling the last thing he saw before he was struck. The silhouette of a huge figure in black.

Using the kitchen bench for support, Luke slowly stood, holding the benchtop until his wooziness subsided. He found a glass in a cupboard, filled it and drank deeply, listening for any sounds inside the house. His head throbbed fiercely, but he could hear nothing. Looking at the time on his phone, he must have been unconscious for only a few minutes. Out in the hallway, he checked the front door then went to the bathroom to look for some paracetamol. The thief must have left and pulled the door shut behind him.

Over the next quarter of an hour, Luke carefully searched the house for the intruder. The upstairs bedrooms were neat and tidy, although the small attic storage room next to his father's bedroom was a mess. The box room may have been turned over by his father's killer, or it may have been a mess for a while. Surely tonight's intruder was most likely an opportunist who believed the house was vacant? If he'd meant Luke any harm, he'd had ample opportunity. Satisfied there was nobody else in the house and that the doors were now securely locked, Luke started to relax. The back bedrooms upstairs showed no sign of having been searched, and one had a spare bed neatly made up.

Back downstairs, Luke went into the dining room to help himself to his father's whisky. He poured a generous portion into one of the crystal tumblers and drank it quickly. Probably not what he needed after the headache tablets and a head injury, but he didn't care. *Should I call the police?* There was no sign of a break in, and he was sure the intruder was long gone. Neither could he give a description of his attacker, other than that he was a very big man, so there seemed little point. If he did call them, he would have to wait until they arrived, and who knew how long that would be. In Bradford, the wait could be hours for a petty crime like this, or they might not even bother, he rationalised.

Tiredness, or maybe the whisky and paracetamol, started to overtake Luke, and the spare bed upstairs became very inviting. He scanned the lower floor again, this time checking the windows, too, and then went upstairs to bed.

The morning light penetrated the curtains enough to wake Luke. 7.35, according to his phone, which was now warning him its battery was almost flat. He climbed out of bed, dressed in yesterday's clothes and went downstairs. The fridge proved a nasty surprise. Some vegetables and a bag of salad had turned into a pungent, dark-green liquid and dripped out the door when he opened it. There was a bottle of milk that had swelled slightly. He found some paper towels to wipe the green sludge from the door before closing it. *A job for the future. Or for someone else.* "All right. Now what to do?" he asked himself aloud.

In a kitchen drawer he found a phone charger that would work and also a couple of unpaid household bills, one of which was the electricity. He rang the number on the power bill and, to his surprise, got through to a real person almost immediately. Ten minutes later, he'd paid the outstanding account, and a reconnection fee, after telling the call centre that the fee was extortionate. The company promised that the electricity would be back on soon. He tried the gas hob and it still worked so he found a saucepan to boil some water, and some teabags, and made himself a cup of black tea. By the time he'd finished, he heard the fridge come to life.

He put his phone on to charge and took his cup of tea upstairs to his father's study. It seemed logical that the study would be the place to search, unless his father had some other safe deposit arrangement or something. Surely Trilby would have said so if he did? *No, there must be something here.* He took the old key and his father's letter, along with the piece of paper with the three numbers, out of his pocket and put them on the desk. He checked the desk drawers and filing cabinet, but none of the locks would take a key like the old one from the envelope. He looked over the walls, rechecked the open safe, pulled out the drawers to look for anything inside that might work, all without success. He studied the wall, tapping the oak panels to see if any sounded hollow. None did. *"Come on, you old bastard, give me a clue!"*

Luke reread his father's letter. The strange, sentimental letter that was so out of character for Geoffrey Shaw. *'... I think of you in our younger days, and I am reminded of a happier time, gazing at the stars together, wondering what the future might hold'.* His father had never talked like that. Was it a clue? The only time Luke could remember ever stargazing with his father had been on a family holiday when he was eight years old. He could still picture it: after dinner, they had walked along the river, bought some ice creams, and found a place to sit and look at the evening sky. Geoffrey had been able to name some of the constellations for Luke. He'd told him that his birth sign, Taurus, would be visible in winter, and had promised to show him but that had never eventuated. *But how is this a clue? A photo from a long-past family holiday in Whitby?*

Scanning the study walls again, Luke saw a vaguely familiar picture of some ruins on a hill, taken across the water. Whitby Abbey. The bandstand they'd sat by on that night was in the foreground. This must be a clue! Luke pulled the picture off the wall, but there was nothing obvious behind it. Undeterred, he took a brass letter opener from the desk drawer and set to work on the panelling. Less than ten minutes later, he'd pried the mouldings from around the panel directly behind the picture, and the square section came loose. With a twist of the letter opener, the oak panel fell towards Luke exposing a cavity behind.

A small brass door revealed itself, with a numbered dial, and a keyhole. The hidden safe!

9

Now midsummer, Bernard pressed on through the plains and gentle hills of the Duchy of Normandy, towards Cherbourg. He knew he had entered a disputed territory. Normandy was still largely ruled by Henry III. However, Louis IX considered it his territory, his grandfather, Philippe II, having won it back forty years earlier. The never-ending dispute between the English and French kings over many generations was helpful inasmuch as it overshadowed the oppressive control of the Church.

The days were long and hot, and his horse was showing signs of exhaustion. It had been a fine companion and would be rested in Cherbourg. From there, Bernard would find a ship's master and arrange passage to the shores of the Kingdom of England, a journey of no more than a week. Bernard himself did not feel as strong as he had at the start of this long journey. His meals had often consisted of little more than grain and water. There were days when his horse fared better than he.

Listless and in need of respite, Bernard arrived in Cherbourg. At the market he traded the horse for supplies and a few more gold coins. Upon reaching the shores of England, he would need the coins to acquire an animal sufficient for the trek that lay ahead. This journey was Bernard's first foray outside of his homeland, and he had no way of knowing how difficult the foreign land would be. He was aware that Henry III was a Frenchman, descended from William of Normandy, and he hoped that would be helpful. He also knew that thirty years earlier, following the appalling Massacre at Béziers, Raymond VI of Toulouse had spent time in England, harboured by his brother-in-law, King John I. King John was also of the House of Plantagenet and kept Raymond VI safe from the Crusades and the Inquisition.

During his long journey, Bernard had decided that not only would he deliver his sacred despatch, his talisman, to the allotted place in the Kingdom of England, but also that England would be a suitable location for the map he was carrying. He could not imagine it being safe in France whilst the Catholic persecutions continued.

Days earlier, Bernard had passed through Rennes, the capital of the Duchy of Brittany. It was there that he had received news of the siege of Montségur. The battle was finally over. Royalist forces had found a weakness in the defences and were preparing to break through and storm the château when the occupants had agreed to negotiate surrender. The terms had been quickly determined. People who renounced their Cathar faith and swore allegiance to the Catholic Church were permitted to leave. The remaining two hundred and ten people were burned alive. The Cathar Perfecti had walked into the pyre of their own accord, as Royalist forces watched.

The messenger reporting the news had not known whether Raymond de Péreille had survived, nor any others of that or any other family. He had also reported that the Inquisition had taken an interest in the survivors, so it had seemed to Bernard that it may have been a mercy if his brother had been burned. Bernard's task, his sacred despatch, meant it would be some months before he would be able to return to his home and learn the fate of his brother, his wife and young son. He could only pray for them in the hope that God had shown them mercy.

He had carried the weight of this terrible news with him from Rennes. He prepared a simple meal of nuts and grains that he'd bought in the Cherbourg market square and ate in a solemn and lonely silence. He then found adequate lodgings in a barn, and soon after nightfall he once again lay in a straw bed and contemplated the life he had. He was exhausted, and the feeling he carried in the pit of his stomach had started to eat away at him. The burden of his mission seemed to be increasingly weighty as each day passed. He was torn between the love of his God and the love of his family. The journey had drained and weakened him.

Thoughts turned over in his weary mind. Could he fulfil his obligation to God another way? *Perhaps if I throw the talisman into the ocean and burn the map.* That, he reasoned, would surely protect the talisman from the Church. And he'd then be free to travel back to find his wife and son, and his beloved brother. He did not know whether any of the other men had been successful in their tasks either. Perhaps it was better that he lost or destroyed the remaining talisman. *What if the Church already had the other three?* It would not be abandoning his calling. It would surely be *protecting* the sacred relic.

He was almost delirious with exhaustion but his mind would not stop. Tears rolled down his cheeks and down on to the straw. He could picture his young son looking up at him searchingly as he'd said goodbye, uncomprehending. He thought of his wife, how she had encouraged him and wished him well, all the while wishing he would stay, though not saying it. He thought of the poor little girl in Poitiers. He thought of her younger brother, her parents, living with the horror of what had been so violently and cruelly done to her. *The ill wind blows strong.*

As he lay on the rough bed, these swirling thoughts led him to resolve that he must complete his task. *This sacred despatch may be the sole purpose of the remainder of my life. The Church must not have the sacred objects, not in these godforsaken times.* One day, there would come a time when the world was ready. When the objects would need to be found and would give meaning to life once again. 'The sacred objects would find their destiny', the legend said. As he finally drifted into a fitful slumber, Bernard knew in his heart that he was part of their story, part of a legend older than time.

10

Gerald Montford closed his laptop and downed the last of his brandy. He was about to ring for another when the antique mantel clock chimed eight. He glanced at his watch, a hand-made George Daniels, for confirmation. Gerald required that all clocks at Montford Hall were precise, and the estate's steward ensured the staff took great care to meet the earl's wishes.

Gerald stood and surveyed his library. It was his favourite room, surrounded by antiques and treasures of the five hundred years of Montford Hall's existence. Five hundred years of the Montfords holding the title of Earl of York. He was proud of his family's long history – more than a thousand years of the House of Montfort. He occasionally toyed with the idea of returning to their original name, an ancestor having anglicised it after the Anglo-French War of the late 1700s.

The library was the room in which Gerald received most of his visitors, although for tonight's guest a different part of the hall served the purpose better. The fire was now dwindling, but he knew that as soon as he left the room, a servant would enter to ensure it was just as he preferred when he returned. Montford expected his staff to meet his each and every expectation, but he also expected them to do so unobtrusively. Most of the staff, particularly the younger women, were happy to stay out of his way. There were the occasional dalliances, but they were often followed by the woman being quickly and quietly dismissed. Montford stood before the gilded mirror above the mantel and admired his reflection. His strong face, piercing blue eyes and neatly combed full head of hair belied his age. Gerald looked like a man ten years younger than his fifty-five years. His hair was slightly greyed at the temples, but careful dyeing maintained his younger look. He pushed his hair back and, satisfied with the effect, left the room.

The cavernous hallway resounded with each footfall as Gerald walked purposefully towards the old chapel. The oratory would be cold and rather stark in comparison to the rest of Montford Hall, and in Gerald's time as earl, it was rarely used. Its choice as tonight's venue was calculated. His guest was a devout man, who for years had venerated his employer. Gerald strode into the chapel to find his guest, dressed from head to toe in black, standing in front of the stone altar. As the huge man turned to face his host, Gerald made the sign of the cross for effect. These meetings were the only time he bothered with such superstition.

"Welcome, my friend," Gerald said regally, embracing his shaven-headed visitor.

Popa nodded respectfully. "I am sorry I cannot deliver what you want," he said, in a gentle, childlike voice that jarred with his imposing physical presence.

"It is disappointing. Our cause is delayed, but I am sure that when the time comes, you will find a way." Gerald chose his words carefully. His power over this man was almost absolute, but he knew that power was inextricably tied to the man's beliefs. He had known him for many years – ever since the Brotherhood had found him as a lost and lonely adolescent. In fact, it was more correct to say that Popa had been given to the Brotherhood.

Born in Ceauşescu's Romania, Tomás Popa grew up in a dystopian state that was unravelling before his eyes. The dictator was executed when Popa was ten years old. His mother was a nun who had been raped by a priest, and Popa spent his early years in a Romanian Orthodox monastery, where he learned that sacrifice was the most important virtue, aside from a blind devotion to God. During the Soviet era, his mother's Church, the Catholic Church, was suppressed by the state. Many of the Orthodox priests and powerful clergy were informers, providing the Securitate information received within the sanctity of confession. Many people disappeared. As a child, Tomás had always been taught that they were taken away because they were not devout enough. They had not sacrificed enough. When he was fourteen, the abbot, a pious and fanatical man, had given him into the service of the Brotherhood. Gerald's father was Grand Master at that time, though Gerald had seen through Popa's fearsome exterior to a simple young man, a simple servant who could be used.

Gerald had befriended Tomás and had told him that his name was to be revered; Tomás de Torquemada was the first Grand Inquisitor of Spain. 'God's soldier and leader of His quest to stamp out heresy.' A few years later, Gerald inherited the Brotherhood's leadership from his father and instilled in Tomás a single purpose for his life: to find the treasure of the heretics, the Cathars, and restore it to its rightful heirs.

"I will," Popa said earnestly, cutting through Gerald's thoughts.

"Tell me, Tomás, what did you find in the heretic's house?"

"There was a man. I didn't expect him." Gerald raised his eyebrows; the only visible sign of his increasing annoyance.

"Who? What was he doing there?"

"I do not know. I did not know what to do. I struck him down and left so he could not identify me."

"Who was he?" Gerald demanded.

"Lucas Shaw was the name on his credit card."

Gerald was surprised. His briefing had mentioned the estranged son but had described him as wayward and of no consequence. Perhaps there was a connection to Lucas Shaw that the Brotherhood had missed. Gerald was about to tell Tomás it was a shame he hadn't interrogated the man, but he checked himself. He did not want to encourage Popa to use his own judgement. He was a simple man, and the Brotherhood's quest was not as simple as Popa understood it to be.

Popa looked intently at Gerald, awaiting guidance.

"Could he have seen you?" Gerald asked.

"I don't think so."

Gerald paused a moment, as he considered what to do next. He would have much preferred to hear a definitive 'no'. "Did you check the house, as we discussed?"

"I went up to the study before I left. Nothing had been touched."

"Very well. Do not worry about Lucas Shaw for now," Gerald said, and the concern drained out of Tomás's face.

"What must I do?"

"For now, my friend, there is nothing for you to do. I feel we are closer to achieving God's will." Gerald smiled at the humble, devoted man before him. "You have served God well, Tomás. You have served the Brotherhood well. The work we are doing is of vital importance, and I am sure God knows of your devotion. There will come a time for you to attend to Lucas Shaw; however, this is not it. I have a different strategy in my mind. You may go."

Tomás Popa nodded his assent and turned to face the altar. He genuflected, uttered a short prayer, made the sign of the cross again and quietly disappeared out into the night.

11

A sense of anticipation once again washed over Luke. This must be the safe his father's killer was looking for! He inserted the key into the lock and it turned, but nothing happened. *How do I open this thing?* He reached for his phone, realising it was downstairs in the kitchen, charging. Taking the stairs two at a time, he almost tripped on the landing but did not slow down. He unplugged his phone and noticed he'd missed three messages. Win.

Hi Luke, are you coming in today?

??? That was just minutes later.

Luke, please call me urgently. Win. The last was ten minutes ago, and there was a missed call. It would wait another ten, he decided, sprinting back upstairs with the phone.

A quick search found some sites with instructions, although he didn't see any for a safe with a combination *and* a key. He left the key as it was, hoping he'd turned it the right way. *At least three turns to the left past zero.* He gave the dial four rotations anti-clockwise, stopping on the number 43. *Two turns to the right past zero, and stop on the second number.* He followed the instruction carefully, stopping on his birthday, 27. *One turn to the left, past zero, and stop on the final number.* Again, Luke dutifully carried out the instruction, stopping on number 70. He scrolled down on the phone. *Then turn the handle downward to open the safe.* "Shit." The safe did not have a handle. He pulled at the door, but it did not budge. "Shit! Shit! Shit!"

He searched once more and found an alternate set of instructions. *Now spin the dial to the right until it stops by itself.* The crucial final step, hopefully. He did as directed and gently pulled at the combination dial. The door opened, just as his phone rang.

"Hi, Win," Luke said, trying to sound pathetic.

"Are you coming in today?" Straight to business. She must be annoyed.

"I'm really sorry, but no, I still feel sick," he lied.

"Luke, this is becoming a serious problem now. I'm afraid I'm going to have to ask you to bring in a certificate from your doctor."

"Oh. Sure, whatever you need," he replied. "I'm sorry I didn't call earlier." Maybe he would be able to charm her when he went back to work.

"I also have to let you know that I've checked your available sick leave and, well, there isn't any," she said. "Will you be back tomorrow?"

"I'm afraid not," he improvised. "I'm still not feeling right and don't want to give this bug to anyone else." *Will she buy that?*

"All right. We need to talk when you get back." She hung up.

Maybe not.

Luke put his phone in his pocket and peered into the old safe. It looked like just a pile of old papers. He put his hand inside and withdrew a sheaf of ancient documents. As he did so, he heard a 'tink' of metal on metal. At the back was an old piece of jewellery or ornament of some sort, made from brass or bronze, maybe. It looked familiar, but he couldn't recall where he'd seen it before. *Looks like a cross with a head,* he thought.

The documents were more interesting. He unfolded the largest to reveal a map. Not the modern day version, but a heavily inscribed medieval map. It encompassed all of Britain and a good portion of Western Europe. There were passages of text that he couldn't read.

Where he could make out a few letters or words, the language looked like Latin. It also had numerous illustrations, some with text, many without. But the picture was too cluttered for Luke to make any real sense of, so he pushed it to one side.

The remaining documents were equally impenetrable. Penned in a difficult medieval script, they also appeared to be in Latin. Even so, Luke's curiosity was piqued, and the look and feel of the cache of documents brought back memories of his studies a decade earlier. He recalled one of his lecturers saying Latin was 'not an altogether bad second language for a historian'. But he hadn't taken the advice and couldn't think of anyone who could help him translate.

Luke could also remember his father shaking his head in disapproval when he'd failed firs- year law and changed direction to take history and sociology. Right now, studying these ancient parchments, history seemed much more useful. But at that time his father had challenged him, asking where his interest in 'the old, the irrelevant and the dead' had come from. Luke didn't know the answer to that either. Looking back, it made him wonder whether his father had known then about these documents, and this eight-hundred-year-old duty that passed down the Shaw family line. Luke's interest in history seemed to have more relevance now. It also made him wonder why he was working in a law firm.

He laid out the documents one by one on the desk and took photos of each. If he could find someone to translate, he could send copies and keep the originals. It then occurred to him that sending these documents over the Internet might not be a good idea. His father, and apparently many generations before Geoffrey, had gone to great lengths to keep them hidden. Perhaps there was another option. Sitting on top of the filing cabinet was a printer and scanner. He switched the device on and it whirred to life.

The old parchments fitted on the flatbed, but the map had to be copied in two parts. It wasn't a problem for Luke, though, and he'd carefully made reasonably good-quality copies of the whole set of documents before his tea had gone cold. Next, he returned the documents to the hidden safe and closed it. The wood panel slid back into place, but it wouldn't stay there. It needed the mouldings to hold it where it belonged. Using the letter opener's blade, Luke was able to push the tiny panel pins back into place and restore the panelling almost to its former state. He wished he'd been more careful when he'd levered them out. There were visible gouges in the timber. "Shit," he muttered, looking around the room. Then he remembered the picture of Whitby Abbey he'd left sitting on the desk. Fortunately, it covered the damage completely.

Satisfied with his morning's work, Luke locked up the house and walked out into the cool morning air. It was almost twelve o'clock when he reached the station.

12

The ocean spray had a pleasing effect. Bernard's skin was red and dry, his lips parched and cracked at each side of his mouth, and the salt stung his eyes. But the gentle spray of the cool waters of the channel between his homeland and the Kingdom of England made Bernard feel more alive than he had in days. Two days earlier, he had found the master of a small cog, an elegant ship reminiscent of the Viking longships of the past. The cog was taking wine and other goods to the markets of Poole on England's south coast. Bernard negotiated an inexpensive passage, having agreed to sleep in the crew's quarters. This morning, with a heavy heart, he made his way through the smoke of Cherbourg's cooking fires towards the port. With a fair wind, he expected to sight land tomorrow.

This voyage, like much of his travel through the Duchies of France, was a lonely one. The cog was an English ship, and the crewmen did not speak French. A quick study, Bernard was already picking up some of the northern language, but when he'd needed to ask a question, they did not understand him. He had tried to use their language, but they were not of a mind to listen. When it was possible, he preferred to stay on deck, although it required of him an alertness that he struggled with. The vast web of ropes that made their way across the deck and up to the two masts were perilously confusing, and Bernard struggled to keep safely out of their way. He would be glad to make landfall, acquire a horse and start his northbound journey. His health had not improved, and even the relative peace of the sea voyage had not diminished his exhaustion.

As he lay wearily on his hammock, Bernard recalled the stories he'd learned years ago of the Cathars of England. Their fate had caught up with them generations earlier. They had been all but destroyed when, in the year of Our Lord 1166, the Council of Oxford had abolished and outlawed Catharism. There were stories of a few surviving perfecti – those who defied the law and secretly carried on their practices.

He was sure there would be people willing to help; Catharism was a devotion that transcended laws, though he knew they dare not reveal themselves to Bernard for fear of arrest and torture. Equally, Bernard could not risk his sacred duty by exposing his beliefs to others. No, he would not risk arrest by trying to elicit help. He would travel unassumingly north, as had long been planned. God would surely preserve his strength and remaining vigour so his task could be completed.

His destination was the ancient borough of York, and he expected the journey from Poole to take two weeks, if he could secure a good enough horse. The House of York was also of the Plantagenet bloodline, originally from the County of Anjou in France. Although it was rumoured that a construction of a large cathedral had commenced some decades ago, York was administered by a sheriff and not by the Church. The Cathar parfait, whom Bernard sought, was known to very few in France, though he had been given counsel that this was a person he must locate and should trust. He hoped he could find her.

After making landfall, Bernard found his way from the port, through the unpleasant odours of piles of rotting fish on the sunlit dock, past the spoiled cargoes that had not withstood the summer heat, and the oppressive smoke from the coal and peat cooking fires. He trudged on into the town, and in the square he was able to acquire an adequate horse after much gesticulating and bartering in a mix of broken French and English. He was still exhausted and now worried, for his malaise had not improved. He'd heard many men say the sea air was a good tonic, although seemingly it had not aided him at all. Perhaps it was the long distance he had travelled.

Now in a foreign land, with people he could not understand, Bernard felt an eternity away from his beloved wife and son. He shook off his melancholy and drained the few remaining warm drops from his goatskin. Finding a trough with water clear enough to see through, he refilled it, slung it over his bony shoulder, wearily mounted the horse and rode slowly to the north-east.

Days later, a rasping wheeze had enveloped Bernard, deepening his growing fatigue and sickness. By the time he had arrived in Oxford, he had noticed with much alarm that his kerchief was now spattered with blood from the wretched coughing. With dwindling funds, Bernard had travelled to Osney Abbey, barely a mile west of Oxford. The abbey, he knew, was Augustinian, and the Augustine canons taught that 'nothing conquers except truth and the victory of truth is love'. He had been warmly welcomed and given his fill of food and water, although in truth his appetite had diminished to a mere fragment of itself.

The journey through the southern counties of this foreign land had not been without trouble. The Welsh to the west had started to push the English back and had railed against Henry III's taxes. Along the way, there had been soldiers and occasional skirmishes, though Bernard, as a simple and poor traveller, had been let alone. He had been warned also that to the north the Scots had amassed a large body of men at the border. It seemed to Bernard there was trouble everywhere.

Two weeks in the abbey did not rid Bernard of the malady, although it did not worsen and the cough seemed to carry less of his blood. The monks referred to his disease as phthisis, a term unfamiliar to Bernard. Whatever it may have been, the ailing had slowly transformed him from the hardy, robust man he'd been at Montségur, into a pale and weakened shadow of his former self. The monks worried that Bernard was losing his mind, often seeing him walking the grounds muttering to himself and tapping something inside his cloak for reassurance. Bernard reflected that his withering transformation had almost certainly started during the siege. All the people imprisoned inside the château had recognised that their plight was increasingly fraught, and hope had dwindled further with each passing day.

During his stay, Bernard had been able to borrow clothing in order to wash his tunic and his heavy cloak, their redolence having become increasingly overbearing. Even in the summer warmth, the cloak had taken two days to fully dry out, during which Bernard had nervously concealed his precious cargo within the borrowed habit. As he'd bathed, he looked in dismay at his wasted limbs, once strong and firm, now bony and weak. After his bath, he had panicked briefly and cried out when he thought he'd lost the borrowed habit with its precious cache. He rejoiced when a monk soon returned it, apologising for picking up the wrong one. The monks told him he should continue his respite, though he knew that was not possible. His despatch was of a far greater importance than Bernard himself. His was a higher calling.

The abbot wished him well for his journey as Bernard prepared to leave the relative safety of the abbey. His destination was still more than a week away, if he were able to make a good pace. During his stay, his horse had fared better than its travel-weary owner. The grasses by the River Thames were lush and plentiful. The abbot's construction of a canal to drive the abbey's mill had meant that the lands between the river and the abbey had been claimed, and the horse had been free to roam the pasture with the other animals.

Bernard slung his goatskin and satchel over his emaciated shoulders, mounted his horse and took his leave quietly, rather crestfallen at having to leave this place of peace, a town where scholars could debate the teachings of the Church, albeit with caution.

13

Fine mist and drizzle greeted Luke back in Bradford, and the excitement he'd felt finding the safe and its cache had slowly ebbed away. After a hot shower, he spent the rest of the afternoon listlessly wondering where his life was going. The implications of Geoffrey Shaw's letter and legacy could be lifechanging. Or not. They could be as much or as little, as Luke allowed them to be. He wished he had someone to talk it through with. Someone he could trust, confide in. He hadn't had a girlfriend for the best part of a year, and that relationship hadn't been particularly serious. The truth, he knew, was that most of his relationships hadn't been deep. He had more or less drifted from one to another, and had been accused more than once of being shallow or having a fear of commitment. He could still clearly remember Emma's parting shot.

His drinking companions were of little use. None of them took anything seriously, and they were not the sort of people to open up to. They were more likely to laugh at him and throw it all back in his face. None of them had offered any sympathy when Emma dumped him. Still, they were company, and he had no one else. A few pints with friends might push the depressing thoughts away, at least for a while. He took out his phone and texted the lads.

Pub? Within ten minutes he had four replies.

Can't. Date.

Yep. Half seven.

Working.

About an hour for me.

Half past seven. That was 45 minutes away. Perfect. He should have enough time to grab something to eat on the way and get to the pub around the same time as the other two. He jogged down the stairs and headed down the street with more of a spring in his step. Even though it wasn't much, he looked forward to some cheerful company and a bit of a laugh.

He reached the pub just before 7.45 to find his two friends already part way through their first beer and ribbing each other. He bought a pint and joined them.

"No chance man, she's way out of your league," Ben said to Nick. Ben's mop of untidy red hair made his incredulous facial expression even funnier.

Nick just sat with a wry grin on his face. "Hey, Luke," he said eventually.

"Lads," Luke replied.

"Nick thinks he's in with a chance. That blonde over there," Ben said, nodding towards the bar. Nick had dark brown hair and a full beard to match. Thoughtful dark eyes made him seem more intelligent than Ben, and he had good chat, Luke reflected. *Better than me,* he mused, even though people said they looked like they could be brothers. Nick might well be in with a chance.

Luke turned his head to see what the fuss was about and saw an attractive blonde looking directly at him. He quickly turned back. "Well, you don't see someone like that every day in this pub."

"No, you don't," Nick replied, climbing out of his seat. He surreptitiously straightened his shirt and went over to the bar.

"A fiver says she blanks him," Ben suggested.

"Not taking that bet," Luke replied, settling in to his chair.

"What's up, anyway?" Ben asked, shifting gears.

By the time Luke had given the most basic of details of his trip to Harrogate, Nick had returned to their table.

"Worth a try," Nick said casually. He shook his head, as if to push the woman out of his mind, and went on to regale the other two with his latest office news. When he'd finished his story, he gulped down the last of his beer. "Last man in, Luke. Your round."

It was their system. Unless they arrived together, they each bought their own first drink, and then the last one in bought the next round.

"All right." Luke stood and went up to the bar. As he waited, the blonde looked over at him again. *Was that a hint of a smile?*

"Your friend's a confident one."

At first, Luke didn't think she was talking to him, but there was nobody else at the bar. "Yeah, he's always like that." She was stunning, and her eyes were locked on his. He couldn't think what to say next.

"You look like a man with something on his mind," she observed.

"I've been sorting out my father's estate today." It was the first thing that popped into his head.

"Oh. I'm sorry to hear that." She gave Luke a sympathetic smile that set his heart racing. "It's not easy to lose someone close, I know. I lost a friend recently." She held his gaze and did not elaborate. He almost said 'we weren't close', but the barman was standing in front of him, waiting, so he ordered his round of drinks.

"Madison," she said, offering her hand.

"Luke. Nice to meet you." Her touch was gentle, her hand warm. His heart seemed to beat faster. "Can I buy you another drink?" Luke asked, looking at her almost-empty glass. *Dammit, that's such a cliché.*

"No, I'm fine. It's kind of you to offer." The barman took Luke's money, and he picked up the three pints. "I just want someone to talk to," Madison said. "Will you come back?" Luke beamed at her.

"I'd love to." *The lads are never going to believe this.* Luke carried the drinks over to Nick and Ben, both of whom had been staring at him as he walked over.

"What the fuck, Luke, are you getting a sympathy vote over there?"

Maybe Ben had been listening after all when he'd talked about his day, although Luke didn't think he'd sounded sad about it. He put the drinks down, passing Ben's across the table. "Her name is Madison, and she wants someone to talk to." Luke picked up his beer. "Being a gentleman, I am happy to help her out." He ignored the gagging sound Ben made, winked at Nick and left them alone, thinking maybe his luck had just improved.

14

Luke lay in bed, reflecting that this night had ended very differently from what he'd expected. At the pub, Madison had been great company. They'd talked for hours, about everything from his father to his work. She seemed sympathetic and interested, and asked him about his mother, about his relationship with his father, and they even talked about his rekindled interest in history. She was a breath of fresh air, also interested in history, and asked about the Harrogate house. 'I just love old houses,' she'd said.

Luke had forgotten all about Ben and Nick and didn't notice what time they left the pub. At least they'd had enough respect to leave him alone. That could have gone either way, but he'd been so fully absorbed in the conversation with Madison he hadn't thought about it. By the time they'd bought their next drink, Luke had started to talk about his anger with his father, and he felt he might have unfairly unloaded some of his baggage on her. But when he asked Madison about her recent loss of a friend, she didn't want to talk about it. 'Oh, it's all right, just that sometimes life doesn't go the way you want it to,' was all she'd said. She had a way of gently directing the conversation, and Luke had been perfectly happy to go with the flow. She made it very easy to talk, and it was just what he needed.

As they'd left the pub, the drizzle started up again. Luke suggested a coffee at the cosy café just up the road, but as they walked, the drizzle turned into rain, and they ducked into a doorway for shelter. They squeezed into the tiny space, and Madison said she was cold, putting her hand into his pocket. Luke put his arm around her, and she leaned forward and kissed him softly. 'I have another idea,' she whispered into his ear.

"Mmm," Madison sighed as she woke up, and pressed her warm, lithe body against his. Her shoulder-length soft curls caressed his chest as he felt her hand reaching down past his stomach. "I'm sure you must have some more energy left for me," she said sweetly.

The morning light poured through the gap between the curtains that Luke hadn't closed properly the night before. He remembered tossing their wet clothing across the chair in his bedroom in their haste but looked over and couldn't see it now. Madison was already out of bed and he could hear the shower running. He got up and eventually spotted his things on the clothes airer in the sitting room. They were dry, so he assumed she must have moved them during the night; hers weren't there. He threw his into the laundry and called out to her. "Hey."

"Hi," she called back. She emerged from the bathroom and they changed places as Luke went in for his shower. He kissed her on the way past, but she cut him short. 'Not now'. As he showered, he looked at the damp walls and the patches of mould on the ceiling of the windowless room, wishing it wasn't quite so bad. When he finished, Madison was in the kitchen looking in the fridge.

"Sorry. I don't keep much here." *Sorry this place is such a dump.* "It's just a place to sleep," Luke said sheepishly.

"That's okay. I'll pick up something on the way."

"Do you have to go to work?" Luke asked. He realised they hadn't talked about her life at all.

"Well, now you don't have to stay in this place if you don't want to."

She ignored his question. "Your father's house sounds lovely. You could live there."

"It's a bit far from work."

"Oh yes, the job you told me you hated." She misread the change in his expression. "Sorry. Not my business."

"It's fine. You're right. I was actually wondering why I haven't bothered to find a better job."

"Do you have any coffee?" she asked.

"No. Just tea." She waited for him to go on. "In the cupboard above the kettle. I'll make it." He went into the little kitchen at the back of the sitting room, found two clean cups and made some tea.

"Maybe it is time for a change," he mused. "I grew up in Leeds, after we came over from New Zealand, and I only moved to Bradford to study. My parents never lived here. My father moved to Harrogate while I was at Bradford University. I suppose I'm still here simply because I never made the decision to leave. I don't even know where home is."

Madison looked at him. Her gaze had a way of getting inside his thoughts. And she was gorgeous, even after little sleep and wearing yesterday's clothes. "You were more enthusiastic last night when you talked about the Harrogate house, and how you felt."

"I suppose it brought back some memories for me. Mum's piano was there. I don't know why my father took it up from Leeds. He didn't play. I still remember Mum showing me how to play chords. The house seemed to have something of her in it, even though she never lived there." He recalled the picture of Whitby, and that family holiday. She nodded silently for him to go on. "I was just reminiscing. Does that sound silly to you?"

"No. I wish I had memories like that. I can see it makes you feel better to talk about it. Tell me more." Madison encouraged Luke to talk about his trip to Harrogate, and how he'd felt when he'd seen the solicitor. Luke just let it all pour out. It was cathartic. He told her about his visit to Valley Gardens, and the New Zealand Garden, but then she had to leave.

"Damn," she said, looking at her watch and cutting him short. "I have to go to a meeting." She gave him a lingering kiss that left him wanting more, then she took her phone out. "What's your number?"

Luke gave her the number, and seconds later his phone pinged with a new message. She watched as he unlocked it and read the message.

Madison. And a kiss emoji.

"Now we can contact each other," she said, walking towards the door. "I'm busy for the next few days, though." And with that, Madison closed the door, leaving Luke staring at it with no idea what to say.

15

Madison's quick departure left Luke wondering. It had been a night he wouldn't forget for a long time, partly because he just needed someone to talk to, but also because she'd made him feel wanted. She was a surprising woman in many ways, although she hadn't told him much about herself. Nonetheless, she'd planted a seed in his mind. Maybe it was time to get out of Bradford and make some changes in his life. With his inheritance and the legacy his father's letter described, things were changing around him. Time to take some control.

For the first time since the previous afternoon, he thought again about the documents he'd found in the hidden safe. He retrieved them from the kitchen drawer, wondering briefly whether Madison had seen them when she was searching for coffee. Probably not, he decided. Surely she would have asked about them? But what to do next? He unfolded the map on the kitchen bench. With no understanding of Latin, he could make no sense of the documents. Studying the map once again, he saw numerous strange symbols and a few passages of the dead language. The most prominent symbols seemed to be spread out towards the four sides. But what did they mean? He needed help but didn't know how to find it. Maybe at the university? Luke didn't know where to begin. He searched 'ancient maps' on his phone and found a great deal, but none of it helpful. Then he tried searching the maps app for something useful and *local*, which yielded more promising results. After trying a few search terms, he'd got the university and the JB Priestley Library, various museums and a rare-book store that sounded interesting. Geo. Sutherland Rare Books, Maps and Antiquities. It was a fifteen-minute walk. Could he risk showing someone there? Or would the JB Priestley be a safer option?

In the end, it was a matter of convenience. The bookshop was much closer. He rationalised that if what he had was truly of some significance, the bookshop seemed far less likely to make a fuss, or to be connected with anyone who might. So he grabbed a backpack and headed out with his printed copies.

Luke surprised himself by whistling as he walked. He thought of Madison and smiled. He'd wanted some human company last night, and he'd certainly had that, and he reflected that it was probably the conversation just as much as the sex. The next time he saw Ben and Nick there would be a lot of questions, and a lot of banter. He chuckled as he remembered Nick being blanked. Luke had expected the same treatment and wasn't even going to bother to talk to her. He shook his head and laughed to himself. *I'm just a lucky guy.*

Most of the shops he went past didn't have numbers displayed, so he wasn't exactly sure where he was – less than a kilometre from his office, but this was not an area he visited. No pubs and kebab shops here. A little further along, he found the place he was searching for. The sign hanging from the awning was a subtle, old-fashioned one, and he almost went right past. In the front window were dusty-looking tomes spread out sparsely on the shelves. The window announced Geo. Sutherland Rare Books, Maps and Antiquities in gold-leaf copperplate lettering.

Even the door was an antiquity. As it creaked open, an old-fashioned bell rang above it. It was empty except for the shop assistant sitting behind the counter, reading. She didn't look up. The air in the room was cooler than outside and had a vaguely familiar aroma. Evocative in its own way and not unpleasant. He closed his eyes momentarily and could imagine the smell of the ancient papers in his father's hidden safe as he inhaled. He opened his eyes to see the young woman looking at him. He smiled at her, but she quickly went back to her book. To the left of the small counter were rows of bookshelves, and in front of those, two tables with banker's lamps. The tables were vacant but the lamps were lit, their green glass shades providing the only colour against the dark-brown timbers everywhere else. It was a peaceful, strangely relaxing place.

Against the opposite wall was a small display case with several map prints and an ancient-looking globe on a brass stand. A sign inside the glass top identified one of them as an eighteenth-century copy of Ptolemy's world map, circa 150 AD. It looked almost like a modern version, except for the ornate drawings of faces around its perimeter and the obvious cartographical errors. Luke could make out the Mediterranean Sea, Europe, Africa and the Red Sea, but it appeared to depict the Indian Ocean as surrounded by land on all sides, and some of the landmasses were unfamiliar. There was a large island where India should be. The antique globe next to the map looked more accurate, and its plaque stated it was a 1960s copy of a late-nineteenth-century globe. Near the base of the case was a neatly typed explanation of ancient map-making techniques and the meanings of some of the more common illustrations used by medieval and earlier map-makers. *I'm in the right place.* He went over to the counter, clearing his throat gently.

The girl behind the counter put her book down and looked up. "Can I help?" she asked in a quiet voice. She looked rather bookish. Her hair was parted in the centre and pulled back tightly. Her black-framed glasses masked her eyes. He could see that she was about his age and wondered why a young woman would choose to work in a place like this. She must like solitude.

"Hi. I'm not sure. I'm trying to make sense of an old map that's been in my family for a while," he started, opening his backpack to pull out the rolled-up A3 copies. "Maybe you can help me out." Luke thought she was too young to be of much help.

She peered at the map as Luke held the sides. She carefully overlaid the copies to show a single picture and took two long steel rulers from under the counter to hold the edges down in place. "Maybe," she said, without looking up. "I studied history and language. Including Latin." She pointed at one of the text passages. Silently she pored over it, leaning towards Luke from time to time as she examined the text. "Do you have the original?" She did not lift her gaze.

Luke wasn't sure how he should answer her question; after all, his father's letter had sworn him to secrecy. Though he knew it would not make sense for him to have come to the shop if all he had was a worthless printed colour copy. "Yeah, I do. It's been stored away for a while." *Longer than you might think.*

"I've never seen this before. The form is consistent with others of its time, but this one is different. And these Latin texts will need some work, I think." She looked up at Luke and he could see a glint in her eyes that wasn't there earlier. "It's quite unusual." Her newfound enthusiasm softened the severe look that her firmly pulled back hair gave her. At first, she had seemed sad, or somehow fragile, but as she held his gaze for a moment before looking down again, he decided she was probably just a little shy or reserved.

"What do you make of the symbols on it?" Luke was fishing. Part of him wondered whether he had some sort of ancient treasure map, and he wanted to know more.

"Symbols like these are very common on medieval maps. I'd have to spend a bit of time on the texts to reliably ... um ... *decipher* them." She didn't look up. "That's unusual," she added, pointing at an illustration near the top that looked to Luke like four columns or pillars. She appeared engrossed in it. "I love maps like this," she muttered quietly to herself. It made Luke smile.

A minute later she looked up at Luke enquiringly. "Did you say it's been in your family for a while?"

"Yeah, I didn't know we had it. It was with some old stuff I just inherited from my father." He couldn't decide whether to tell her more or not. She seemed very genuine, and if she could translate the Latin text that would be really helpful. Luke knew he couldn't do it himself so had to ask *somebody*.

"I'm Luke, by the way."

She looked at his hand for a moment as he reached out to shake hers. "Oh, sorry. Michaela." Her skin was cool to Luke's touch. She gave him a brief, self-conscious smile as they shook hands.

"What would be involved in getting this properly translated?" He was expecting her to give him a price to consider, as he weighed up how much he should tell her.

"It's not something we normally do, but I'm happy to help you. This could be a significant find. It might be quite valuable." She held his gaze for longer this time, and he could see nothing in her eyes other than genuine curiosity. He made his mind up to trust her.

"That would be brilliant. Thanks." He grinned at her. "How long would you need?"

"A few days. Possibly a week."

"Okay, great. Um, how much will this cost?" He would pay for it from Geoffrey's money but didn't want to get a shock later.

"Don't worry about that. I'll just do it in my spare time," she said. "I like this sort of thing."

Luke was surprised but tried not to show it. "That's very nice of you. I don't mind paying you for your time."

"No." She shook her head, and a braid of dark-brown hair gently tossed from side to side.

"Would you mind keeping this to yourself? I don't know what I have yet ... or what I want to do with it, so ..." His voice trailed off as he hoped he didn't sound foolish.

16

The nights had become much colder, and Bernard found it difficult to sleep, even when the weather was dry enough to coax a fire from the abundant wood. He had been in the forest north of Nottingham for two days and his supply of food was very low. He'd finished the last of his bread although still had some chestnuts he'd gathered the previous day. The weather had been poor last night, so he had not been able to roast them in the coals of a fire. The meagre portion of the bitter raw nuts he had been able to eat had made him feel ill.

In the town he heard rumours of outlaws roaming this wood, but he had encountered no one. Bernard also noticed that as he travelled further north, the language had changed subtly. He had picked up enough of the unfamiliar English tongue to barter for supplies, but there was a different nuance to it here. Different words and more guttural sounds. He assumed these lands must once have been visited by someone other than the French.

Nightfall approached, so Bernard found a place to rest, a little way off the beaten path in a stand of oaks. He tethered his horse and set about building a fire. He felt weak and light-headed, and knew he needed a meal. He gathered dry twigs and pine needles, and some sticks and small branches, then set to work with his flint and steel. Soon he had a small but tenuous fire started, and carefully added larger twigs, blowing gently on it until it took hold. He was tempted to make a large pyre but knew that would only serve to attract the attention of anyone nearby. The moderate blaze was as large as he dared make it, and while he warmed his weary bones, he placed the remaining chestnuts into the outer edge of the glowing coals.

A short while later, with a little perseverance, Bernard removed the shells of the sweet, fleshy nuts, in his haste burning his fingers slightly. It was worth the effort, as he was able to enjoy his first reasonable meal in several days. With his last remaining energy, he gathered some small branches, made a simple shelter using a low limb of nearby oak tree, and cleared a place to sleep. His exhaustion had all but consumed him, the only thing driving him on being his precious artefact. As he lay on the cold earth, he thought once more of his wife and son. With an omnipresent chill in his heart, he turned his back to the dwindling fire, willing its weak glow to warm his aching bones.

The approaching dawn brought the sound of leaves rustling and a twig breaking. Bernard was instantly alert, although the aching in his back impeded his movements. He turned his head slowly and carefully, straining in the dim twilight to see what had startled him. The horse was still tethered to the tree and did not seem to be anxious or spooked. Half expecting to see the rumoured band of outlaws come to rob him of his meagre possessions, Bernard looked through the trees for anything that did not belong. He winced as he turned and was relieved to lock eyes with a large deer standing by an oak across the clearing.

Bernard relaxed and exhaled, dropping his head to his chest. As he moved, the spell was broken and the deer darted quietly away into the forest. The majestic beast had nothing to fear from Bernard. He had not killed an animal nor eaten meat since he had adopted the Cathar faith decades earlier. In any event, he had been forewarned that the hunting of deer was forbidden, except by the express permission of the king.

After a deep drink from his goatskin, Bernard pushed himself up onto his feet, untied his horse and, with more strength than he knew he had, mounted the beast and returned to the path.

As the sun broke away from the horizon, Bernard crossed the River Meden and left the King's forest. The terrain had become less difficult, and the closeness of his destination spurred him forward. The horse would be well rested in York, so he quickened the pace. The weather was pleasant and a light breeze cheered him. The day's travels were uneventful, and he encountered very few fellow travellers. Recognising a foreign voice, they treated him warily, quietly nodding and riding on. Along the way, he passed orchards where he found apples on the ground outside the stone walls, along with some almost ripe walnuts. It was a meal he could eat without pausing his horseback journey.

The hours passed quickly, and Bernard reached York, just south of the River Ouse, as dusk approached. A light rain had just started to fall, and the little remaining vitality within him was spent. He felt he could travel no further. He would need to find lodgings for the night.

He passed through a gate in the old stone wall, and the smell of the town assailed his senses. The air was thick and fetid. A little way on, he saw rows of houses that were small and crammed together, and many had offal and other waste tossed carelessly outside. He rode slowly on, towards the tower of the cathedral he could see in the distance. As he crossed the river, he stopped for the horse to drink and to refill his goatskin.

Across the bridge, the houses were larger and the pungent odour less overpowering. Bernard was tempted to follow the directions he'd been given to find the parfait, although worried that he was so exhausted he might make a mistake. In this foreign land, in a town where a magnificent cathedral was being built by the church, a mistake could be fatal. He came upon an inn and decided that lodgings for the night would be wise. He could begin his search the next morning. He tethered the horse at the trough and opened the inn's door, mustering the best air of confidence he could.

As he entered, the conversations hushed slightly as people turned to look. A few of the patrons gave the weary traveller a nod, and most went back to their lively talk. There were no unoccupied tables and few unoccupied chairs. He would have to ask to share, thereby revealing his foreign origin. As he made his way to a table with only one man seated, he saw the large pig skewered in the centre of the cavernous hearth. Next to it was a row of fowl slowly roasting. He saw no sign of any vegetable. A meal in this place would consist of little more than ale.

His lament was interrupted as a plump and curvaceous woman accosted him, suggesting she had a room at the back. She reached for his crotch and Bernard turned and fled, much to the amusement of the men seated near where he had been standing. The woman called something after him, prompting them to laugh more loudly, but Bernard was not familiar with the words.

Outside, he ambled back to the trough to find his horse was gone. Presumably taken by an opportunistic thief. His shoulders slumped further. *What now? Am I being tested?* He surveyed his surroundings, deciding that pressing on towards the square, in search of better food and somewhere to sleep, was his safest option. Pulling himself together, he tried his best to shrug off the aches in his bones, and trudged in the direction of the tower. The square wasn't far. After finding suitable sustenance, he noticed one of the signs he was looking for, a marker for the parfait. He made a snap decision to find her tonight.

He sat on an unused hitching post and quickly ate, pausing to open his leather satchel and withdraw the slender manuscript. It was as he'd remembered; after the marker he'd seen, there were three more pointers, all leading him towards the 'rose and mortar'. Unfortunately, there was no indication as to the meaning of rose and mortar. It seemed an odd combination. Nonetheless, Bernard carefully followed the directions and found himself in a narrow, cobbled lane reminiscent of the fetid streets he had first encountered. In the pale moonlight and drizzle, visibility was poor. He walked the length of the lane, finding only a rudimentary sign for the mortar and pestle, possibly a symbol for a healer. Cold, wet and still coughing blood, he thought he needed a healer's help, but he knew if he stopped now, he would not have the strength to continue without resting first.

He steeled himself and searched again along the cobblestone path, squinting into the darkness for a sign of a rose, but found nothing. He resolved to give it one more attempt before returning to the square to seek safe lodgings. He'd been to the end of the lane and back, studying dwellings on both sides, and was almost ready to give up when, more by chance than skill, he found what he sought. It was on the front of the cottage with the mortar and pestle sign. Above each of the tiny front windows, carved into the architrave, was a small, but beautifully intricate rose. He could not be sure that he had found the right place, but he was spent and sure he could go no further.

He called out, almost from sheer relief, and knocked at the same time. Presently, the door opened, just a crack, and Bernard saw the face of a middle-aged woman framed by the yellow lamplight behind her.

"Yes?" she said warily.

Bernard uttered the message he was told to give. The woman started to close the door, and Bernard repeated his message, this time more slowly. The woman stopped.

"I am Bernard de Péreille," he said weakly. "I have travelled far." Bernard slumped to his knees and fell forward.

17

For the first time in several days, Luke remembered to check his mail. Usually it was nothing more than advertising and bills. He unlocked the mailbox to find an invoice-sized envelope and a brochure from a nearby discount store. The envelope had an official-looking coat of arms on the front. Another notice about his late tax return maybe. Luke was tempted to throw it out with the junk mail, but upon closer inspection he realised it wasn't from the British Government – it was from the New Zealand Government. With the events in Harrogate, not least his being attacked in his father's house, he had forgotten to chase up his earlier enquiry.

He tore the envelope open hastily to find an official letter, and a copy of a birth certificate. His birth certificate. Lucas James Colley, born in Lower Hutt, New Zealand, 27 April 1987. He'd always known his middle name to be Geoffrey, after his father, not James. His birth mother's name was Susan Elizabeth Colley, and she was born in 1970. Her occupation was recorded as 'student'. She would have been seventeen when Luke was born. Barely even middle-aged now, assuming she was still alive. The section for his father was blank.

The possible implications started to flow into his mind. *It was the eighties. Women weren't forced to give up their children, were they? Why did she abandon me? Was she simply too young? How had she felt? Is she still alive and well? Is she married now? Does she have any other children? Do I have brothers and sisters?* Too many questions. She was born in 1970. Perhaps that was the 70 in the safe combination. *But how would Geoffrey have known that?*

He picked up the letter. It was from Oranga Tamariki, the Ministry for Children. It said his birth mother had authorised the release of his birth certificate should he ever come looking for it. She'd done it very soon after the adoption. He sat on the couch and let out a long sigh. *Now what?* He didn't know what to do. Or how to feel.

Before finding the letter, he'd spent most of the afternoon sitting around in his flat, thinking. He mulled over his options. *Should I get out of Bradford finally? To Harrogate? Or back to Leeds? Or London? And what about work?* He would have to go to work on Monday, and Win was going to be annoyed. He hoped he hadn't pushed her too far this time. He knew she bore the brunt of the partners' irritation when they needed IT support and he wasn't around. And there was Madison. A memorable night in a lot of ways. But she'd left this morning in a way that made him wonder what the future could hold. He knew very little about her.

This morning, at the rare book shop, he'd risked trusting the shop assistant. Hopefully that would lead to further insight into the map. *Hopefully.* Maybe he should have given her the other documents, too. Well, he could do that next time they met. She'd said maybe a week to translate and decipher it; all he could do was wait. So wait he would. Back to work on Monday, back to the routine of his life, and just let the next few days or week unfold around him.

But the letter had changed all that.

Feeling restless, he went into the tiny kitchen to make a cup of tea. While it brewed he surveyed his humble abode. Very humble. In fact, depressing. *How did life get like this? Just drifting from one day to the next, rudderless?* Luke decided to treat himself to a nice dinner, albeit a solitary one. He finished his tea, put a jacket on and headed down the street towards the city. There wasn't a huge choice in his area, so he ultimately settled for a curry. *I need to get out of here*, he thought.

After his dinner, he walked back home and, almost without thinking, stopped in at his local pub, hoping for a bit of company. But it wasn't to be. Saturday wasn't their night. Friday was the lads' regular big night. He bought a pint anyway and sat on the last vacant bar stool. For the first time in as long as he could remember, he *noticed* people. The pub wasn't as noisy as a busy week night, though there were a few rowdy groups. But as Luke scanned the room he saw a surprising number of people drinking alone. Sad, lonely-looking people, many of them just staring into their drinks. *Am I going to be one of them?* He looked at his reflection in the mirror behind the bar. *Am I already one of them?* A depressing thought, but one that sparked something in him. *I don't have to be.* He quickly finished his beer, more from habit than thirst, and left.

For a Saturday night, he was back at his flat unusually early. And unusually sober. He reread the letter from the children's agency in New Zealand and studied his birth certificate again. It was a tangible connection, although a tenuous one, to his history, and to his birth mother, Susan Elizabeth Colley. The agency's contact phone number was on the letter, and he was about to call when he realised it would be Sunday morning in New Zealand. Would they have any further information anyway? It seemed their last contact from Susan Colley had been when Luke was probably still in nappies. How would they know where she was? And would they tell him? Then he searched online, scanning the Wellington phone directory for S Colley. Nothing. There were no Colleys in Wellington. *Dammit, she must have got married and changed her name, or moved away. Or died.*

He tried a wider search, this time looking for anything in New Zealand, and third from the top there was an S Colley in the directory. Did he miss her the first time? He searched again for S Colley without specifying a location, and sure enough, there it was. S E Colley in Lower Hutt. He felt a lump in his throat. *Could this be her? Have I found my biological mother?* He wrote the phone number down and looked at it. *What do I say? 'Hi Mum, it's me, your son'?* Maybe he should call her in the morning. *No, then it will be night over there. Too late?* A silent debate raged on in Luke's mind, until he realised he was procrastinating. *Just do it!*

"Hello." His call was answered on the third ring. A woman's voice. He tried to picture her, unsuccessfully.

"Um, hello. Am I speaking to Susan Colley?"

"Yes, Sue speaking. Who is this?"

"Um, my name is Luke Shaw, I'm calling you fro-" He stopped short as he heard her sudden intake of breath. "Lucas Shaw, calling from Bradford," he continued. There was silence at the other end. "Is that Susan Elizabeth Colley?" He knew the answer before he'd finished asking. There was a brief pause.

"Yes," she replied in a faint, shaky voice.

"I think I am ... I might be ..." He wished he could see her face.

"My son," she completed. Luke could hear her quietly sobbing. "I've always hoped ..." She spoke through her tears.

"It's ... amazing. To hear your voice. Six weeks ago I didn't know my mother wasn't my real ... my birth mother. And now I'm talking to you."

"I'm so sorry I gave you up. I wanted you to have a better life. I ..." She sounded distressed. "Were you happy? *Are* you happy?"

"Yeah, I guess. Mostly. Mum died fifteen years ago, and my father, well, struggled a bit." Luke chose his words carefully, he didn't want to worry her.

"Your father? Is he ...?" *Did she know him?*

"He died two months ago. He'd written me a letter telling me I was adopted. We hadn't talked for a while."

"Oh dear, I'm sorry to hear that."

"It's all right." Luke wanted to be able to give her a hug. This was difficult over the phone. "Could I come to meet you?" It was a spur-of-the-moment idea, and Luke knew as he said it that his voice sounded like a child's. "If you need some time, I'll understand," he quickly added.

"I don't need any time. I would love to see you."

18

The woman helped Bernard into the warm house. "You are ill," she observed. Bernard responded by coughing violently, and as he coughed into the kerchief, the woman noticed the blood. She looked him up and down, taking in his withered limbs and sallow, gaunt face and rheumy eyes. "Phthisis," she said, shaking her head. "You must rest. I am Eleanor. My mother named me for Eleanor of Aquitaine, a king's wife, born near your home." Eleanor must have recognised Bernard's accent.

She led Bernard to a thick carpet in the corner of the room, on which sat a mattress of straw. As Bernard lay down, he looked upon the woman, thinking that she reminded him of his wife, although older. Hers was a faded, but peaceful, understated beauty.

"God brought you to my door." She left the room, taking the blackened kettle from the fireplace.

Bernard heard her working in the next room, perhaps a scullery. Across the small room, the low fire in the generous hearth slowly burned lumps of peat, infusing the lamplit room with a strangely sweet smell. He also took in a subtle herbal aroma, perhaps emanating from the next room. Eleanor returned with a large cup of a steaming, greenish-brown liquid and handed it to Bernard.

"Drink slowly," she said. "It will help you." She said the words matter-of-factly, without overt sympathy.

Bernard drank the warm, bitter potion as instructed.

"Good. Now, when was your last meal?" she asked.

Bernard answered weakly, "I am not hungry."

She ignored his answer and went into the scullery, returning a moment later with a small bowl of a thick broth made with onions, parsnips and herbs that did not smell familiar.

"Eat," she said firmly.

Bernard awoke as the dawn's early light penetrated the dark room. Eleanor sat on a bench near the hearth, occasionally stirring a metal pot hanging over the small fire in the hearth. For the first time in many days, he felt rested. Eleanor went into the next room and returned with a cup of the green concoction, and Bernard dutifully drank the liquid.

"You have made a difficult journey," she said blandly.

"Yes. A dark wind blows across my homeland."

"And mine. We must live in the shadows." She handed Bernard a bowl of a thick porridge made with barley. As he started to eat it, he realised that his appetite had also begun to return.

"I see that my tonic has soothed you, but I also see that you have lived with the phthisis for some time. It consumes you." Eleanor spoke unemotionally. For her, Bernard's condition was merely the will of God. He would live or die as God pleased, and death would free his soul. Strangely, her manner made him more comfortable. It was the way of the Cathars. Bernard knew he did not have much life left in him, and he needed to know that he could trust the woman.

"There is a magnificent edifice being built in York," he ventured.

"It is not magnificent. It is immoral. Good men have died for powerful men who desire ornaments." Her expression spoke to Bernard of her repugnance. *A good sign.* Then her face changed; perhaps she feared she had said too much.

"Such monuments are all over my homeland also. Many have died." Bernard quietly uttered a lament in his native language.

"Yes. It is a travesty," Eleanor replied.

"You speak Occitan?"

"I spent some years in Toulouse and Carcassonne when I was younger," she explained. "Carcassonne is where I learned the healing."

Bernard decided to test whether he should trust her. "I have travelled very far for my cause," he started.

"Yes. It is written in your eyes."

"The church is too powerful," he said.

"Yet it seeks more power."

"There is an ancient knowledge it seeks."

"Wealthy men seek money. Powerful men seek power. It is the way of this wicked mortal world." Eleanor spoke the words with a deeply felt sadness in her heart. "Yet our wisdom," – here she spoke of the gnostic traditions – "comes to us from the ancients. It cannot be taken, it must be given."

Bernard was satisfied that he had heard enough to trust Eleanor of York. "This knowledge is as old as time. It has come from a lost golden age, an age of harmony."

"An age that seems distant," she bemoaned.

"I travel with one of the four talismans of the ancients."

Eleanor's face indicated to Bernard that she had guessed as much. "You have brought it to a place where the church grows stronger."

"I have brought it *from* a place where the faithful are slaughtered." Bernard's tears welled up as he pictured his wife and child, and his beloved brother Raymond. "The talisman must be concealed. It must be safeguarded for when its time comes," he said vehemently, coughing as he did so.

"I have thought about this," Eleanor said, confirming that she had indeed guessed the purpose of his arduous journey. "I know of a place."

Bernard nodded, hoping he had sufficient strength remaining to make the talisman's final journey.

"It is two days' walk," she said, as though reading his thoughts. "We can leave tomorrow, when more of your strength has returned."

"I have funds enough for horses," Bernard told Eleanor, showing her the pouch of coins. He was not confident he could manage two days' walk. She nodded. For the remainder of that day, Eleanor ministered to Bernard in her no-nonsense, impassive way, instructing him to eat and giving him another of the bitter green infusions with his evening meal. Bernard wondered about this woman's life, but his questions did not yield much. She mentioned a daughter who had married a farmer from a nearby village, but ignored Bernard's subsequent question as to whether she had a husband.

Soon after dawn the next day, Bernard and Eleanor walked to the square and purchased two horses. They were not young beasts but were adequate for their journey. The seller had agreed that he would buy them back if they returned in good health in a few days. Bernard had rested well the previous night and felt strong enough to make the journey, though he knew in his heart that his illness was not improving. Eleanor's tonic reduced the light-headedness and sweating, but little more. Even so, Bernard was pleased when she put some of her herbs into her satchel for the journey.

They travelled east and the sun warmed Bernard's face as they slowly rode. The town soon gave way to orchards and farms, and then open fields and forests. By late morning, they had crossed several rivers and streams, some forded and some requiring a careful wade across. With the sun almost directly overhead, they stopped to eat near a shaded copse. Lunch consisted of walnuts and a hard goat's cheese that Bernard did not much care for. Eleanor refilled their goatskin flasks in a stream nearby. Bernard had some difficulty mounting his horse, his strength once again sapped, but with Eleanor's help, they were soon on their way again, turning to the south.

By late afternoon, they reached a wide estuary, which Eleanor explained was where the River Ouse met the sea. She told Bernard that they were in the town of Hessle, where there was located a church protected by the Poor Fellow-Soldiers of Christ and of the Temple of Solomon. Bernard was shocked – the Knights Templar were well known for their role in the Crusades. They were responsible for thousands of Cathar deaths. Eleanor watched his face, and as he mulled over her logic for choosing this place, she saw a weak smile forming. *It's perfect! Right under the noses of the Catholics. They wouldn't think to look here.*

"It is suitable?" she asked. Bernard nodded. "I chose this particular church for many reasons. I know the priest died recently and has not yet been replaced, and I know the bishop does not make the journey to the coast very often. We should not be disturbed if we wander through the building to 'pay our respects'."

Bernard considered Eleanor's thinking to be sound. They entered the church, making the Catholic sign of the cross as they did so, albeit unnecessarily since the church appeared unoccupied. They walked around the inside of the building, around the transept and even the vestry, looking for somewhere that would remain undisturbed. It soon became apparent to both that there wasn't be a suitable hiding place within the body of the church itself.

"The crypt?" Bernard asked. They found the stairs that led to the building's undercroft and, underneath the altar, the crypt. There was evidence of work being done on the cellars, but, likely due to the late hour, it was now empty and quiet. Inside the crypt, a mason had evidently been inscribing a stone coffin, leaving his tools behind when he'd finished for the day. Bernard wearily sat on the edge of the empty casket, while Eleanor searched the crypt's alcoves. At the western end, under the altar, she found a small alcove with a dusty, decades-old sarcophagus resting on a plinth. She called Bernard over, and he struggled to his feet to hobble towards her.

It was a Templar knight's coffin. The alcove was a confined space, and neither of them could stand fully upright, but they could make out the Templar Cross, with its four equal arms, chiselled into the stone top.

"Will this suffice?" Eleanor asked.

"It's perfect," Bernard replied.

Eleanor brought the mason's tools over, and with a supreme effort they were able to lever the coffin lid up just enough to create a small gap. They let it fall back while Bernard removed the talisman from its hiding place within his cloak. Eleanor looked upon the object, an ancient ankh, in awe, before they prised up the stone lid again and slipped it into the Templar's sarcophagus, next to where the knight's skull would be lying.

Bernard's arms ached, and he was sweating even though it was cool in the crypt. He pushed his ills to one side and strained to use the mason's chisel to etch a simple marker into the stone surface above the Templar Cross. Later, he would have to inscribe a cross, along with his already-determined coded clues, into this location on his map. He dropped the mason's chisel as he realised he was completely out of breath. The ache in both his arms had turned into a more pressing pain, and he staggered out of the alcove. Eleanor picked up the tools and quickly returned them, covering the disturbance in the dust around the Templar's alcove as best she could. Bernard now struggled for breath.

Eleanor knew Bernard's condition was dire, but she also knew they needed to get out of the undercroft. They could not draw anyone's attention to their presence here. She helped him, half pushing him, up the stairs and into the nave. He cried out and put his hands to his chest, just as a young priest walked in. The man looked terrified and ran towards them as Bernard fell to his knees. Bernard pulled Eleanor close and thrust his satchel into her hands.

"The map, inscribe the map with the ..." Bernard gasped. He clawed at his chest as the priest reached them, and slumped forward onto Eleanor's feet, eyes half open in a hollow, unseeing stare.

19

When the boarding call came, Luke was deep in thought. The last two days had been a whirlwind, but as he waited in the long queues at Manchester Airport, doubts had started to seep in. He'd said 'could I come to meet you?' without even thinking, and Susan had sounded delighted he'd said it. *But what about my life here? What about Madison? Will she call? Will she just move on, disappear as suddenly as she appeared? And work, well, I've totally screwed that up.*

Yesterday morning he had gone into the office earlier than usual and found Win. He told her he would need more time off. He'd started to explain about finding his birth mother, but before he finished, she was rolling her eyes. 'I've given you every chance, Luke,' she'd said. 'We need someone responsible and dependable in this job. I can't just give you time off on a day's notice.' He lost his temper, calling her an insensitive cow, before storming out. Half an hour later, he calmed down and realised she was right, and she had given him plenty of chances. He knew he'd gone too far. He knew it when he booked his flights on Sunday morning without bothering to check. He called her to apologise, but she said she would expect his resignation. He could hear one of the partners in the background telling her off about something not working.

So, newly unemployed and feeling apprehensive, Luke boarded the long flight to Auckland, from where he would change for the hour-long flight to his birthplace, near Wellington.

Just over a day later, Luke climbed out of a taxi outside a small, tired-looking weatherboard house near the Hutt River, having checked in and left his suitcase at a Quality Inn a few kilometres away. At the front of the property was a large tree shading the front yard. The tree was not familiar to Luke. Its short trunk separated into a gnarled tangle of branches almost where it emerged from the ground. Overhead power lines crossed the driveway to the house and the one next door. The number on the weather-beaten letter box confirmed he was at the right address. Its front yard consisted of a neatly mown, but partly brown, dead lawn, although by the front porch were flowerpots on a stand providing a welcoming display of colour.

A slim woman with grey streaks in her mousy-brown hair emerged through the front door, her face breaking into a wide, unrestrained smile. She almost ran towards him, and Luke could not help but return the smile as he went to her. She hugged him tightly, tears streaming from her eyes. "I can't believe it," she sobbed into his shoulder.

Luke almost cried with her. The feeling in his chest as he hugged her was one he hadn't felt since his mother had died.

"I can't either," he said. "I didn't know ... I just got the letter on the weekend, and ..."

"Thank you so much for calling me. I can't tell you what this means to me. I've never forgotten. I've never forgiven myself for giving you up." She hugged him again, and he felt her tears on his cheeks.

"I'm really happy I called. And that I'm here." He beamed as she released her embrace, and he looked at her face again. A kind face, but there was loneliness in her eyes. He wondered what the intervening years had been like for her. "There's so much to catch up on," he said.

"Come in, come inside," she invited. "Have you eaten?"

"Yes. I'm fine, thanks."

"A cup of tea then?"

"Perfect." Luke followed her into the house, and into the small front sitting room. It was simply furnished, with just one picture on the wall, above the gas fire, and very few ornaments. A bookshelf against the wall was quite full. She brought in a tray with two cups, a small, cracked jug of milk and a sugar bowl.

"Thanks ..." He didn't know what he should call her. She'd said 'Sue' on the phone. In the end he settled for 'Mum', a little self-consciously. Her face lit up as he said it, and she started to cry again. He took the tray from her, set it down on the coffee table and gave her another hug. During the long flight, Luke had imagined how he might feel, how this reunion with his birth mother might unfold; he had worried that it might be awkward, or tense, or could go badly. But it was none of those things. He wasn't prepared for how he would feel. As he held his sobbing mother, he felt nothing but a blooming warmth in his heart. His tears finally flowed. It was a release he'd needed for years.

Over the next several hours, they told their stories to each other. Sue described the heart-wrenching events that culminated in being forced by her parents to give her baby up. She had been in her final school year, and Luke's biological father had dumped her as soon as he found out she was pregnant. She knew there wasn't much choice, but it had broken her heart. Her parents and Luke's grandparents had known each other back in Leeds. The two families had emigrated in the same year, and she had known Geoffrey Shaw, albeit distantly. His father had suggested the 'solution' to her parents, and they had jumped at the opportunity. It had been a very quick adoption. A social worker had taken Luke away while she slept, still in the maternity suite. She'd fallen asleep holding him and had woken up alone. She had never forgotten the feelings of loss and emptiness. She cried once more as she told the story. She kept telling herself it was for the best, but she had never recovered emotionally. Nor had her relationship with her parents. She couldn't bring herself to forgive them, and when they moved back to the United Kingdom a few years later, she refused to go with them. Her life was in New Zealand.

Her son, even though she could not see him, was in New Zealand.

Then, when Luke was seven, she'd heard his adoptive family were moving back to Leeds. By then, she was married, so moving across the world hadn't been an option. The Shaws had made it clear they would not be telling Luke he was adopted 'until he was older and able to understand' so had cut off any chance of contact.

"I tried hard to make my marriage work. We both did. But I think I was carrying too much baggage. In the end it didn't work out. We lasted just over five years, but ..." She paused to reflect a moment. "He was a good man, but, well, it was complicated."

Luke could see there was more to the story, but she didn't elaborate. "I'm sorry to hear that."

She saw the concern in his eyes. "Don't worry," she said. "There have been happy times, too. And I've always had you in my heart."

Luke told her about his adoptive mother and the happy years of his childhood. He told her he understood why she'd had no choice but to give him up. He wanted to ask why she hadn't tried to find him but didn't want to upset her. Instead, he told about his visit to Valley Gardens and the accidental discovery of the New Zealand Garden, and its symbol of new life, the koru. "It made me feel more connected to New Zealand. I still have good memories," he said.

"It's wonderful to hear those words. I've wanted to hear you say that ever since I gave you up."

"I don't know why my father never told me I was adopted. We didn't get on all that well, but I just don't get it. He thought it was important enough to write me a letter to be delivered after he died but never told me face to face."

"Maybe he just didn't know how. It's a complicated thing. Everybody reacts differently, I think," she suggested.

"I guess so. But now I'll never know. Now I've got no living relatives in England."

"Oh my God, how could I forget?" She put her hand up to her mouth. "You have an aunt. My sister Lisa." His eyes opened wider. Sue disappeared into the kitchen, returning with a box full of papers. "Lisa Williams. She kept her married name," she said, rummaging through the box to find an old letter. "Here it is. She's in Castleford. Or was, ten years ago. I think that's quite close to you, isn't it?"

"Yeah, about an hour on the train, I think."

"We don't keep in touch, I'm afraid. Just seem to have drifted apart," Sue said wistfully. "She has two girls, so you have cousins, too."

"Oh, do you have any pictures?"

"No, I don't. I'm sorry." Luke hoped he hadn't upset her, exposing another wound in her troubled life. Susan assured him it was all right and said she had something special she wanted to show him. She went off down the hallway and came back with an old music box. She opened it and withdrew a faded photograph of a girl with a baby, in a hospital bed.

"You were a few hours old. Lisa took it secretly and gave it to me later. My parents wouldn't allow it." Susan had been an attractive, bright-eyed young girl. The beatific smile she wore told Luke that she'd loved him. Luke stared at the picture, as he wondered what a childhood with her might have been like. It almost brought more tears to his eyes. He asked to take a photo of it.

The hours he'd spent with her passed quickly, their meandering conversation having taken them into the late afternoon. Luke's tiredness from the flight started to bite, and he yawned. "Sorry," he said. "Long trip. I probably should go, get an early dinner and get some sleep." He stood.

"I'm so glad you came, Luke. It's been a wonderful day." Susan went out with him, stopping under the shade of the big tree. "If you'd come at Christmas, you would have seen this tree in all its glory. It's a pōhutukawa. It has lovely crimson flowers in December."

"It's beautiful." He took his phone out. "I should get a ride."

"If you feel like walking, you can get back to your hotel along the riverbank. It's a nice walk."

"That sounds good." She took him through to her backyard and opened the gate to reveal the riverbank path. They hugged one more time. "Can I see you again tomorrow?"

"After work? I get home about five."

"Dinner then?"

They made their arrangements, and Luke left her standing by the gate, smiling.

20

The map had captivated Michaela. Perhaps it was partly because of Luke's odd request. When people of her age came into Sutherland's, it was usually to ask for a cash price for an old heirloom they'd found. But instead of asking its value, he'd wanted to know more about it. He appeared genuine, if a bit of a charmer, although when he asked her to keep it to herself, she thought she'd fleetingly glimpsed a lost little boy in his eyes. She took it home with her that same day, and after cooking herself some dinner, she cleared her small desk and set to work. She took a notepad from the drawer and spread the two A3 pages out on the desk, carefully aligning them to make a single image.

At first, it had looked like a typically embellished medieval map, but the Latin phrases that were carefully penned in various places offered the promise of a mystery to be solved. The illustrations also seemed to her to be more purposeful than was often the case. She had seen many ancient maps where the map-maker had aggrandised his work by adding beautiful pictures that had little meaning. Often they depicted mythical beasts or hidden treasures and were drawn in places where real cartographic detail was missing.

But this map had specific illustrations of objects, and the most elaborate of them were located next to cities and towns. The larger sections of text were close to these places. There were also areas with very little detail, and the map-maker had made no attempt to disguise his lack of knowledge with an extravagant sketch of a dragon or suchlike. It was as if these bare sections were simply *unimportant*. She took a photo of it, and then on her laptop, she overlaid it with a current map of Western Europe. The detail in it was approximately accurate, as anyone might have expected, but it was what was *not* there that surprised her. Looking at England, the City of London was only roughly drawn. Far more detail was, of course, known about London at the time than this cartographer had bothered with. The City of York was drawn in more detail and even had an illustration of York Minster. Then looking at France, she found the same thing. Paris was noted, but only the main routes in and out and the city wall were depicted. The cities of Toulouse and Carcassonne, like York, were shown in greater detail. It didn't make sense. Nor did it seem logical to her that the map-maker had not identified himself. That was most unusual. She rubbed her eyes and went into her kitchen to make a cup of tea.

Thinking that the sections of text might help her understand the strange map's anomalies, she started to work on translation. With a bit of effort and very close scrutiny, she was able to copy out each of the five prominent Latin sentences carefully. She then took a fresh page from her notepad and started the painstaking work of translating them from centuries-old Latin into modern English. The first passage she tackled was inscribed near York. As it gave up its meaning, she was disappointed. It appeared to be a religious warning, not uncommon for the period. On her first sheet of paper, under this first Latin phrase, she wrote in English:

The fate of man is dependent upon the forces of evil being kept at bay.

The next passage was written on an area of light cartographic detail in south-eastern France, near Carcassonne. It, too, seemed consistent with the custom and practice of the time. She finished the last of the cup of now-cold tea, and wrote her translation underneath the Latin:

[The tokens] are as old as time. [They] belong to a lost golden age.

They were just superstitious warnings. She looked at her watch and was surprised to find it was almost one am. Feeling disheartened, she set it aside for tomorrow and went to bed. There was still quite a long way to go before she would have something to share with Luke. But although she was tired, sleep would not come. She wondered where the map had come from. How had he obtained it? 'It's been in my family for a while,' he'd said. Perhaps it was just a fanciful drawing. But that was hard to believe; clearly a lot of work had gone into it, and its maker must have been a well-educated man to know Latin. Or maybe a priest? Eventually she went to sleep with those thoughts churning around in her head.

Michaela didn't like Sundays. Stuck at home with nothing to do. She'd lived in the same flat ever since moving back to Bradford after university in Manchester. She had stayed because the rent was affordable, and she could put money aside towards buying a place of her own. The few friends she'd kept in touch with were in Manchester and they rarely saw each other. The last time she'd been out with them, one of her girlfriends had tried to set her up with one of her single male friends. The night had ended with an awkward misunderstanding, and Michaela had been very embarrassed by the whole thing.

She could visit her parents, she supposed, but that had been somewhat strained, too, ever since she broke up with her boyfriend almost a year ago. He had been concealing his emerging drug habit from her, and she found out when she caught him stealing money from her. She'd felt betrayed, let down in the worst way. When she'd told her mother, instead of support, or at least sympathy, her mother said it was her own fault. 'You should have seen it coming. Your friends are all going nowhere. Why can't you do better?' When she'd reflected on it, she realised that all her life she had been criticised and taught to expect to fail.

She went out to pick up some groceries, but also just to get out of the flat for a while. After shopping, she treated herself to a freshly squeezed fruit juice at one of the new cafés that had recently sprung up. They were a definite improvement to the area, but she knew they probably also prompted her latest rent increase. The weather started to turn, so she hurried back, not quite getting inside her building before the rain came. She climbed the two flights of stairs to her flat and let herself in to shake off the wet and the cold.

After lunch she went back to the map. It seemed less exciting now, the text passages probably just religious warnings of little significance. But there were still three blocks of Latin to translate, so she sat at the desk and continued from where she'd left off the previous night. The next passage she chose was written on the Atlantic Ocean, just north-west of Lisbon. It did not come easily. Her first attempt didn't seem to make any sense, but after almost half an hour of writing, checking, erasing words and rewriting, she was satisfied it was correct:

No man may look upon more than two [tokens] else his life will be forfeit.

What could that mean? And 'tokens' again. Was that the right word? She made herself a cup of tea as she listened to the rain gently caressing her sitting room window.

The next Latin passage proved to be just as cryptic. It was inscribed upon the mountains near Florence – another important city that, inexplicably, was not depicted in as much detail as the smaller Siena to the south:

Scatter [the tokens] to the four winds, else disaster will strike.

It didn't make sense. *Am I missing something?* She finished her tea as she looked at the first four phrases again. Thinking purely literally, she was still happy with her work. The final passage, overlaid on the eastern Mediterranean, near Barcelona, was the briefest, but it was slightly different from the rest. It was also partially obscured by a blemish on the image, possibly a stain or some old damage to the original map. She was sure it was some kind of warning, but she wasn't content with her efforts so far. It needed more work. She decided to come back to it later.

She could not determine whether the locations the creator of the map had chosen for the text were in any way significant. All the Latin passages were inscribed on areas without much cartographic detail, so it could simply have been the cartographer finding convenient places to write. But why not just put them all together? Perhaps over the large, sparsely drawn Bay of Biscay? Or the Mediterranean? There didn't seem to be any logic to it. And these *tokens*? Is that what the map's maker had meant?

Michaela had translated the phrases literally, relying on her knowledge of the dead language. She knew that would be the usual approach of any trained academic, any translator. But she also knew there were other important factors to consider. She had told Luke she studied history and language. That was true, but her degree had been a joint honours degree; history and linguistics. Linguistics gave her a different perspective. She could draw upon her training in history also, allowing her to take into account the evolution of language over time, as well as the context and social norms from the period in which it was created. The choice of particular words and phrases by the map's creator would have been influenced by his beliefs, the events and norms of the day, and the way he perceived his intended audience.

With that in her mind, she now looked at the translated passages again. The first thing that struck her was the repeated Latin word *signum*, which she'd translated as 'token'. She'd put it in brackets because it could mean many things. Token, sign, image or idol, omen. It could be an object, or it could be prognostic, like 'a sign of things to come'. The third statement included the words 'look upon the *signa*', so *objects* or *tokens* seemed likely. She hadn't written 'amulet' because that should be *amoletum*, although an *amoletum* was an object whose purpose was to avert evil. But in the third and fourth passages, it appeared that these objects could be dangerous. Keep them apart, or 'life will be forfeit', and 'scatter [them] to the four winds to avert disaster'. *Can they be used for good **and** evil?* She crossed out the word 'token' and replaced it with 'talisman'.

During the Middle Ages, people believed in superstition. They believed in the power of good and evil. They believed in magic. *So, I've got references to objects that could avert, or create, a disaster? Are these mythical objects?* But they seemed real in the text. They had to be scattered to avert disaster. Satisfied that she'd done her best on the context for the phrases, she went back to the final passage. Her first attempt, she decided, was the best alternative, and the words she'd written gave her a chill:

Fate will be appeased by blood.

21

A cool breeze made for a pleasant stroll along the Hutt River path. On the way, Luke passed a group of boys throwing a rugby ball, and one of them passed it to him. He threw it back and they laughed good-naturedly at his wayward pass. Rugby was not Luke's game.

"Thanks, bro," the boy called, nodding at him.

Luke grinned back. "Cheers."

A little way further along, he found the right gate and let himself into his mother's backyard. He walked along the driveway around to the front door and knocked.

Susan opened the door with a wide smile. "Sorry, I'm not quite ready. Come in." She showed him into the sitting room. "I won't be long," she said over her shoulder, as she headed down the narrow hallway.

Luke went over to the bookshelf and saw that his mother must have a keen interest in history. There were a few novels, but the top two shelves were mostly lined with history books. They all looked worn, possibly bought second-hand, but one stood out. It was entitled *The Four Pillars of Gnosis: A Brief History of the Cathar Faith*. In the Bradford bookshop, Michaela had pointed out the drawing of the four pillars on the map, saying it was unusual. Coincidence? He picked it up and examined the table of contents. Pillars of the Gnostic Beliefs,

Philosophy, Science, Mysticism and Art; Gnosis, Dualism and the Emergence of the Cathar Faith; King Henry II and the Council of Oxford; Albigensian Crusade; Persecution and Execution; Legacy of the Cathars; and the list went on.

"Are you interested in history?" Susan asked, as she entered the room carrying her handbag.

"All my life," he nodded. "I've never known why. Until now." He grinned at her.

"Me, too. I wish I'd studied it at university, but things just never worked out that way. Did you study?"

"Yes. My father pushed me into doing law, but I hated it. Switched to history after a bad first year."

"Why don't you take it? The book," she offered. His questioning look prompted her further. "Really. Please. I've read them all. They just gather dust now."

"Well, thank you. I'd love to. Shall I get us a ride?" he added, taking out his phone. "I've found us a restaurant in Jackson Street that the hotel said was very nice." He gave her its name. "Do you know it?"

"I've heard of it, but I don't eat out much. It sounds lovely." On the way to the restaurant, Luke insisted that dinner was his treat. At first she argued, but when he said it was actually Geoffrey Shaw's treat, she reluctantly accepted.

The restaurant was quiet, with a cosy ambience, and the food excellent. They talked at length about their lives, and Susan had a gentle way of asking questions as she built up her picture of Luke's life. The conversation gave her a sense that he was at a crossroads of sorts.

Luke hadn't wanted to press her, but it seemed to him that her life was rather lonely. He worried that he was the cause, but her reassurance was vehement. "You're not to blame yourself. I've never blamed you, and I've never regretted having you," she said determinedly. She put her hand on his. "I'm so grateful you found me, and came all the way here. It means a lot."

"I wish I could stay longer. My flight home is tomorrow night. When

I booked I didn't realise I'd be in the air almost as long as I'd be here!"
Luke was torn about staying; his flight was booked, but he supposed he
could change it. But he knew things needed to be done back at home.
His father's house, the map and Michaela, *a job*. And of course, there was
Madison. He was disappointed that she hadn't contacted him. *Maybe I
should text her.*

Susan broke into his reverie. "Is something the matter?"

"No. Just thinking about all the things I should be doing. I'd rather
stay, though," he said earnestly. "And I'm glad I came, too. Do you think
you'll ever visit the UK?"

"Maybe one day." *It would be nice to visit Lisa*, she thought. Although
she wondered whether she could afford the trip. Her job at the local
council didn't pay very well.

Luke was staring at her. "I hope you don't mind me asking, but I have
to know. Why didn't you look for me?" He'd only known her for two days
but already cared enough that he didn't want to upset her. *But I have to
know.*

Susan took his hand and took a deep breath. "I got pregnant at
sixteen, and your father dumped me. I think we both had huge pressure
from our parents, but he made it clear he was having nothing to do with
it. They wanted me to get an abortion, but I wouldn't. It was a traumatic
time. Then, when I'd finished school, I moved out of my parents' house
and got a job. I often thought about looking for you, but the adoption
agency had made it clear you were no longer legally my child and I had
no rights. The Shaws didn't want me in your life." She noticed his
expression change. "I think they just wanted what they believed was best
for you. It wasn't spiteful or anything like that," she explained.

"Yesterday, I said my marriage breakdown was complicated. Well,
when you would have been about six years old, I got pregnant again. My
second baby died in childbirth." Luke squeezed her hand and looked at
her, encouraging her to continue. "There were complications, and I was
left unable to have any more children. That was the beginning of the end
for my marriage. Less than two years later, we divorced. We didn't have

much, and the divorce left me with nothing."

It was a harrowing story. She paused again, as if deciding whether to go on. Luke waited, his face filled with concern.

"I fell into depression for a while and found it hard to work. By the time I pulled myself out of that, I think you would have been nine or ten. I made a decision that I wouldn't push myself into your life. You had your teenage years ahead, and your education, and I just thought it wouldn't be fair." There were tears in her eyes again.

"Thank you for telling me. I know it wasn't easy," Luke said softly. "It means a huge amount that you didn't abandon me. Ever. Even before I knew I was adopted, I think I've always known there was something missing from my life. Now I know it was you."

A waiter brought tea, breaking the moment.

Then Susan looked Luke directly in the eyes. "Luke, have you ever thought about what your legacy will be?" He had no response. "You're young. You have a lifetime ahead of you," she went on, as Luke silently reflected that she was only seventeen years older than him. "Don't be like me. The world won't notice when I'm gone. I'll leave no footprints."

It seemed a sad thing to say, but she didn't look sad. She looked indomitable.

22

The priest solemnly administered the last rites to Bernard. Eleanor watched as the man did his duty, all the while thinking Bernard would have been horrified. Receiving a sacrament from his oppressors was a cruel irony, and one that Eleanor had no choice but to play along with. Nevertheless, she could not allow him to be buried here as a Catholic so informed the priest she would return his remains to his village. She also wanted to search his clothing to ensure nothing important was left in the hands of the church. The priest accepted her explanation that she and her cousin, who had been unwell for some time, had come to Hessle to pay their respects, but she now had to return immediately to her husband and children. She would take her cousin back to his village for proper burial.

Eleanor traded Bernard's horse for a small cart to transport his body. At the church, the priest helped her load him onto the cart, and she slowly rode back towards her home in York as the evening light started to fade.

"May God rest your weary soul, Bernard of Languedoc," she said softly to his corpse behind her. "You've completed your duty."

Two hours later, Eleanor led the horse off the track and into a sheltered copse. She diligently searched his clothing, finding nothing other than the sack of coins, and then, with much difficulty, dragged Bernard from the cart. Next, she removed a plank of wood from the side of the cart to use as a spade. As a parfait, she knew what was required to safeguard Bernard's soul. She made her peace with God for the untruth she'd spoken earlier and started to dig the soft earth. An hour after that, sweating and dirty from the work, she was satisfied she had dug deep enough. She manoeuvred Bernard into his grave, shrouded in his heavy cloak, and filled it in, uttering the necessary prayer.

Eleanor mounted the horse and rode until she reached an orchard, leaving the cart on the track outside for the crofter to find the next day. The moon was full and the sky clear, which helped her make her decision to carry on all the way to York. The clear sky meant it would be a cold night, and the full moon would guide her. She had tucked her satchel inside Bernard's, along with the map. She now needed to determine what she should do with it.

Eleanor reached her humble home before dawn, tethered the horse and went inside. She would sleep later, but for now, she set a fire and prepared some barley porridge, positioning it in the hearth to slowly cook. She hadn't eaten since she shared the simple lunch with Bernard yesterday. *Poor man.* She had no doubt that he had pushed himself too far in order to achieve his quest. She knew little about him, other than that he was a good man, unrelentingly focused on ensuring the fate of the talisman and the fate of all people with it.

She took his map out of the satchel and unrolled it. At first, it made no sense to her. Then, as she examined it in the dim candlelight, it began to speak to her. It was beautifully and carefully drawn, and inscribed with imagery and symbols. At the lower edge, there was a Latin inscription she recognised, although she did not read Latin. Anno Domini MCCXLIII. The Year of Our Lord 1243.

She began to recognise familiar locations in France, as well as parts of Bernard's trek through England. York was marked, and there was an ankh symbol next to its name. Perhaps Bernard had intended to conceal his talisman in York. *That will need to be corrected,* she thought. 'Inscribe the map with the ...' was all Bernard had managed to say before he slipped away. The *what?*

The earthy aroma of the porridge, tinged with the gentle sweetness of the peat fire, beckoned Eleanor to the hearth. She stirred the pot and tasted it. *It will do.* With the small bowl of gruel, she sat at the table and studied the scroll closely as the early morning light slowly grew stronger. The ankh had no apparent reason for being there, so that fact alone made it stand out to her. Then she found a second symbol, and the picture started to make sense. *I know what I need to do.* The new location of the *philosophy* talisman needed to be coded into the map, in a way that a Cathar, a follower of gnostic tradition, would be able to understand but a non-believer would not.

As a healer and purveyor of all manner of herbal treatments, Eleanor also knew how to make dyes. She set about concocting a suitable ink to inscribe the map for a distant Cathar descendant to find and decode. She was not a scribe and did not know how to write but knew of the technique. A large sewing needle, the type used to sew leather, would serve as a stylus. After some practice, she found she could draw a simple ankh reliably, as well as a Templar Cross with a tiny marker in its left, or western, point. Next, she practised changing Bernard's York ankh so it resembled something else. With some perseverance, she found she could make it look like a flower, which she hoped would make it appear to be merely an illustration of the map-maker, perhaps to signify gardens in York. *Yes, that should suffice.*

By noon, she had inscribed the map to her satisfaction, carefully drying the parchment near the hearth. Her remaining problem was how to safeguard it. Eleanor did not believe it should stay in York. Her daughter was not devoutly of the faith, and Eleanor did not think highly of her son-in-law. Bernard had not given her any indication of his plans, *if he'd had any.* The only thing he seemed to be completely clear about was that nowhere in France was safe from the eyes of the church. Eleanor had a sinking feeling that the Kingdom of England was soon to be the same.

The map was a precious key to the location of the sacred objects. She felt a huge weight, a weight that she realised Bernard had been carrying for some months. The scroll must be protected and preserved for the right hands, perhaps many generations from now. But she was conflicted also, just as Bernard had told her he had felt some weeks earlier. Would the kingdom, and all other kingdoms, be safer if she simply destroyed the map and Bernard's parchment? *Perhaps so.* She worried that in the hands of a power-hungry church, it could change the fate of the world. It could place knowledge and domination into the hands of those who were not worthy. Those who would use it against others for their own ends. Eleanor understood that the talismans spoke of a long-forgotten golden age, where authority and knowledge were shared, where the secrets and mysteries of gnosis were for the good of man. A time and a place far distant from the kingdom, Eleanor knew.

In the end, she could not bring herself to destroy the key to something so profound. She must find a solution. Perhaps further north there would be a safe haven for it. There was unrest, that was certain, but the church had not achieved the same pervasive control as it had south of the Roman wall. The northern hordes had not been fully tamed, not by the English, or the Romans before them. Theirs seemed an older and more earthy tradition, one with which Eleanor felt an empathy.

Yes, tomorrow she would once again leave York and travel north into the land of King Alexander. She set about sewing the map and parchment into her cloak to ensure its safety. She fed the horse tethered outside, knowing that the next day it would take her on the most important journey of her life.

23

The man in the mask slowly walked towards her. She stared at him, horrified, but could not look away. She couldn't move; her legs were weighed down and her arms pinned to her sides.

"*Vos scitis a veritate. Oportet te mori.*" He whispered the words to her. "*Vos scitis a veritate. Vos scitis a veritate. Oportet te mori. Oportet te mori.*" You know the truth. You must die.

"Why?" She tried to shout the word, to implore him, but could not speak. Her heart was racing. She had never felt so afraid in her short life. The man in black kept lumbering towards her. Inexorably. In his hand she could see a long iron object. The end glowed a burning red. She could smell smoke.

"*Vos scitis a veritate. Oportet te mori. Vos scitis a veritate. Oportet te mori.*" He was almost upon her.

With every ounce of her remaining strength, she struggled to move her restrained limbs, but to no avail. She opened her mouth in a silent scream as he reached her. Somehow her restraints were replaced by the vice-like grip of his hands.

"*Vos scitis a veritate. Oportet te mori.*"

She was rigid with fear as he pressed the iron poker into her chest.

She sat bolt upright in bed, fighting off the duvet she'd been wrapped in. 3.10, according to her bedside clock. Bathed in sweat and with an aching head, she sat in the dark, alone and shaking. *Just a bad dream*, she told herself. *But it was so vivid.* Michaela did not have dreams like that. She turned on the lamp, half expecting to see someone lurking in her room. After her breathing had almost returned to normal, she climbed out of bed and went to the kitchen for a glass of water. The heating had been off for hours and the flat was chilly. She shivered, only partially from the cold. *That was awful. It must be the map.* All those hours poring over the mysterious Latin phrases and the drawings of strange objects must have affected her.

She went into the bathroom to wash her face and looked in the mirror. With her wavy hair out and without her glasses, she thought her face looked somehow softer. Maybe she should try that occasionally. *Or maybe it's just my poor eyesight.* She washed the sheen from her skin and gently shook her head to let her dark-chestnut hair touch her shoulders. *No, it's just not me.*

Spooked by the nightmare, she rechecked her front door lock before returning to the kitchen to make a cup of cocoa. She hoped that would help her relax and get back to sleep. A happier sleep. It must have been that last phrase she'd translated: *Fate will be appeased by blood.* That was the logical explanation.

The next morning she woke before the alarm, still unnerved by the nightmare. It had taken her a while to get back to sleep, but at least she'd managed to get a few more hours. Before going to work she tried a couple of searches on the Internet for any similar maps but didn't find any. She'd been reluctant to key in the exact Latin phrases, simply because Luke had asked her to keep it confidential, and she'd promised she would. He had seemed very serious about that. But it meant her searches were oblique and therefore less useful. Still, she had other options.

The old door creaked open, ringing the bell to announce her arrival to the silent, empty shop. She was half an hour early, but that wasn't unusual. She loved the shop. She loved its ambience, its smell, the way sounds echoed around the high ceiling. She loved being surrounded by history. After withdrawing the rolled-up A3 pages, she put her handbag in its usual spot under the counter, tucking the map in neatly next to it. Then she started up the computer, a rather incongruously modern object rudely placed amidst the antiquity. Her first search was of the digital catalogue. It was a formality; she didn't expect to find what she wanted in it, but it was a logical place to start. If she was lucky, it might save her a lot of time. Unsurprisingly, she was not lucky.

Next were the old catalogues. Four large, dusty volumes stored in the back room, with hand-written records dating back to George Sutherland himself, the original proprietor in the mid-1800s. During the morning she pored over the four tomes, marvelling at the beautiful handwriting of the first hundred years of records. After the Second World War, the ink became less faded, as the handwriting progressively worsened.

There was only one interruption. The door creaked and the bell rang, but it wasn't Luke. A large man in a black coat came in and she gasped. "Sorry. I must have been deep in thought," she said quickly. He had an enquiry about selling a rare third-edition *Jane Eyre*. Michaela had to explain that the shop already had two, one at £299 and the other in better condition at £395, and no one had shown any interest in either. Sorry.

She had no luck with the old catalogues, so after lunch, she took the map out and unrolled it, resting the heavy steel rulers at each end to hold it in place. If a customer came in, all she had to do was move one of them and it would roll itself up again. She looked at it more objectively. Not studying the words, but their placement on the map, instead. It didn't look like sheer coincidence to her. The five cities or towns they were written near were definitely drawn in more detail than other cities which, at the time, should have been more important. There were illustrations also in four of those five locations. That mysterious caption near the top, *The Four Pillars, what does that mean? There's a distinct theme starting to emerge here.*

Next, she studied the illustrations. Ignoring for now the more generic of them, such as crude ships upon the seas, in case the reader had any doubts as to what he was looking at. It was here that Michaela saw the flaws in her hypothesis. There were four unusual and salient drawings, five if she counted the picture of the four pillars, but only three of them were situated with the Latin inscriptions and the most accurately drawn cities. York had a drawing of a flower, whereas Hessle had a beautifully drawn ankh. But Hessle itself was not mapped very clearly, and there was no inscription near it. It didn't quite add up.

24

"I'm going to be shattered when I get home," Luke muttered to himself as he waited to board his flight, yawning. "Maybe I'll give myself a couple of days off," he chuckled. His smile lingered. It had been a wonderful couple of days, and he felt more buoyed up than he had for years. Probably not since his university days. It had been genuinely heart-warming.

Last night he'd dropped his mother home after a lovely meal and a deep conversation that had started to cement their relationship. He'd promised the driver a tip as the man had patiently waited while Luke hugged her and said goodbye. He told her he would try to visit again soon, and they'd both choked up a little. The book she'd given him was in his backpack, still in the paper bag she'd found for it.

After boarding, he retrieved the book and opened it, not quite sure where to begin. He hoped it would yield some useful information about the map; if indeed the 'four pillars' reference was relevant at all. *May as well start with the introduction ...*

The term *gnosis* comes from Ancient Greek. Gnosis means knowledge. More specifically, many references cite both spiritual and experiential knowledge.

In ancient times, throughout Byzantium and Persia, and subsequently Ancient Greece, four pillars of knowledge were recognised. Science, mysticism, philosophy and art were all intertwined. The great philosophers, Socrates, Plato, Aristotle and others, all understood science, theology, mysticism and the arts. These giants crafted holistic philosophies still relevant and practised today.

They teach us that in a golden age of man, there was no conflict between science and religion, or philosophy and art. These were the four pillars upon which noble and enlightened societies were created. It was believed that without all four of these pillars, a balanced understanding of the world could not be reached. It was also believed that through knowledge, great insight and inspiration could be found.

Gnostic belief and tradition seems to have continued underground from its origins in the Byzantine and Persian Empires, long before Christianity and Islam emerged, until the late medieval period.

Its earlier origins are the subject of legend, and few facts are known. These legends hold that during a long-lost golden age of mankind, the four pillars – science, mysticism, philosophy and art – were equally revered by a society free of evil. Knowledge was venerated most of all, enlightenment being vested in the four pillars.

The first leg of his return journey, Wellington to Auckland, was only one hour, and before he'd finished the first chapter, the pilot announced they were commencing their descent. Luke put the book away and closed his eyes. On the next flight he would search for something directly relevant. During the brief stop in Auckland, he switched his phone back on, but there was no message from Madison. He decided he would text her as soon as he got back home. Just over an hour later, he boarded the long-haul flight and settled back in to his book, flipping through relevant sections to search for something useful.

King Henry and the Council of Oxford

The Cathars had not been strong in England; however, in the late 1150s, a group of Cathar faithful had escaped persecution in Europe and established a small community. Within no more than a few years, this community had expanded as the Cathars managed to convert some of the local people. As their influence grew, soon the Church learned of their exploits and became deeply concerned. At the Council of Oxford in the year 1166, the bishops of the Council ordered the banishment of the Cathars and handed them over to King Henry II. Henry was reputed to have had each Cathar man, woman and child branded then cast out, ordering his subjects to leave them to die.

Albigensian Crusade

By the middle of the 12th century AD, the Cathar faith had grown stronger and developed a foothold in Albi, near Toulouse in Southern France. Towards the end of the century, the community had grown large enough that the Catholic Church's dominance in the region was under threat. Pope Innocent III made numerous attempts to stifle and control the faith but met with little success.

Innocent III wanted stronger action, and the murder of the Papal Legate Pierre de Castelnau, in 1208, provided the catalyst he needed. He declared a crusade against the heretics. For the next three decades, Cathars were hunted and persecuted by the Church and the French nobility. Innocent's enticement of promising the Cathars' lands and possessions to any nobleman taking up arms had proved very effective.

During these Crusades, tens of thousands of Cathar faithful, men, women and children, were massacred. The Albigensian Crusade also played an important role in the creation and institutionalisation of the Dominican Order, and the Inquisition, during the 13th century. The Inquisition underwent two name changes during the 20th century, becoming the Congregation for the Doctrine of the Faith. Like the Dominican Order, it continues to this day.

Luke rubbed his eyes. It was getting late, and he could barely keep them open. It continues to this day. The notion stuck in his weary mind. Before putting the book away, he quickly thumbed through the chapter entitled Legacy of the Cathars. The closing paragraphs caught his eye:

There are many stories of a legacy, or even a treasure, of the Cathars. Many of these legends suggest that the fortress of Montségur was the hiding place of this legacy, at least until the siege of 1243–44; however, no evidence has been found to support these stories.

Treasure hunters have unsuccessfully pursued a mythical treasure for eight centuries. The notion of a Cathar treasure appears flawed, inasmuch as the Cathars made great sacrifices in their lives, took vows of poverty and rejected all material possessions.

25

"You're back." *Madison. How does she know?*

"Hi. Yeah, just got back to my flat. How did you know I was away?"

"I missed you," she cooed. "I was going to message you yesterday, but I could see you were off the grid. Lucky guess." Her tone was playful. "I want to see you. Tonight."

"Sure. I'll look forward to it." Luke tried to sound more enthusiastic than he felt. It *would* be great to see her, but sleep was what he really needed. They made their arrangements and Madison ended the call. He finished unpacking his suitcase and sat down for a cup of tea, with the Four Pillars.

Sleep had not come easily on the return journey, and when it had, he dreamt of the Inquisition. An interrogation. Men in black robes asked him questions to which he did not have answers. They suggested answers, and if he agreed, they accused him of something else. If he disagreed, they accused him of lying; of sympathy for the devil, of being a heretic. The logic was circular and the dogma impenetrable. There was no reasoning. And all the while, they heated fire irons with which to torture or brand him. He'd woken with a start and hadn't been able to sleep for the rest of the flight.

After his cup of tea, he closed the book and put it on the kitchen bench. He'd been engrossed in the little he'd read but just couldn't concentrate. He would come back to it in the morning. The book was also a connection to his birth mother and their shared interest in history. He ordered a pizza delivery. Large size, in case Madison wanted a slice or two.

Luke awoke to soft kisses on his neck, marvelling at the energy Madison had. It was apparently limitless. He'd only been asleep a couple of hours. He put his arm around her neck and pulled her closer.

"So, why did you leave me?" she teased, surprising him as she stopped kissing and rested her head on his shoulder.

"It was a snap decision." He told her about phoning Susan and deciding on the spur of the moment to visit her. Madison listened quietly as Luke explained a little of Susan's story and how he'd felt. He wanted to tell her that it had made him feel good about himself, but he didn't think she'd understand. Madison was a woman who *always* felt good about herself.

"I thought you might have moved up to Harrogate by now. You seemed to like the idea," she said, with an abrupt change of subject.

"Still thinking about it," he said. "Thinking about a lot of things. I might ..."

Madison's interest had apparently waned; she interrupted him with a kiss on his mouth that was filled with promise and intent, as her hands reached under the covers.

The sound of the shower running stirred Luke from a deep sleep. At least it was daylight this time, and he felt slightly more rested. He checked the bedside clock. It was just after seven am.

"Still no coffee, I assume," Madison said, as she walked into the bedroom naked.

"No. Just tea." *And probably no fresh milk.* He watched as she dressed, then got up to shower. "I think I'll go up to Harrogate today," he announced. "There'll be paperwork to do for my father's will, and I suppose I'd better get started on cleaning out the house."

"That sounds like a great idea. Maybe it would be good for you to find out more about your father. And who knows, you might unearth some exciting long-lost family secret." She opened her eyes wider in mock surprise.

Like 'the Collection'? The thought flashed across his mind briefly, but he held back. "He was a boring man," Luke replied with a laugh.

"Tell me about the house," she encouraged.

So Luke told her about Geoffrey Shaw's stately home on York Road. About walking up from Valley Gardens, the leafy streets, how different it was from Manningham Lane. She appeared to be genuinely interested. He told her about the 'pretentious' antique furniture his father had collected, the expensive whisky and crystal glasses, the antique four-poster bed.

Madison checked her watch and said she had to go. That was her way, it seemed. She kissed him and gave him a hug. As she did, she bit his earlobe and whispered in his ear. "Fuck me in your four-poster bed."

And with that, she was gone.

26

On the way to Harrogate, Luke phoned the solicitor's office. The receptionist told him Mr Trilby wasn't in at the moment but was due back within in a few hours at most. A legal clerk would be able to assist him when he arrived. As the train approached its destination, he closed his eyes, still weary from his travels. And the tireless Madison. He smiled at the thought of her. She was a woman who knew what she wanted and seemed to be accustomed to getting it.

He climbed the steps and entered. Once again, he marvelled at the absence of oak, marble and gilded furnishings.

The receptionist remembered him. "I'll let Harry know you're here," he said cheerfully. "Please have a seat."

Luke sat and waited, expecting to see an unhappy, overworked clerk; a person who took orders from self-important lawyers, fixed the IT systems and did the filing. Instead, he was met by a serious but pleasant young man a few years his junior, carrying a box file.

"Harry Greenwood. Please to meet you." His handshake was firm, and he looked as though he enjoyed his work. Maybe this law firm was different. Luke introduced himself, and Harry showed him into a small meeting room. The clerk opened the box and withdrew some papers.

"I'm sorry Mr Trilby isn't here. He's due back just after lunch.

Fortunately, there's not much left to do." Harry placed some forms in front of Luke. There were little sticky flags that said 'sign here'. Harry started to explain each one.

"Don't worry, Harry, I've seen a lot of these before. I used to be a solicitor's slave, too." He grinned at Harry, who returned a polite but confused look. *Maybe they do treat the juniors better here.*

"Do you enjoy your work?" Luke asked.

"Oh, yes. Mr Trilby and the other partners are very good to work with." Harry paused, looking as though he had something on his mind. "I knew your father of course. He was a good man to work with, too. I was very sorry to hear he, er, died."

"The firm I worked for in Bradford wasn't like that," Luke replied, steering the conversation away from his father.

"Most of the partners here are Freemasons," Harry said. "You know, tolerance, respect, equality, and all that."

"My old work wasn't like that. I don't think the partners there have heard of any of those things. Arrogance, chauvinism and hierarchy. I've no idea about Freemasonry, but if it's about the things you said, then I doubt it. They never talked about it."

"They don't here either, but occasionally you hear things. Your father was a Mason too, did you know?" Harry asked.

"No, I had no idea. I'm afraid we didn't talk much."

"Oh, sorry to hear it. He talked about you sometimes. Told me you were a legal clerk, like me."

Luke shook his head slowly. "That's what he wanted, but technically I wasn't. I studied history, not law. But to be honest, I'm surprised he even knew."

"Yes. Mr Trilby always said your father was a good man who took his responsibilities very seriously," Harry said.

Luke finished signing the last of the papers and pushed them back across the table towards Harry. "I think that's it."

"Thanks. Let me just check with Mr Trilby." Harry took out his phone and stepped out into the hallway.

As he waited, Luke pondered what to do next. He would have to clear out the house if he was going to sell it. He couldn't picture himself living there, but equally he couldn't see himself staying in his flat in Bradford. Lately the flat had seemed so much more depressing. He also thought of seeing his birth mother again. Such a long way, but maybe if she wanted to come to the UK, Luke could help her out with Geoffrey Shaw's money. *If* she'd accept that.

Harry returned with another small cardboard box labelled 'For Lucas Shaw – personal'. "These are your father's personal effects. Mr Trilby said you should take them."

Luke opened the box to see a folder with some papers, and a few bits and pieces. Underneath the folder sat a walnut tray embossed with a Union Jack, holding a bottle of ink and his father's old fountain pen. Luke remembered the pen from his childhood. His father had told him it was the same as Winston Churchill's pen. He closed the box and looked up to see Harry's troubled face.

"Terrible business." Harry shook his head.

"*Law?*"

"No. Sorry. Your father's murder. Especially *that* way. I'm sorry."

"A burglary?"

"Oh." Harry's face at once registered concern and horror. "Didn't the police tell you?"

"They notified me, then interviewed me, but no, they didn't give details. 'Killed during a burglary' was all they said." *What the hell?* Harry looked like he would have eaten his words, given a chance. "Tell me what, exactly?" Luke demanded.

"A policemen told me your father was … tortured. Burned with a fire iron." Harry shuddered and shook his head. "The police said his killer presumably wanted information. I'm sorry."

Luke shook his head in shock. *Tortured. What the fuck?*

Harry was embarrassed. "I shouldn't have said anything. I assumed you knew."

"What information? About a case, his work?" In his heart, Luke knew the answer. The safe was opened, but the Collection was in the other hidden safe. *That, he obviously did not reveal, even under torture.*

"The police didn't know. We don't think it related to any of his work, and Mr Trilby said Mr Shaw never took files home." Harry waited as Luke digested it all.

"I just assumed he must have surprised a burglar and been stabbed. Not a premeditated attack. Heat of the moment." Luke was still reeling. *Could the man who'd struck Luke in the kitchen be the same man?*

As his mind raced through the implications, Luke's world started to turn inside out. At first, the Collection had been nothing more than a relic of the past. Some old documents his father had taken way too seriously. The map had been a mystery, a puzzle to solve. It was an adventure, nothing more. But now it seemed clear his father had been murdered for it. It took on a level of malevolence that shook Luke. "And his murder? I have to ask, how was my father killed?"

Harry looked at his shoes. Eventually he forced himself to meet Luke's eyes. "He was stabbed through the heart with a fire poker." Luke could tell there was more. He waited for Harry to continue. "The police found him pinned to his chair with it." The pair sat silently in the small room for a few moments as Luke tried to make sense of what he'd just heard. "I'll get you a glass of water," Harry said, pleased to have something to do.

Luke's face had turned pale as he pictured his father's study. The desk chair was missing, and the carpet had been pulled up. Now he knew why.

27

LEICESTER, KINGDOM OF ENGLAND, APRIL 1555

Sitting alone in the richly furnished, panelled library of the depleted Montfort Estate, Henry Montfort pondered his unexpected inheritance. His family had lived through the indignity of Henry VIII's excesses, and his confiscation of most of their land and titles as a direct consequence of the family's allegiance to the Catholic Church. Within days of his father being laid in the ground, Henry had been given a letter and a key.

Henry was a loathsome young man, disliked by the estate staff for his extravagance and arrogance. His tutors thought him dim-witted, always daydreaming and staring out the window, coveting a regal life that was no longer the Montforts'.

The estate's seneschal, a calm and stoic man of Henry's father's generation, considered the father foolish to entrust the Brotherhood to such a fanciful, ill-disciplined boy, but he did not voice his views. The seneschal knew Henry was his employer's only son, and the decision was not one for discussion. He had presented the young man with the letter and the key, as instructed. He was to guide the lad as best he could.

Henry read the letter once again. The Brotherhood of Amaury. His unexpected destiny. He, Henry Montfort, was now the Grand Master of the Brotherhood of Amaury, a secret organisation founded more than three hundred years ago for a sole purpose – to recover the treasure the Cathars had stolen three centuries earlier from its rightful heirs, the Crusaders, led by Simon de Montfort. In his father's own words, the Cathars' treasure would 'bring immeasurable power to the man who held it'. His father's letter also referred to a 'recent important acquisition'.

Henry now turned his mind to the parchments and the small section of a very old map that lay on the table next to his father's letter – the contents of the locked drawer the key had opened. The documents dated back to the thirteenth century, and many were in Latin, a language Henry did not understand, in spite of his tutors' best endeavours. Henry's father, however, with the seneschal's help, had spent considerable time translating them. He had left notes that referred to his ancestors' belief that the Cathar treasure dated back to a golden age, before 'the known history', a time when men knew great power.

Treasure. A golden age. Great Power. It was intoxicating. That, surely, was Henry's destiny. Restoration of the family's lands, wealth and standing. With a Catholic queen on the throne, now was his time. He read and reread all his father's notes, including the manuscript with the map. His father had referred to an unusual symbol. Something out of time and place. He called it an ankh. Henry's father believed this ankh was an important clue to the location of the treasure.

Henry picked up the map and studied it. He now wished he'd listened more to his tutors instead of considering the lessons a waste of his time. But scientific and esoteric learnings had not interested him, especially when he saw the world as his for the taking, and his time was better spent in the chamber of the upstairs maid.

The map was an elaborate sketch of the whole kingdom, with simple illustrations of ships in the southern sea, livestock and various flora on the land, major towns with their cathedrals, and an intricate coat of arms. In the north, just above the inscribed name York, was the mysterious ankh that had so excited Henry's father.

He spiritedly rifled through the notes, eventually finding a translation of one of the parchments. It referred to the map. Evidently it had been in the hands of the Brotherhood for three hundred years, having been furtively copied by a monk who believed it to be of some arcane value. The monk had hastily copied it from the map of a northbound traveller who had seemed obsessed with it. The monk knew of the ankh as a symbol of life and strength. *This has to be the key to its location,* Henry thought. *But why has no one yet found it? Surely it must be secreted somewhere within York Minster?*

Henry rang the bell, and presently a servant arrived. "Fetch the seneschal," he ordered, and the servant scurried away.

When the steward arrived, Henry demanded to know when York Minster had been built. The seneschal turned to the library bookcases immediately behind Henry and scanned the shelves, patiently retrieving a large volume. He soon found the reference and informed his master that building had commenced in the year 1220. A check of the monk's document revealed that the map had been copied 'in the year of our Lord one thousand two hundred and forty-four'. *So, the cathedral had been under construction for a generation when the traveller's map was found. Perfect!*

Henry made a snap decision. He instructed the seneschal to arrange an audience with Queen Mary.

YORK, KINGDOM OF ENGLAND, JANUARY 1556

The seneschal had once seen young Henry as impetuous, grasping and foolish, but since his father's death, he had transformed himself into a driven man, forceful and single-minded, albeit with the same venal qualities. The grey-haired steward had been dumbfounded when the young man had demanded an audience with the queen, but he had set about arranging it, and with the family's known Catholic associations, the seneschal had managed it. He had coached Henry unremittingly in court etiquette, and Henry got what he wanted. The royal court would likely have been expecting a request for reinstatement of the substantial confiscated lands and rescinded titles, but instead Henry had asked for a lesser title and a comparatively modest estate near York. Queen Mary had granted his wish, having recently confiscated a suitable estate that her father, Henry VIII, had gifted to a vehement supporter of his Reformation.

And so it was that the Montfort family regained their status, and Montfort Hall was designated. Before the harsh winter months, Henry, Earl of York, had moved his household into Montfort Hall, some eight miles north-west of York, along the River Ouse. A perfect location for Henry to begin his search of York Minster for his rightful inheritance. The idea of wielding an ancient power, lost for centuries or possibly millennia, consumed Henry. He was resolute and fanatical, and imbued the same zeal in other members of the Brotherhood.

With the seneschal's help and guidance, Henry had reinvigorated the Brotherhood of Amaury, and ignited in its small, elite membership, a hunger for the power and wealth the Cathars' treasure would surely bring them. Henry had also proved to be charming and persuasive when he needed to be, and had enticed the Archbishop of York to allow the Brotherhood to 'seek greater enlightenment within the minster'.

28

As he opened the front door, Luke felt a new nervousness. The York Road house had somehow taken on a more sinister aspect, now he knew his father had been tortured and murdered here. As he walked from the solicitor's office, Luke thought it likely his father's killer now knew who *he* was. Since he had had the opportunity to kill or interrogate Luke but hadn't done so, it was logical that Luke wasn't in any immediate danger. The house had already been thoroughly searched, although the man hadn't found what he wanted. He could be back, Luke supposed, but, more likely, he'd decided the Collection must be hidden somewhere else.

In the upstairs study, Luke couldn't help but picture the awful scene: his father sitting at the desk, eyes open but unseeing, his blood dripping onto the carpet as his body was held firmly in place by the iron poker. He sat in one of the other chairs, feeling unsteady. A subtle but distinct noise downstairs broke through his thoughts, and he was suddenly alert. He stood as quietly as he could and looked out through the doorway. Silence. He slowly crept down the stairs, avoiding the creaky floorboards in the entrance hall. Still not a sound. *At least this time it isn't dark.* Cautiously peering through each doorway, he checked every room, finding nothing untoward. He then opened the cupboard under the stairs, stepping back in case someone jumped out. But there was no one. *Old houses make noises sometimes,* he reasoned, trying to keep his apprehension under control. He rechecked that the front and back doors were locked and jogged back upstairs.

Next, after removing the Whitby picture, he opened the panel and, with some concentration, managed to open the hidden safe. 43-27-70. *Are the combination numbers all significant in some way?* he wondered. 27, his birthday. 70 could refer to Sue's year of birth, although that seemed a bit of a stretch. But if they were, what was the significance of 43? He took out the original map and the other documents, leaving the piece of jewellery, or whatever it was, in the safe. Then he carefully closed the door and put the panelling back in place.

He took the old documents down to the kitchen, sitting them on the table next to the box of his father's personal effects. Maybe another look would help, though he still didn't know what to look for. He unfolded the map and examined it again, but it did not give up any secrets. He took out his phone and dialled.

"Sutherland's," answered a soft voice.

"Hi, is that Michaela?"

"Yes, speaking."

Luke could hear the reverberation from all the timber in the old, high-ceilinged shop. He could almost smell its ambience. "Hi, it's Luke Shaw. I came in last week with an old map. Um, I'm just calling to see if you've made any progress."

"I'm glad you called," she replied. "Yes, I have. I think there's something special and unique about your map. I've finished most of the translation, and, well, I have some ideas I can discuss with you."

"That's great. Could I call in, say, tomorrow morning?"

"Yes. We open at nine."

"How about 10.30?" Luke wanted to give himself enough time to get back to Bradford. *If I spend another night here.* They agreed the time, but before ending the call, Luke wanted to warn her to be careful. But how?

"Please remember to keep it to yourself," he said awkwardly.

"Of course!" She sounded irritated.

"Okay, I'll see you tomorrow then." He pushed the cache of old documents to one side, wondering what Michaela had discovered. 'Something special and unique about your map,' she'd said.

The file box Harry had handed over included some fairly recent correspondence and paperwork, but towards the bottom of the pile, Luke found a couple of old photos. One of his mother that must have been taken a year of two before she died, and one family photo when he was still at school. Right at the bottom was an envelope neatly addressed to Lucas Shaw. Yet another posthumous letter?

It was fifteen years old and written on thick, cream-coloured paper. It must have sat amongst his father's papers, unsent, all that time. *If he wasn't going to send it, why did he bother to keep it?* Luke started to crumple it, thinking angrily that the old man should have just *talked* to him. But he thought better of tossing it out and opened it, as much from curiosity as anything else. It had marks and creases in the paper that implied reading and rereading. Had his father agonised over sending it? Or reviewed and rewritten it? Like the others, it was in Geoffrey Shaw's elegant and careful hand, presumably with the replica of Winston Churchill's fountain pen.

Dear Lucas,

I write this letter with a hope that we will be able to talk openly about these matters, but at the present time it is not possible. These last few years have been difficult for both of us. I want you to know that I understand your anger. I know I have not been the father you have needed, and for that I am truly sorry. I hope that one day you will understand, and you will be able to forgive me.

I also write this letter in the knowledge that there is something you need to know, and following the death of my darling wife, your mother, whom I miss more than I can put into words, it is important that I don't leave it to chance.

During your mother's illness, you accused me of being cold and distant. You were right. Your mother knew me well enough to know that I was afraid. I do not write this to make an excuse, for it was inexcusable, but to help you understand. All my life I have been taught to hide my fear. My legal training reinforced that. I was not the father or the husband I should have been. I am truly regretful that I cannot be the father you have needed. It is not in me.

I have not often shown it, but I have loved you all of your life, even though I am not your biological father. Your mother and I wanted to start a family very much but could not have children of our own, so we adopted you as a baby. I want you to know that we have always loved you as our own.

Your mother and I agreed that we would tell you after your eighteenth birthday. We made our decision to keep this from you until you come of age. We know many stories of adopted children who have struggled with their self-worth and their identity, as a direct result of finding out they were adopted. We both wanted to protect you from that.

I hope that one day you will forgive me, and that you will not blame your mother. Whether right or wrong, our decision came from our love for you.

Your loving father,

Geoffrey Shaw

Reading it brought back memories of how Luke had felt at the time. Grieving the loss of his mother, confused and hurt by his father's distance, and angry with his father. And the whole world. He'd spent many years, perhaps almost all of his twenties, like that.

But Geoffrey Shaw *had* cared. He'd been *afraid*. He'd been lost, just like Luke had been. *Why couldn't he tell me?*

Luke sat back in the kitchen chair and closed his eyes, still holding the letter. Through all the intervening years, since his father had written this letter, Luke had carried a bitterness within himself, and a silent, corrosive anger. His father had *let* him carry it. Had let it destroy their relationship. Something started to well up inside. Not anger this time. No, he, Lucas Geoffrey Shaw, owned his own emotions. Whatever his father had felt and done was because of who and what he was. But whatever Luke had felt, *he* owned that himself. He could have been more understanding. He could had been more sympathetic and supportive of his father for what he was going through. Instead, he'd blamed. He distanced himself. His father had lived the last fifteen years of his life without his wife, and without his son. That was just as much Luke's fault.

Tears welled up as he gripped the letter. His emotions were in overdrive, shifting from anger or frustration, through to a terrible sadness and sense of loss. He was reliving the grief cycle all over again, although this time it was different. "You old fool, you should have talked to me," he said aloud to the lonely kitchen.

He cried for the loss of his father for the first time. He also cried again for the loss of his mother. It felt raw, just like it had all those years ago.

29

A servant quietly entered to bring Gerald Montford his usual glass of brandy. It gently lapped back and forth in the glass as it sat in the copper brandy warmer on its silver tray. The tiny tongue of flame beneath the glass flickered as the servant closed the door on his way out. In ten minutes, Gerald expected his guest to arrive. A wealthy, powerful man and as close an acquaintance as Gerald allowed, Sir Richard Beaumont was a useful ally. Albeit, he had strong ambitions, and was also one to test Gerald's patience from time to time.

An ongoing point of discussion was Beaumont's son. As the Brotherhood's Grand Master, Gerald must choose a successor, and with no heir, it had to be someone outside the Montford family. Edward Beaumont was an obvious choice, his father had said many times. 'He's ready for it. He has the right breeding and the right characteristics,' Richard declared. Gerald Montford thought Richard had it right on two counts – Edward was certainly from a good family, and he was a brutish young man – but he was not ready. In spite of being inducted into the Brotherhood, he possessed neither the intellect nor the instinctual cunning required to lead it.

An impeccably dressed butler entered the room, softly clearing his throat as he stood by the door, waiting. Gerald sipped his brandy and glanced over, raising his eyebrows to indicate permission to speak.

"Sir Richard has arrived, my lord."

"Send him in," Gerald replied regally.

The butler disappeared, returning a moment later with a large man in an expensive but ill-fitting dark tweed suit. He was the antithesis of Gerald Montford. The two men were of similar age, but Beaumont looked ten years older, and the excesses of his avaricious life had taken their toll. His grey hair had receded considerably and was currently combed over to give the appearance, at least from a great distance, of a full head of hair. His moustache was neatly trimmed but sandwiched between ruddy jowls that almost reached his ears.

They greeted each other as the butler snapped his fingers. A servant appeared with a whisky decanter and tumbler for the new arrival. He poured a generous measure, and Sir Richard helped himself.

"Gerald, the perfect host, as ever," he said.

"Richard. You are always welcome." Gerald smiled for his guest. "What brings you to Montford Hall?" Gerald hoped it was not another play to gain acceptance of the young Beaumont as his heir.

"We are close, Gerald, close to achieving our goal."

The map.

"I can almost feel it. Finding the sentinel was a masterstroke. My hat is off to you."

Gerald waited for Beaumont to continue.

"As I say, we are close, but we are not there yet. What is your plan?" It was bold of Beaumont to ask such a direct question of the Grand Master.

"Rest assured, my dear Richard, when Shaw died without revealing his secrets, I put plans in place immediately. Surely you would expect nothing less."

"Indeed."

"But as has been our way for centuries, the Grand Master decides these matters." Gerald again waited for Beaumont to declare his hand.

"Of course. It was unfortunate that Shaw died so quickly." Sir

Richard shook his head. "The search of the house?"

"Do not concern yourself, Richard. The house was thoroughly searched. Twice. Popa does not give up easily." Montford gave a wry smile; he understood Popa's methods well, having spent years grooming him. "Shaw clearly had a hiding place elsewhere. The guardians have lived in the shadows, in fear of us, for five hundred years. They are weak," he sneered. "We will find it."

"Shaw has a son," Beaumont ventured.

"Yes." Gerald snapped. "And?"

"Have you questioned him?" Beaumont pressed boldly.

"Are you questioning *me*?"

"No, I ..." Beaumont gave Montford an obsequious grin and changed tack. "Of course not. I was going to offer my help."

At last, the man is finally getting to the point. "Richard, tell me how might you be able to help?" Montford stared at his guest, and the man started to sweat.

Beaumont knew that openly challenging the Grand Master was likely to result in a disciplinary measure. Perhaps even a visit from Popa.

Gerald pressed a button to summon a servant.

"My dear Gerald, with great respect, perhaps Edward might be of some use." Beaumont sounded nervous.

Good, Gerald thought. "Oh?" He raised his eyebrows and waited, wondering how Richard might contrive a use for his graceless son.

The servant returned and Montford nodded towards his guest. As the servant poured, Beaumont signalled for him to continue, until the tumbler was half full. He picked it up and drank deeply, watching as the man meticulously refreshed Gerald's brandy, replaced the tea-light candle in the warmer and balanced the glass carefully in place. "Edward could interrogate the Shaw boy," he said hastily, as the servant left the room.

"Why would I want that? Popa will question him, if that becomes necessary."

"*If* it becomes necessary?" Beaumont's face became ruddier as he grew bolder. "We know Shaw was the sentinel. It is necessary *now*, surely."

"Do you question my judgement?" Montford demanded, his anger now rising.

"Well, no, I ..."

Montford strode over to his guest and struck him across the face with the back of his hand. Blood erupted from Beaumont's lip. "If I think Edward useful, you will be the first to know, Richard. I suggest you leave now."

Beaumont finished the whisky, wincing as it stung his torn lip, turned and left.

Gerald looked at the blood on the back of his hand. The sight of it pleased him.

30

Michaela left her flat early again. Lately she had been waking up before the alarm, usually with the old map on her mind. There was something strangely compelling about its mystery. Ever since her nightmare, it had also worried her. She was reasonably sure it was a key to ... well, she wasn't sure *what*. The peculiar illustrations must be significant, but how? A treasure map? But why go to such lengths to hide and obscure, yet at the same time record details? Why have a map at all, if this treasure isn't supposed to be found? The conundrum troubled her. *Does this map lead to something terrible?*

She let herself into the shop, leaving the closed sign on the door. It was not quite eight thirty. She put the rolled-up A3 pages under the counter and made herself a cup of tea. *What will I say to Luke?* She didn't want to sound foolish. She had no doubt the map was special, but its translation could be interpreted in different ways. A key, a story, a *warning*. She also recalled what he'd said on the phone. 'Remember to keep it to yourself.' At the time, she was annoyed; did he think she would be indiscreet? Careless? But later it crossed her mind that maybe he knew it was special, too. Maybe he even had a sense of its potential danger. *Or is that foolish as well?* She took her notes from her handbag. The 'four pillars'. What were they, and how did they fit with the illustrations? And the dream she'd had. Surely that was just coincidental, prompted by working on the translation late at night? But it had seemed so real. She shuddered at the thought of it.

A knock on the door brought her back to reality. An old lady stood outside, peering in at her. 9.10.

She quickly opened the door. "I'm sorry. I forgot to change the sign." She spent the next twenty minutes helping the woman find what she wanted. It was a welcome distraction.

Shit!" Luke sat bolt upright. 8.55. He hadn't set an alarm. If he was going to get to the bookshop by 10.30, he needed to be on a train in half an hour. Having a flat in a shared building on a busy road, Luke rarely slept in. He wasn't accustomed to the quiet of the old house in Harrogate. No neighbours through the wall or ceiling, no trucks outside, no shouts from rubbish collectors. It was eerily peaceful.

He had a quick shower, dressed and, before going downstairs, quickly surveyed the study. He was about to lock the front door when he remembered the old documents he'd left on the kitchen table. "Shit." He checked his watch and decided to go back and put them in a kitchen drawer. Safe enough. Who would look there? The house has already been searched thoroughly anyway.

As he walked briskly to the station, people in the streets surprised him by saying 'good morning' and nodding politely to him. *This is not Bradford.* Sitting on the train, holding an insipid cup of coffee, he started to wonder what the rush was for. He supposed he could have called ahead to say he was going to be late, but Michaela was doing him a favour, and he was grateful to her. It crossed his mind that the old Luke wouldn't have cared and just turned up late. But he wasn't the old Luke any more. The slump he'd been in, probably for years, was lifting. Once again, he felt a sense of anticipation, of excitement, in his gut. He was looking forward to finding out more about the map. What was it that Michaela had said? That the map was *unique and special*?

He strode towards Sutherland's with a spring in his step that was out of character. *10.35. Near enough.* He pushed the door open, and Michaela looked up at him from the counter.

"Hi. Sorry I'm a bit late."

"Hi, Luke. That's all right. It's as quiet as ever in here."

"Well I'm sorry I didn't call you earlier. I've been away. It's a long story."

She gave a half-smile that encouraged him, raising her eyebrows very slightly.

"To New Zealand," he explained. Her eyebrows went up a little further. "Spur-of-the-moment thing." He realised that must have sounded crazy.

"You spontaneously flew 12,000 miles?" She looked genuinely curious.

"Yeah." *Well, in for a penny ...* "Long story, but the day I came in to see you, I got a letter about my mother. My birth mother. I just found out I was adopted a few months ago. Anyway, I found her, and spoke to her that night. I just decided I had to see her." He felt foolish, but Michaela's face showed nothing but kindness and empathy.

"That's really sweet," she said wistfully. "I wish ..." She stopped short and looked down at the counter. "My mother and I don't talk much."

"It was like that with my father. My adoptive father."

"Families ..." The same wistful look crossed her face again. "Do you think you'll visit your mum again?"

"I'm sure I will. We haven't made any plans yet, though." It occurred to Luke that he'd talked more about his life in the last ten minutes than to any of his friends in the past ten years. She was a good listener.

"It must be nice, finding your mother like that. Especially now."

"Now?" he asked.

"I'm sorry." She looked down at the counter, embarrassed. "You said you'd inherited the map from your father. I just assumed ..." Her cheeks coloured slightly.

"Oh. Sorry. I mean, thanks. You're right, yeah, he died a couple of months ago."

"I'm sorry," she said again, this time holding his gaze.

"Thanks, Michaela, it's nice of you to say."

"Micky."

"Micky. I like it."

"Do you want a cup of tea?" she offered, with a self-conscious smile.

"Yeah, that'd be great. Just black is good." She handed him the documents from under the counter. He looked surprised. "Don't worry, I haven't let them out of my sight," she added quickly. "Were you worried about them?" she asked as she went into the tiny alcove behind the counter.

"Not about *them*. Things have happened around these documents. Bad things. Could be coincidence, or ..."

Micky brought out two mugs of black tea, teabags still in, and put them on one of the little tables, next to the banker's lamp. "Do you want to sit here? We can talk freely, the owner's away for a few days." She went back to get a saucer for the teabags as Luke thanked her and took his seat. "I'm convinced there's something unique about your map. I've translated some things that worry me." She sat opposite Luke, her braid swinging gently from side to side. Her hair was pulled back tightly, and Luke wondered how she would look with it out. Up close, she had a kind face.

"Me too," he replied. "Just before I called you yesterday, I found out that my father might have been murdered by someone looking for this map. I know it seems crazy, but it's possible."

31

Micky was shocked. For her, the map had already taken on some sinister qualities. But *murder*? That was a whole new level. Luke's words unsettled her.

"I'm not exactly sure where to start," she said as she unrolled the map. Luke held the edges down as she reached for the rulers. "Maybe here." She was pointing towards the drawing of the columns. "The Four Pillars. I've been wondering if this might be a legend or a kind of title. There's a theme. *Four* pillars, *four* distinct illustrations, near areas of Latin inscription, *four* towns drawn in great detail."

Luke studied the map. She could be right, but there were a lot of towns and villages depicted. "Which four towns?"

"Here, for example." She pointed out York.

Luke looked more closely but couldn't see what she was implying. "Why shouldn't York be shown in detail?"

"Look at London," she replied.

It took him a few seconds to grasp her point. "Yeah, I see what you mean. London has way less detail than York. That *is* weird."

"Exactly. Now here." She pointed out a town north of Lisbon. "I think it's Tomar. It's a *small town*." Luke stared and whistled as the significance registered.

"It looks more important than Lisbon on this map!" He was starting to get excited.

"It's odd, isn't it?" Micky was absorbed in the mystery. "Now here." She pointed out a town south of Florence, again depicted in greater detail than Florence, one of the most important cities of medieval Europe. "And the last one, down here." A region of Spain near Barcelona.

"That's actually amazing. I'd never have thought of that," Luke said.

"Well, my theory isn't perfect, but I'll come back to that soon." There was a gleam in her eye. She took out a handwritten sheet of notes and put it on the table. "All these areas have these Latin inscriptions." Again she pointed out the area near York, with its Latin passage. "This one says 'The fate of man is dependent upon the forces of evil being kept at bay'."

"Is that unusual, though?" Luke asked.

"No, you're right, It's not," she started. "It's ... kind of ... when you put them together." She read out the others: "The talismans are as old as time. They belong to a lost golden age; No man may look upon more than two talismans or else his life will be forfeit; Scatter the talismans to the four winds, else disaster will strike; and finally, Fate will be appeased by blood." She looked at his face, trying to gauge his reaction.

"What are these talismans?" he asked.

"I don't know yet. Maybe the illustrations are a clue."

"Okay," he said, although it sounded to Micky like a question.

She thought she was losing him. *Is this all just too farfetched?* "I know. Some of this is a bit of a stretch. Maybe I got a bit carried away with it." She started to feel foolish, and Luke noticed her face colour slightly.

"I don't think you got carried away at all," he encouraged. "There's other stuff I haven't told you. I've learned a lot over the past week. I don't even know where to begin." He shook his head, trying to clear his thoughts. He needed her help, and he knew he had to trust her. He *wanted* to trust her, she seemed so ... genuine. And *he'd* found *her*, almost at random, not the other way around.

"First, there's my father's will. He left me a letter with clues to find this map." He made quotation marks in the air with his fingers. "Clues that only I would understand. They led me to a hidden safe, where I found this, and an old bit of jewellery.

"The letter also told me about something else I'd inherited," he continued. "A *duty*. For centuries, my family have apparently been the guardians of the 'Collection'. He just never told me its purpose, and now I think he was killed for it. And I think his killer attacked me in his house." Luke touched his head where he'd been struck. "It's still sore a week later."

Micky looked horrified. "But how could that ..." She didn't finish the question, as the implications sunk in.

"I can't be sure. Like I said before, I only found out how he died yesterday. Until then, I believed it was a burglary gone wrong. It all got me thinking that this map is dangerous." A customer entered the store, and Micky stood to help her.

While he waited, Luke checked the map once more. The Four Pillars. She'd said maybe it was the map's legend, or title. He thought of the book he'd borrowed from his mother. Another coincidence?

"Sorry about that," Micky said, sitting down again as the customer left the shop.

"Don't worry about it. I was just thinking about my flight back home. I started reading a book I borrowed from my mother. She's interested in history, too. It's called *The Four Pillars of Gnosis: A Brief History of the Cathar Faith*. I even had a dream about it. About the Inquisition. I was being interrogated by zealots. Anyway, do you think these four pillars are the Cathars' four pillars?" he asked, pointing at the illustration on the map.

"It's definitely possible. The area and the timing seem right."

"The timing?"

"Mid-thirteenth century. Here." She pointed at the bottom of the map. "Anno Domini MCCXLIII. The Year of our Lord, 1243."

Forty-three. The last number of the safe combination. Simple and easy to remember, as long as you have all the information. Impossible to guess if you didn't.

"Here, too," she continued, touching the map near Carcassonne, next to the Latin phrase she had translated as 'The talismans are as old as time. They belong to a lost golden age'. "The Languedoc. It was a Cathar stronghold." She took a breath, as if to say something, but stopped short.

"What is it?" he prompted.

"Twelve forty-three. I'm pretty sure that was the year of the siege at Montségur." They both looked at the map, and Montségur was literally on her fingertip. "I've been wondering why there's an inscription here but no illustration. Could Montségur be the *origin* of these mythical talismans?"

"But *what* are they?" Luke asked.

"The illustrations. They could be a clue. Look." Micky excitedly pointed out the drawings she'd decided were the most important and prominent. The first was the one in Portugal. It looked to Luke like a pocket watch. "I think it could be an astrolabe. It's an old instrument used by astronomers and navigators. And here ..." She pointed to a sketch near Siena, Italy that could have been an artist drawing a lion's head. "A lot of effort has gone into that one."

"What could that mean?" Luke asked, confused.

"What were the 'four pillars'? In your book."

"Um, mysticism, philosophy, science and art. Shit. Nice one." He grinned at her. "Those two could be science and art, couldn't they?"

"Yes! I think they could be," she said, quietly pleased.

"And the other two?" Luke enquired.

"Well, that's where my theory doesn't seem to work." Her enthusiasm waned slightly. "I can't make out the picture in Catalonia, and here in York there's only a flower."

Luke studied the map once again. The illustration near Barcelona didn't look like anything familiar. A strange, circular symbol. As he looked at the York flower, Micky drew his eye towards Humberside.

"And this doesn't fit." She was pointing directly at a beautiful drawing of the piece of jewellery he'd found in the safe. "It's an ankh."

Luke quickly pulled his phone out of his pocket. "I knew I'd seen it before. It's this." He showed her a photo of the artefact, and her jaw dropped. "It was in the safe. With the map and stuff. I guess it's part of the *Collection*."

Micky shuddered.

"Are you all right?" Luke asked.

She looked pale. "It makes this seem so *real*. I'm a bit freaked out, I suppose. I *thought* this might be a kind of treasure map. Like a key to a puzzle. But maybe it's a puzzle nobody would want to solve."

Luke waited for her to continue.

"I wasn't going to tell you, because it sounds crazy, but I had a nightmare after working on the map. I don't have those. I don't dream, or at least I don't remember them. But now it makes more sense. There was a man in black coming towards me. He was speaking in Latin. '*Vos scitis a veritate. Oportet te mori.* You know the truth. You must die.' I woke up when he stabbed me with a red-hot poker."

"Fuck me," Luke blurted out. "Sorry. That's exactly how my father was murdered."

32

"What does it all mean?" Micky asked, her brow deeply furrowed. Luke shrugged, shaking his head. "No clue."

"Do you know where it came from?"

"Only that the Shaw family have had it for generations. But the Collection isn't just the map and that ankh. There are other papers." Luke took out his phone again and showed her the photos of the other ancient documents. "I should've given you these last week." He shook his head. "Didn't know what I had."

"Could I have a closer look at those?" Micky asked.

"Yeah, sure. I'll message them to you."

"Over the Internet? Are you sure?"

"Hmm. You're right. I've got copies at my flat. The originals are in Harrogate." *In the kitchen drawer.* Luke looked over at the computer. "Printer?"

Micky showed Luke the printer tucked away in the alcove behind the counter. It took him less than a minute to connect his phone to it and print copies of the other documents.

"Do you have any photos of the map?" she asked.

"Just these." He tapped the A3 pages. "Why do you ask?"

"I can't quite make out this bit of text." She pointed out the short passage written on the Mediterranean shore near Barcelona. Luke could see that the original had been damaged somehow. A small part of the inscription was missing, and a blemish obscured some of what was there. "It's the phrase I've translated as 'Fate will be appeased by blood', but I just can't be sure."

"Sounds like a warning to me. I'd have to go up to Harrogate and get the originals. I left them there because I don't have anywhere safe to store them."

"Okay. I've got plenty of homework to keep me going here anyway," Micky said, looking at the newly printed copies. "But," she mused, tilting her head to one side, "if the ankh *is* one of the four pillars, why isn't it in its hiding place in Hessle. Or York? Why did your father have it?"

"I guess we'll never know," Luke replied.

Micky clearly wasn't satisfied with his answer. She examined the map again. "Let's see what we do know," she said without lifting her gaze.

Luke sat down opposite her at the little table.

She was absorbed in the map. "It seems clear that the ankh *was* in Hessle. If I'm right about the clues on the map, it should be in York, so I don't really understand what happened there. But here," she stabbed the map with her finger, "it's quite clear." She abruptly stood and went over to the counter, returning with a magnifying glass. She quickly inspected other parts of the map, then returned to Hessle. "This church. Why would a tiny village in East Yorkshire have a detailed drawing of its church when most other places don't?"

Luke didn't know what to say. He just watched and listened as she became more aminated, poring over the illustration of the Hessle church.

"What could this mean?" she asked, pointing at the left side of the drawing. There was a tiny cross with four equal sides.

Luke thought for a moment, recalling his mother's book. "A Templar Cross maybe?"

"Let's see if we can find out more about this church," Micky said, taking out her phone. A moment later she found what she was looking for. "There was only one church anywhere near here in the twelve hundreds. It the All Saints Church. There's a site here about its *Templar* history."

"But the Templars were *Crusaders*. Weren't they the ones persecuting the Cathars?" Luke asked.

"Hmm. True. But what else could this be?" She continued scrutinising the map. "I still think you're right. A Templar Cross. Somewhere on the west side of the building." She thought for a moment. "Whoever hid it would have chosen a location that would be safe for centuries. What better than a church?"

"That was nearly eight hundred years ago." Luke hated to dampen her enthusiasm, but it seemed like such a long shot. "Needle, haystack."

"I think we can narrow it down even further." It appeared her enthusiasm would not be dampened. She showed Luke an image of the original floor plan of the church. "We can ignore all the new bits. Your haystack is a lot smaller than you think."

Her excitement was contagious. She was right. A cross, or something Templar, in a small, eight-hundred-year-old portion of a relatively modest church. Not impossible. Although the ankh must have been removed in the distant past, presumably by one of Luke's father's ancestors. Still, wouldn't it be great to find that the map's clues are real.

Micky must have had the same thought. "How far is Hessle?" They both grabbed their phones. "Hour, hour and a half, maybe," she said, getting in first. "Maybe you could go there to take a look."

Luke stared at her. The ankh couldn't be there, but it would be good to confirm Micky's theory. "Okay ... You could come, too, if you wanted to."

Micky was taken aback. "Oh, no, I don't think ..." She felt very tempted, but her mind suddenly flooded with all the reasons why not. "I have to work. The owner is away. I can't just close the store," she said lamely.

"That's okay," he said. "I understand." He didn't want to press her; she seemed slightly embarrassed. Even so, he felt disappointed. He reflected that this morning's discussion had been one of the most enjoyable conversations he'd had in a long time.

33

Robert Schaw trudged through thick snow back to his home, looking forward to the warmth of the large hearth in his library. He had attended a meeting of the newly formed Master Masons, an assembly committed to the values the stonemasons must uphold, coupled with traditional mysteries long associated with the craft. Robert's younger brother, William, was Master of Works for King James VI, and the Grand Master of the Masons' assembly. For Robert, it was more the traditional mysteries than the mason's craft that had attracted his interest.

Robert had sworn an oath that he would never speak of his responsibility as guardian with any other. The Master Masons were a means for him to hear tell of developments pursuant to his calling. Tonight, he heard word of such a development. One of the masons had returned from his stonework at York Minster and told a story of the Brotherhood of Amaury's relentless search of that edifice. The Brotherhood had been galvanised in recent years, through the leadership of Henry Montfort, an arrogant and ruthless man. Henry had spent more than two decades meticulously scouring the minster for a treasure Robert knew he would not find.

Tonight, of most concern to Robert was a conversation the mason had overheard between Henry and another man. Henry's lack of success at York had now led him to seek the original map of Bernard de Péreille. Montfort had evidently come to realise that the replica must be incomplete or have contained transcription errors.

The Schaw family had long been guardians of the map. As the eldest of his generation, Robert had inherited that obligation from his father, as it had been for generations. Robert knew of Bernard's journey, and of the sacred talismans scattered to the four winds by the Cathar faithful. Bernard's map, safely hidden within a secret panel in the Schaw manor house library, had been inscribed with a warning many decades, or possibly even centuries, earlier. He knew the power of the four pillars, and that in wicked hands, the fate of man would be in jeopardy.

As he approached the Schaw manor, he also considered the other disturbing tale he'd heard that evening. The true location of Bernard's talisman was to have major stonework completed in the spring, and this would include rebuilding the oldest part of the crypt. It was not the guardian's task to hold the talisman – his was merely to protect the map – but Robert knew he must now decide whether he should seek to retrieve the sacred object or to accept the risk that it would be discovered, or destroyed, during the works.

Robert sat in his grand library, tempted to retrieve the old map from its hiding place, eager to understand whether it held a clue as to how Montfort might have been misled. *Is it possible changes were made after it was copied by the monk centuries ago?* With a knock on the heavy timber door, a servant brought whisky and unobtrusively stoked the fire.

"That will be all for this evening," Robert said, dismissing him. The servant nodded and left Robert alone with his thoughts. Robert slowly sipped his whisky as he reflected on the lonely role he had inherited. It seemed there was work to be done, and yet he could speak of it with no one, not even his trusted brother William. As Master of Works for the king, William's counsel would have been helpful. Robert had been considering for a while that Hessle may not be the most suitable location for the sacred talisman. He had heard stories of the estuary flooding the town and the sea almost reaching the church. The King's Master of Works would certainly have sight of how serious the risk to the church was.

Once the main house was all quiet, Robert locked the library door and retrieved the map, together with the delicate old parchments stored with it. He spread the documents out on the desk and studied them. It was difficult in the lamplight, but it was something he dare not do in daylight. With his eyeglass and some perseverance, he found what he sought. A symbol of a flower near York had been modified. One of the inks had faded more than the other. He could see that, at one time, the symbol could certainly have been an ankh.

So, it seems the Brotherhood have a map ... Mercifully, theirs must show the original incorrect location of the English talisman. But could it be a full copy of Bernard's map? If so, perhaps the Brotherhood already have the other three objects! It was a horrifying thought, that these sacred artefacts, so brilliantly hidden away right under the nose of the church, might already been in malevolent hands.

Robert took his eyeglass and carefully scrutinised the other talisman symbols on the parchment. None appeared to have been altered in any way, unlike the York ankh. Part of him was pleased the map was accurate, though part of him was deeply troubled that it now seemed possible to him that the Brotherhood had a copy with the correct locations for three of the four pillars.

With another thought in his mind, he examined the depiction of Hessle very closely. *Could it, too, have been added later, after the map had been copied?* With a meticulous comparison of the inscription and illustrations around the north-east of England, he determined that Hessle had been an original part of the map, including the All Saints Church. The fact worried him, because it was plausible that, in desperation, the Brotherhood could simply start searching every thirteenth-century structure depicted. There were not that many, and he knew little about the resources the Brotherhood had at their disposal. He knew only of Henry's lust for the treasure, and that under Henry they had grown stronger.

Robert's last hope for the protection of the objects lay in the nature of the parchments accompanying the map. He knew that some of these documents had not existed prior to Bernard's death. One of these described the investiture of the first sentinel, the responsibility vested in the Schaw family. Another was Bernard's travel journal. The cache had been safe with Robert's family for three hundred years, and he felt confident in the assumption that the copy of the map was made during Bernard's travels, when the original had been much more exposed.

It was logical that *only* the map had been copied. Most people were not literate, especially in Latin, and hand copying documents was an arduous and time-consuming task, whereas copying a map primarily required drawing skill. In Bernard's time, maps carried a magical quality, a promise of adventure, or treasure, so an obvious choice.

The parchment that now had Robert's attention was much more ordinary – one evidently penned by Bernard at or near the end of his journey. The handwriting was shaky and difficult to read. Being written in the hand, and imperfect Latin, of an educated layman, it did not appear to carry the same weight as the map and the other documents. As a scholar himself, Robert had learned Latin and was able to painstakingly translate. The parchment spoke of an unfinished journey south from Montségur, and as Robert translated, a smile slowly crept over his face.

34

With the mid-afternoon sun shining brightly, Luke was glad of the shade of the big old trees and the gentle breeze coming off the estuary just south of the railway tracks. The town of Hessle was lovely and peaceful. On the train journey, as he'd approached the station, he had glimpses of the Humber Estuary, with its brownish water and rocky shoreline. According to the map, All Saints Church was about a kilometre up the Station Road. His path took him past some stately homes and the occasional well-maintained terrace. He turned left onto Southgate, heading towards the town centre, soon emerging onto a major intersection. There were a couple of elegant old Tudor pubs, and he could see a large stone church building ahead.

On the left side of the building, Luke spotted an open door. He followed the path between the hall and the old church and entered. The building seemed to be open to the public, but empty. It was a beautiful structure, but as Luke looked around, he saw little that he could realistically date back eight hundred years. Other than the stone walls, nearly everything else looked to be more eighteenth or nineteenth century than thirteenth. The altars, the pulpit, the pews and even the older memorial plaques – all of it looked to be centuries too young. Micky had suggested looking for a cellar or a crypt. 'That's more likely to be older, and seen fewer tourists and less change over the years.' Good advice, if it *had* a cellar. He looked around, but didn't see any obvious stairs leading down. His phone pinged.

I want to see you tonight. Madison.

Sorry. Out of town.

Shame. You know what I want. A kiss emoji. *Where are you?*

Castleford. He'd say he was visiting his new aunt, if she asked.

Tomorrow then. The four-poster. A wink emoji.

While he'd been texting, a sexton had walked in and was looking at him with disdain.

Unperturbed, he beamed at the man. "Hi. My name's Lucas, John Lucas," he improvised. "I'm a historian researching a lead from an early medieval manuscript. It suggests there might possibly be an old Cathar artefact located somewhere in your beautiful church. Do you mind if I take a look around?"

"We are open to the public, so please feel free. I've never heard any such story before, and I think it's highly unlikely that a thing like that would ever have been here, but we do date back to those times, I suppose."

"Perhaps there's a cellar, or a similarly old part of this amazing structure?" *Am I laying it on too thick?* "May I ask your name? I'd like to be able to give you credit if we're able to publish."

The man brightened up a little, and handed Luke a card.

"There *is* an undercroft. We don't usually open that for tourists, but since you're a historian, I suppose there's no harm. The stairs are to the side of the nave, just over there."

Luke eventually saw what the man had pointed at. A low stone wall separated the narrow stairs from the nave. From a distance, it blended into the main wall, almost concealing it. "Thank you so much," Luke said, turning towards the stairs.

"You mustn't touch anything, of course."

"Of course," he called over his shoulder. "Thanks."

Down the stairs, he found himself in a cellar, poorly lit by tiny highlight windows set deep into the stone walls. Arches all around him held the tonnes of stone above in place. It *looked* old enough. What had Micky said? 'You'll be looking for something *Templar* at the west end of the oldest parts, maybe in a crypt.' *Now, which direction is west?*

It took a minute to get his bearings, and he worked out that the west end was, in fact, an old crypt. *Perfect. But now what?* He carefully studied the walls using his phone light but found nothing helpful. Most of the tombs around him had very worn inscriptions carved into them, and he couldn't make out any names or even letters. They all had the traditional Christian cross on them, not the equal-armed Templar Cross. He scratched his head as he walked around the undercroft again, making sure he'd got his sense of direction right. There were various piles of old junk, broken pews and the like, but nothing as promising as the crypt. And he was sure that *was* the west side. At the far end, there were still a couple of dusty and very plain-looking alcoves with unadorned tombs. He'd dismissed those at first because they seemed so insignificant, but now he remembered that the Templars took a vow of poverty, and that's exactly what their tombs should look like.

Sure enough, carved into the top of the furthest back sarcophagus was a Templar Cross. No name, and no other inscription of any kind. But as Luke studied it, he saw a mark near the far end, at the head. He couldn't quite get his head over it to see it properly; the alcove was just too small. But he could get his phone in. After a few attempts, he managed to get a good flash picture of the marking. *An ankh!* His heart started beating faster, and he wanted to look inside. He knew the ankh couldn't be there, but his curiosity was in full flight. Rummaging around the old junk in the cellar, he found two short lengths of timber that he thought might help him lever up the stone lid.

He examined the lid for a good place to wedge his timber in and found some old tool markings, perhaps where his ancestor had removed the ankh centuries ago. With all his strength, he had just managed to lever the lid up no more than a centimetre when the sexton found him.

"What on earth are you doing?" the man cried.

"I ... I just ..."

"You'd better leave now, before I call the police." The sexton was clearly agitated.

Luke imagined that nothing like this had ever happened to the man before. He must have looked like a grave robber, or some kind of fetishist.

"I'm sorry," was all he could say, as he quickly climbed the stairs and left the church.

The old pubs on Southgate looked inviting, but he decided he'd better leave the village in case the sexton saw him again and changed his mind about calling the police. He'd get a pint and something to eat back in Bradford. As he strode back to the station, he consoled himself with the fact that he already had the ankh. Opening the tomb was just to check, and perhaps a morbid curiosity.

The sexton was still shaken when the phone rang in the church office. The caller's number told him it was the Archbishop of York's office. He hadn't been intending to report the incident, since there had been no visible harm, and he would have to admit that he'd been taken in by the young man. But the Archbishop's Chief of Staff could tell something was wrong, so the sexton told him of the young man's strange request and the attempted desecration of an ancient Templar tomb. "The oddest thing is that when I checked it for damage, I found an old Egyptian symbol, an ankh, etched on that sarcophagus. But it looked as though it had been there for years."

35

I found it!

Luke's phone rang almost immediately after he sent the text. "Hi."

"Hi. It's Micky."

"I know."

"Oh. Of course. You found it? Found *what?*"

"A Templar tomb with an ankh carved into the top! And it had some chisel marks where someone had opened it before me. Maybe my ancestor. It was amazing."

Micky listened intently as he told her all about his trip, the search, how he followed her suggestions to find the tomb and the hidden ankh drawing. He knew he sounded like an excited child, but he didn't care. "I've got some photos of it."

"I'd love to see them," she said, sounding every bit as keen. A momentary pause as Luke thought about suggesting they meet tonight. "Maybe tomorrow? Would that be all right?" she asked, tentatively.

"Yeah, that'd be good," he said, slightly disappointed.

They agreed to confirm in the morning and ended the call. Luke smiled to himself. Today had been one of the best days he could remember. Talking to Micky about the Collection had further rekindled his interest in history, and the trip to Hessle was *fun*. An *adventure*. He wondered fleetingly what it would feel like to be Indiana Jones.

It was just after eight o'clock. Time for something to eat and maybe a celebratory pint or two. On the way down to his local, Luke found himself whistling as he walked. He grinned as he greeted the lads in the pub.

"You look dangerously cheerful. That blonde must have agreed with you," Nick said. "I still can't believe your luck."

"You're just jealous that she fancies me," Luke retorted.

Ben and Josh laughed. Their drinks were almost finished, so he bought a round, as was their custom. He also ordered himself a meal.

"You dumped us like old rubbish," said Ben.

"And you'd have ignored her, I suppose," Luke shot back.

Nick just grinned. He'd have done exactly the same thing, and they all knew it.

"I was just helping a girl out."

"Out of her clothes, I'm sure," Ben replied.

"Are you jealous, Ben?" Nick asked, and Ben's face coloured, almost matching his mop of red hair.

"Now come on, lads. I told you she fancied me. That's all I'm saying," Luke said evenly.

Ben quickly recovered his usual cheerful demeanour and recounted for Josh the night last week when Nick got blanked and Luke got lucky. "She's an absolute stunner," he said. "Way out of Luke's league."

"Fuck off," Luke said good-naturedly. The lads were not going to spoil his mood tonight.

"Well then," Josh observed, "you're back to your old form, then."

"What old form?" Nick asked. Nick had moved up from Halifax three years ago and had met Ben when they both worked for the same bank. Luke, Ben and Josh had known each other since their university days.

"Our Luke here drank and shagged his way through university," Josh said, rather uncharitably. They all laughed loudly as Luke's pie arrived with a side of mushy peas.

A few months ago, Luke might have been annoyed with Josh. But not tonight. He was still buoyed up by the great day he'd had. He laughed along with the boys, too, even though it wasn't fair. In fact, it was only half true. The drinking half. He'd certainly drunk more than his share, but his time at university was often lonely. He'd just lost his mother, his relationship with his father was strained to say the least, and he'd had nobody to confide in. Sure, there had been the occasional girlfriend but, if he was honest with himself, they had been brief and superficial relationships. It wasn't like Josh had made out.

"Fuck you, Josh," Luke said without animosity, as he smeared the peas on top of the pie.

"So you're still seeing her?" Ben asked.

"Yep," he replied, with a mouthful of food. As he said it, it occurred to him that his heart wasn't in it. Madison wasn't the sort of girl he could talk to about yesterday's adventure. Or about much else. She just wasn't interested in how he felt. She'd asked questions about his father, but it was always on her terms, and every time he'd talked about himself, she'd changed the subject or she'd had to leave.

"Lucky bastard," Ben said.

As the others made various lascivious comments, Luke recalled his discussions with his birth mother and yesterday's conversation in the bookshop. Those had been like talking to old friends. Talking about their common interest in history. Comfortable in each other's company and not trying to be anything other than who they were. He didn't want to talk about his sex life; tonight he wanted to talk about his *discovery*. But even if he could trust the lads, or Madison, to be discreet, he thought there was no point. They wouldn't be interested, or would just find ways to poke fun at him.

36

"Edmund!" Henry bellowed to his son from his bedchamber. "Edmund! Where are you, boy?" Henry's impatience and irritation had grown steadily since the previous autumn when James, Henry's firstborn and favourite, had died from the Black Death. Edmund and his mother had been spared. In his lucid hours, Henry cursed the plague. He would not have missed the younger boy, nor his mother, had they been taken, but he'd had high ambitions for James.

"Yes, Father." Edmund's fresh face greeted him, his unruly reddish-brown hair falling over his eyes.

Henry looked at his son with distaste. At barely twenty years of age, although tall and physically strong, the boy was not ready. Edmund was a disappointment to him in many ways, but he knew he had no alternative.

"Sit." Henry motioned towards the armchair nearest the oversized four-poster bed, and Edmund obediently sat. He looked upon his father's sallow face, its pale skin intersected by a web of red lines like the fine cracking in an old painting. Henry's physician blamed the old man's dietary and drinking excesses for his appearance, but Henry did not care. Of more concern to the physician were Henry's periods of muddle and

159

delusion. These increasing spells of madness the physician attributed to the 'French Disease'.

"Boy, I have no other choice left. You are now my sole heir, and I must bequeath upon you a duty of great importance." Henry looked critically at his son. "You are weak, and the task will test you. It is my hope that it will make a man of you." Henry paused, as if to gather his thoughts. "For centuries, the Montfort family has had a great calling. We are destined to regain a great power. The prize is near, I can feel it. When I leave this world, you will lead the Brotherhood of Amaury as my heir."

Edmund heard his father's words, though his mind wandered. He had not heard his father speak of a brotherhood before. *What is this?* 'Great power', 'the prize is near'; these words swirled around Edmund's mind. He was not weak, as his father had declared, he simply didn't care. There was little about his father's life that interested Edmund. He had all the money he needed and, since his father had ignored him for most of his life, he could do as he pleased. But this was new. 'Great power'. *What might I do with great power?*

"The Brotherhood is close to obtaining one of four great and powerful talismans, and you must now show your mettle and lead my brethren." Henry laid his head back on the overstuffed pillow for a moment. "Fetch the seneschal. He will guide you." He closed his eyes and waved his son away.

Edmund sat a moment, wondering what use the ancient steward could possibly be but, even with his father's weakened state, he dared not challenge him. He stood and left the room to find a servant. *Great power. Is this real, or one of father's increasingly frequent delusions?* Certainly Henry was feared by many, Edmund had seen it in the eyes of men who had come to his father's regular evening gatherings.

The servant returned with the white-haired old man a few minutes later, interrupting Edmund's thoughts.

The seneschal set his steely eyes upon Edmund, who found himself unexpectedly taken aback. "So, Henry has told you," he said, in a strong voice that belied his age. The familiarity grated upon Edmund. The old servant should know his place. Edmund was about to admonish him, when he turned and walked towards the library. "Come," the old man said, and Edmund felt obliged to follow.

In the library, the seneschal invited Edmund to sit and then took a key from his waistband to open a small panel built into the vast bookcase. Edmund watched as he withdrew a bound manuscript and a parchment. As he laid the parchment on the table, Edmund saw it was a map of the kingdom.

"You are now part of an age-old quest," the old man started, looking Edmund squarely in the eyes, in a manner unbecoming of a servant. "We have been seeking to restore a great power to its rightful owners. It is as old as the ages and has lain in the hands of the unworthy for many centuries. Fools who are afraid." The seneschal paused, staring at Edmund. The young man could not hold the eyes of this servant who spoke like an equal. Edmund was tempted to slap him for his insolence, but there was something compelling, a strength, in his expression that stopped him. Edmund did not fear the seneschal; he knew he could easily kill him, but he could see the old man had a use after all. It was becoming clear why Henry had kept him on in the household long after he was able to continue its stewardship.

"We are close, but Henry will not see our present task through. That will be up to you." The old man's eyes challenged Edmund.

"How do you know Father will not see it through?" he demanded.

"I have known Henry his whole life. I have known many things in my long life. This I can see clearly. I have seen his disease before. The Great Pox will take him soon." The seneschal picked up the bound manuscript and started to patiently explain its contents, inducting Edmund into the Brotherhood as one might teach a child. As the old man spoke, Edmund resolved that he would prove his cold, distant father wrong. He would *enjoy* his new-found authority.

The seneschal told Edmund of Henry's relentless search over the past three decades for the York talisman, a search now widening further. He also explained the tantalising implication that somewhere there must be a more accurate map than the one in their possession.

As he listened to the old man's words, Edmund reflected that his life had just become much more interesting. He resolved also that he would seek out his father's physician and find out how long Henry would be standing between him and his new destiny. He would find out when the Great Pox, the affliction he'd heard the physician name as syphilis, would kill Henry.

37

The alarm went off as Micky sat at the kitchen bench eating her breakfast. She'd woken early again and already showered and dressed, but had forgotten to switch it off. The thoughts in her mind went in two different directions: on one hand, she was excited that Luke had found hard evidence that the map truly was a key to a lost treasure of some sort; on the other, she was worried that whatever the 'treasure' was, it might be dangerous, or at least it might have bad people chasing after it.

She finished getting ready for work and made a cup of tea. It would be good to hear more about the find at the All Saints Church yesterday. And she wanted to see Luke's photos. The implications of finding the ancient etching of an ankh were still sinking in. Luke sounded genuinely happy that he'd had a successful trip, and she was delighted her detective work had paid off. Ever since Luke had walked into Sutherland's and shown her the map, she'd been captivated by it. It was just the sort of historical mystery she loved. The romance of it was one of the reasons she worked at Sutherland's.

Last night, she had made a start on the other documents. Without at least starting the translation, it was impossible to tell which might be more important, so she'd just dived in. The first turned out to be a thirteenth-century travel journal, chronicling an arduous northward journey from Montségur through to York. It was an interesting piece of history and a glimpse of early medieval life but, other than an occasional vague reference to a 'quest', there was nothing significant in it. Translating its four small leaves took her until close to midnight. She then made a start on the next document, written during the time of the Reformation, three centuries after the journal. It consisted of two beautifully inscribed sheets of cream-coloured parchment bound together. It turned out to be compelling enough to keep her up until one am. It told of the Brotherhood of Amaury, a fanatical religious group borne out of the Inquisition.

This morning, Micky had been tempted to go back to it before she went to work but instead decided to continue at the shop, hoping it would be another quiet day. Still a bit early to text Luke to confirm their meeting, she thought, so she flicked through the newsfeed on her phone. Something caught her eye, and she scrolled back. It was a headline that shocked her:

Grisly Murder in Historic Hessle Church

She read the story underneath and it made her blood run cold. She started to text Luke but changed her mind and called him instead.

"Hi," Luke said, still half asleep.

"Hi. Sorry to ring this early. There's something you need to see."

"What's up?" He could hear the anxiety in her voice.

"A murder. In Hessle. I'll send you the link and call you back." Click.

Wow, she must be worried. His phone pinged, and he clicked on the link.

Peter Collier, clergyman and church sexton, was brutally murdered in the Parish Church of All Saints in Hessle last night. A police spokesperson stated that an investigation is under way, but at this stage there is no apparent motive. Humberside Police would like to hear from anyone who was in the vicinity of the church between 9 pm and 11 pm.

Collier is alleged to have been beaten and badly burnt before being stabbed to death, according to an unofficial source. Police are also seeking a young man seen leaving the church grounds yesterday afternoon, to assist with their enquiries.

The phone rang again.

"Holy shit," Luke said breathlessly. "That must be the guy I talked to. He threw me out."

"What?"

"Don't worry. I'll tell you later. But, *fuck*, I don't ... what does ... *fuck!*"

"Are you okay?" Micky asked softly.

"Are *you* okay? This is seriously disturbing."

"Yes. Are you going to call them?"

"Who?" Luke asked, as he started to realise what she meant.

"The police. They're looking for you."

"You're right. Shit. I lied to him. The sexton. Told him I was a historian. He caught me trying to open the Templar's casket and told me to get out or he'd call the police. How's that going to look?"

"Maybe he didn't tell anyone. I suppose this could be unrelated."

"Beaten, burnt and stabbed. Just like my father. Must be related," Luke said glumly.

"If he'd reported you, the police would probably have found you by now," she offered.

"I gave him a false name. God, that's going to look even worse."

"Really? I'd never have thought of doing that," Micky said. "Anyway, aren't you in the clear? Weren't you back in Bradford last night?"

"Oh, yeah, you're right! I was out at the pub last night with a few mates. From 8.30 to about 11 pm." He sounded relieved.

"Do you think it might look worse if you don't call them?" It was a gentle nudge, and he took the hint.

"I think I will. Good idea. Can I call you back later?"

"Okay. Do you want to meet for coffee or something?" Micky felt a bit awkward, but she was keen to see his photos and tell him where she'd got to with the other documents.

"Yeah, that'd be great." He looked at his bedside clock. "About eleven?"

"Okay, see you then."

38

The spring sunshine had brought with it the sweet aroma of cherry blossoms. The trees in Robert's garden were in full bloom, surrounding him in a sea of soft pink flowers as he sat on a stone bench under the largest of the trees, sipping a tankard of cloudy pear cider. The drink had been warmed with a fire iron, and gently steamed in the cool evening breeze.

Robert smiled to himself as he reflected on his journey to the Shire of York. The task he had set himself might have been a lengthy affair; however, he'd been lucky. Perhaps fate had intervened. Once he'd settled into suitable lodgings in the village of Hessle, he spent several successive evenings venturing into the old church, and searching through its most ancient parts. By the third night, he determined the crypt was the most promising. The task would have been easier by daylight, and he had almost resolved to gather some stonemason's tools the next day to allow him to search for hidden cavities in the stone walls. But he decided on a final search of the coffins in the numerous hollows of the crypt, first, and set about examining them by candlelight.

He was close to admitting defeat when he found the crude inscription of an ankh on a Templar coffin. A clever hiding place – right under the noses of the Catholics. With considerable effort, he was able to lift the stone lid and prop it open enough to rummage around the old bones. He knew he'd found it as soon as he felt the cold metal in his hand. He also felt an exhilaration that perhaps came from relief at the end of his search, or perhaps somehow from the talisman itself.

He quietly left, confident no one had seen him. Back at his lodgings, he secured the talisman around his neck and under his clothing with a cord. His task now was to protect the ankh as well as the sentinel's map and documents, and to ensure the whole cache was safely passed down to his future heir.

At that thought, Robert pictured his father telling him, just a year before, that he must find a suitable wife before he was too old. At the time, Robert did not know of his future calling as sentinel, but now he understood the importance of his father's words. Approaching his thirtieth year, Robert knew his life was likely half over. He wondered what life would be like with the sounds of children in his large house. He tried to picture himself initiating his not-yet-conceived son as sentinel, in the manner his own father had done.

As dusk slowly fell, these things filled Robert's mind. The cherry blossom's delicate scent filled his nostrils, and the cider warmed his belly. His duty as sentinel had taken on a new meaning now he was also holder of one of the four sacred talismans. It had become a weightier calling. Although he felt confident that the Brotherhood of Amaury could not know of the ankh's new location, his new responsibility did not cheer him. It had been fate that had taken Robert to the Masons' meeting two months earlier, and mere serendipity that a fellow Mason had mentioned the overheard words of Henry Montfort. The Brotherhood was now on the trail of the original map of de Péreille. Years of fruitless searching had convinced Henry that his own copy must be incomplete. The Brotherhood's men continued to search in York, scouring other old structures and the city's four old gates, although some of their number had been diverted to other locations shown on Henry's map. It was only a matter of time before they reached Hessle, and Robert grimaced, realising the lodging-house landlord would surely remember his tall visitor from Scotland.

Robert had taken the precaution of travelling under an assumed name, but the Brotherhood had proved its resourcefulness more than once. It was a troublesome thought, although Robert took comfort from his discovery in Bernard's parchment, the document he had carefully translated on the day he decided to retrieve the Hessle talisman. The cache of documents chronicled Bernard and his fellow monks' travel south from the Château Montségur. The old parchment penned in Bernard's shaky hand recorded a decision one of the monks had felt compelled to make. During his journey, several days south of Catalonia, the monk had encountered bands of Moors making trouble for the Catholics. The Moors were an enlightened people, encouraging knowledge and tolerance, but they had become frustrated with the Church's unremitting dogma and fanaticism, occasionally lashing out in violent skirmishes. Both sides regularly attacked and destroyed the homes and structures of the other, particularly religious edifices. The monk had concluded it was not safe to follow the original plan to conceal his talisman at the southernmost edge of the Catholics' domain.

Bernard had composed his parchment carefully and did not give the new location of the talisman, merely referring to its 'origin'. Robert read and reread the parchment and its accompanying documents thoroughly, but there was nothing in them, nor on the map, that gave Robert any indication of the origin of the talismans. There were only references like 'ancient mysticism' and 'as old as time itself'. The parchment also contained a few sentences of apparently meaningless religious homages and a vague reference to Solomon. *Could that mean the talisman's origin is the Holy Land?* No matter, Robert decided, this news meant the Brotherhood's map must show the location of only two of the four talismans. At least two of them must be safe. Once again, the thought brought a smile to his face.

39

Eventually, Luke managed to get through to a detective constable at Humberside Police. The conversation started uncomfortably, with the detective pressing Luke for his reasons for being in Hessle and visiting the church. Luke barely had time to answer each question before the detective fired another. He also asked Luke about his line of work, his interests, his friends, and how any of that related to the church or the dead man. Luke's answers did not seem to convince him, but after taking Luke's friends' names and numbers for checking his whereabouts the previous night, the man relented a little. He also asked Luke not to travel too far in case he could further assist with their enquiries. He did not give Luke any details of the murder, and Luke felt he dare not ask too much, for fear he might draw attention to the Collection. *Would they believe him, or do anything about it anyway?*

After the call, Luke went out to buy a coffee, and clear his head. The sexton's murder, seemingly in the same manner as his father's, had shocked him. Thoughts of that murder, his own nightmare, and Micky's too, filled his head. He, at least, was no longer a suspect, but that did not mean he wasn't in danger. He couldn't help but wonder if his visit to Hessle was related to the man's death. *Did I cause it somehow? But how could that be?* If it wasn't related in some way, it was certainly a bizarre coincidence. Yesterday's adventure now had a dark tinge to it, and he started to question whether he was getting into something that might be over his head. *Way* over.

Checking his phone, he also realised he was late for Micky. *Eleven o'clock, dammit.*

He sent her a text.

Running a bit late, sorry. Lunch instead?

Okay.

Great. See you at about 11.45.

Half an hour later, he went down to Market Street, arriving at Sutherland's just on time. As he opened the door, it occurred to him that Micky would have to close the shop if they were going to have lunch. Maybe he should have bought something instead. But the answer to his thought came in the form of a severe-looking woman in her mid-sixties behind the counter. He'd forgotten Micky had said the owner would be back today. The woman raised her eyebrows as she observed Luke. He wasn't their usual sort of customer.

Micky appeared from the small alcove, pulling a charcoal jersey over her blouse. "Do you mind if I go a little early?" she asked the woman.

"No, dear, that's fine." She appraised Luke, as if deciding whether he was a suitable lunch companion for Micky.

"There's a café just down the street," Micky offered.

"I'm in your hands."

The café had started to fill, but it was before the rush and they found a table near the back. Luke told Micky about his call to the Humberside detective. They were both still shaken by the murder, wanting to know if it was the same as Luke's father's death, but a web search didn't yield any new information.

"Wish I knew what we're getting into," he lamented.

"I've done some work on two of the other documents," Micky said. "It was a quiet morning, and Mrs Sutherland's been busy in the back with a box of books she brought back from Belgium." A young girl came to take their orders. After she left, Micky leaned a little closer, speaking quietly.

"One of the parchments was written by a man who might be an ancestor of yours. Of your father's, I mean. Robert Schaw. As far as I can tell, he was a Scottish Freemason. His document is about a fanatical religious organisation called the 'Brotherhood of Amaury'. They originated in the 13th century and were named after Arnaud Amaury, an abbot, papal legate and inquisitor." She explained that Amaury was the man who, at the Massacre of Béziers in 1209, had ordered the slaughter of thousands of men, women and children. The legend held that the Crusaders could not distinguish the Catholic faithful from the heretics, so Amaury ordered them to kill everyone. Luke's eyes widened as she told the story.

"So this Brotherhood's namesake is a mass murderer," he said starkly. "I recently read that the Inquisition is actually still going today, although with a different name. Maybe the Brotherhood of Amaury is still around too." A grim look passed between them before Luke changed the subject. "Do you want to see the pics of the Templar coffin?" He took his phone out.

"Yes, please." Some of her enthusiasm returned as she flipped through the photos. "There can't be much doubt, then, that this is all connected. And real."

"You said you worked on two of those documents. Was the other one of any use?"

"A 13th-century journal. Very interesting for me ..." She paused, and Luke was sure there was a twinkle in her eyes. He waited for her to explain, but her serious expression quickly returned. "... but not very enlightening for us. It's a record of a journey from Montségur to York, where it just seems to stop, unfinished, in 1244. Your ancestor's document from 1584 was more helpful. It says that the Brotherhood's sole purpose is to find a treasure which it considers its property. Something stolen from Crusaders in the twelve hundreds."

"Good to know that my ancestors were helpful."

"And *mine*. The travel journal belonged to *Bernard de Péreille*. He doesn't say it, but I think he was a Cathar." Luke's browed furrowed, as he looked at her. She was clearly enjoying herself. "My last name is *Perrell*. It's an anglicised version of de Péreille." She said it with a perfectly beautiful French accent.

"Do you speak French?" Luke asked impulsively.

"Yes," she replied rather shyly. "It's quite common for linguists to speak multiple languages. I did a year of my studies at McGill in Montréal. Anyway, I knew about my family history before I'd seen these documents, but this morning I was able to join the dots and go back a couple of centuries further. I'm pretty confident that Bernard was my direct ancestor." She took off her glasses to clean the lenses, and Luke noticed her amber eyes positively gleaming as her enthusiasm showed in her unguarded smile.

"You've heard of the Albigensian Crusade?" she went on.

"Yes."

"And Montségur? The siege there was one of the later atrocities during that Crusade." Luke nodded, encouraging her to continue, as their food arrived. He looked at the small sandwich and was pleased they'd also accepted the girl's recommendation of an antipasto plate to share.

"Bernard was the brother of the Lord of Montségur, Raymond de Péreille," Micky went on. "He disappears from the historical record after the siege. Raymond, and Bernard's wife and son, escaped that awful pyre, but it's widely believed Bernard was burnt to death with the others. I think this document means that Bernard also somehow escaped to make the journey to York."

"With the ankh and the map." Luke shook his head in disbelief. "That's amazing, that your family and mine are both connected to this. I don't believe in 'fate', but what are the odds?"

"Oh, that reminds me," she said, moving on, "I've been mulling over that last phrase I wasn't sure about. The one I thought was 'fate will be appeased by blood'. Without the original map, it's a bit hard to be sure, but I think it might be more like 'finding fate, or destiny, through blood'."

"Either way, a pretty nasty warning," Luke said, finishing his sandwich, and eyeing the last wedge of Brie on the little shared plate.

"There's more in the map, too. There's something in it I don't understand, about 'the song of the mystics'. It doesn't make sense yet. But I've been looking at it all again, more holistically, and thinking about how people communicated in the early Middle Ages, their superstitions and traditions and the like. I can't quite put my finger on its underlying meaning, I mean *overall*, but it does seem like a warning that this power, or whatever it is, is *very* dangerous. That's why it was 'cast to the four winds'." Micky paused, leaving the thought hanging in the air, while she finished her salad.

Luke considered her words in silence. Deep in his gut, he knew this wasn't just a historical curiosity to be solved. There was something more, something dark, to it.

"I'll fight you for that last piece of cheese," he said, to lighten the mood. Micky looked up at him cheekily. She quickly picked up the Brie and popped it into her mouth with a grin. They both laughed.

"Well, this is cosy," Madison said, surprising Luke as she leaned in front of Micky to plant a long kiss on his lips. "Hope I'm not intruding," she said dismissively.

"Hi," Luke said, caught off balance. "Ah, this is my ... friend, Michaela."

Madison gave Micky a brief smile, assessing her as she did so. "Madison."

"I'd better get back to work now," Micky said awkwardly, standing. She quickly left the table and paid for her lunch.

40

"Did you miss me?" Madison was in a playful mood. As Luke paid the remainder of the café bill, she bit his earlobe again, whispering, "You know what I want." The cashier looked at both of them, barely hiding his look of distaste.

"I was going up to Harrogate today; do you want to come?" He gave in to his own weakness.

"Ooh, yes." The sweet smile, and a naughty-girl look in her eyes.

"I was going to go to Valley Gardens before dinner," he said, ignoring her tease. "I love the New Zealand Garden there. Do you want to see it?"

"Aww. I have something I need to do first, sorry. I'll meet you for dinner. Do you know a place?" Luke suggested the gastropub he'd eaten at the first time he went to the house. "Sounds perfect," she said, waving over her shoulder as she left.

Luke turned and walked in the other direction, back towards his flat. This time he would remember to pack a change of clothes and some toiletries. As he walked, he thought of Micky's translation of the map's warning, and of the Brotherhood of Amaury. *Could they still be in existence today? Surely not.* But there was no denying the two murders. Before Madison had interrupted them, he'd wanted to ask Micky more about her ancestry, too. It was incredible that she was directly connected to the Collection, especially when it had been pure chance that he'd found Sutherland's, rather than a university library or somewhere else. It was an awkward goodbye, too. In fact, he hadn't even said goodbye. He quickly texted her.

Sorry about that. Can I call you tomorrow?

After putting some things in his backpack, he left for the station. No response from Micky. Maybe he would just call in to the shop tomorrow. With the original documents.

He boarded the train for Harrogate, musing that no matter how hard he tried, he couldn't picture Madison ever catching a train or a bus. It just seemed to be beneath her.

Madison walked into the Crescent Road bar and several customers, both male and female, followed her in with their eyes. She wore a thigh-length khaki knitted dress that hugged her trim figure. "How were the gardens?"

"Peaceful. They're a connection to where I was born," Luke said thoughtfully. "In fact, while I was there, I got an email from my birth mother. She wondered if I'd talked to her sister. I'd told her I would."

"Oh." Her tone said 'question', but her face said 'don't bother'.

Luke answered anyway. "I might visit her tomorrow."

"What, in New Zealand?"

"No, her sister. In Castleford."

"Oh, I see." She reached for the menu as a waiter came over.

"Have you thought any more about moving up to Harrogate? It's much nicer here," she said, silently condemning the area where he currently lived.

"I don't know. Not sure it's for me." Madison asked Luke about his father again, and they chatted until dinner arrived. Luke noticed that even though he described his father as cold and distant, his anger had dissipated. Within himself he was starting to rethink the complex man who was Geoffrey Shaw. He was surprised at himself, and surprised at how cathartic the conversation was, as Madison gently nudged him to talk about it. The waiter returned to take a dessert order, but Madison sent him on his way. *Apparently it's time to leave.*

As they walked the quiet streets to York Road, Madison took Luke's hand. A comforting gesture he hadn't expected. "It's a beautiful house," she said, as they went up the neat gravel path. "Looking forward to the tour," she added.

Luke took her through the downstairs rooms, pointing out his mother's piano. "She wanted me to have lessons, but I wasn't interested."

Madison took his arm and pulled him towards the stairs. Upstairs, she strode into his father's study. He followed her in. *Shit.* The Whitby picture was on the floor, leaning against the wall. He'd forgotten to put it back. She looked at the panelling but didn't seem to notice anything. He was glad and wasn't quite sure why. Perhaps the Collection was just to be between him and Micky.

"Nice room," she said, turning towards the door. Luke followed her into his father's bedroom. "Ooh, this *is* nice." She pulled him towards the four-poster and unzipped his jeans.

Luke awoke in an empty bed. 3.20, according to the clock on the bedside table. He felt uncomfortable in the four-poster. His father's bed. Madison hadn't cared in the slightest. She appeared to have no inhibitions at all. It had started to rain softly. He thought he heard her moving around out in the hall, but it was difficult to tell.

"Oh, hi," she said, as she quietly came back in. "I found the bathroom. You need to warm me up." She felt cold as she climbed back into bed. She must have been up for a while.

Madison was already in the shower when he woke in the morning. It was only 7.30. It seemed to be her way. She was an early starter, not interested in morning small talk. "Hi." She came back in looking as radiant as ever.

"Hi. Any plans today?"

"Yes. You? Did you say last night that you'd be visiting your aunt in

Castleford?" Madison asked, putting her earrings in.

"Yes, I hope so. Probably later this morning, and then back to Bradford tonight."

"I'd better dash. My ride will be here soon." She kissed him and went downstairs. He heard the front door close and looked out the bedroom window. Just outside the house next door she climbed into the passenger side of a new-looking black Jaguar.

Maybe even the ride-share vehicles are upmarket in this area.

41

All was quiet in the lodging house. It was early summer in the village, and the lodgers were out enjoying some unexpected hospitality at the inn. Two strangers followed them there, then parted company, one going into the inn after them, where he paid for their drinks and started regaling them with stories of his recent exploits. Outside on the road, the other outsider marvelled at how easy it was to ensure he had time alone with the landlord. As he quietly entered the house, he put on his black mask.

The landlord sat in front of the large hearth, turning and half standing, startled, as the man in the mask cleared his throat. The landlord was a small man with a slight stoop. He stood, placing a hand on the back of the chair for support, looking up as his unwanted visitor towered over him. "What do you want?"

"I want your help," Edmund replied, looking around the room. He casually walked to the hearth and picked up a fire iron, thrusting it into the glowing coals. He was surprised at how alive he felt. This was his moment. Since his first meeting of the Brotherhood, Edmund had been waiting for his chance to prove his worth as leader, and to start to demand the respect his father had commanded.

Henry had passed away just three days after telling Edmund of his legacy, just as the old seneschal had predicted. With the seneschal's guidance, Edmund had called the Brotherhood together and had learned two important truths. The first being that one of their number had been successful in his search for possible alternative locations of the talisman, now that York Minster had proved fruitless. This man had found Hessle to be a place of interest. He'd heard tell of a stranger staying in the village for some days, poking around the town and visiting the Church of All Saints late in the evenings. Edmund told the assembled men that he would personally visit Hessle to investigate, and as he spoke, he learned the second important fact: the men of the Brotherhood did not deem him worthy. It wasn't in their words; none dared to challenge a Montfort heir. It was in their faces. Edmund resolved that night that his actions would need to be decisive.

"I have no rooms available, but I will help you." The landlord tried to maintain a calm demeanour but was unnerved by the black mask. He'd seen one before. An executioner's mask. He remembered the Scotsman who stayed with him. A gentlemen, unlike this brutish intruder.

"Yes, you will."

The landlord moved towards the door and Edmund grabbed him by the collar and shoved him back into his chair. Fear registered in his eyes, pleasing Edmund.

"What do you want?"

"Some weeks ago, you harboured a man who had come to Hessle to search for an ancient treasure," Edmund said boldly. "*My* treasure. Tell me his name."

"But I don't remember the names of all my lodgers. There are too many." The man's voice had become shaky, and Edmund decided he was being unhelpful. He glowered at the landlord, moving close enough that he could see the small beads of sweat forming on his weathered face. The landlord averted his gaze in a fearful silence. He briefly closed his eyes and could recall the pleasant evening conversation, in this very room, with the Scotsman, but could not recall his name.

Edmund retrieved the hot iron from the fireplace and brandished it at the landlord. The man squirmed and tried to push Edmund away, but he was simply too strong. Edmund locked his huge hand around the man's throat and pushed him back into the soft chair. With his free hand, he pressed the glowing iron to the man's cheek. The man screamed, and the smell of burning flesh excited Edmund.

"Stop, stop. Please. I'll remember it," the old man pleaded, sobbing.

"Tell me now!" Edmund moved the iron towards his eye, smiling as the man looked at its smoking tip in abject terror.

He desperately searched his memory for the name the lodger had given, as the heat from the iron singed his eyebrow. "William Roberts!" the landlord screamed, as Edmund blinded his left eye.

"Ah, good. Your memory is improving. And what did this William Roberts find?" Edmund asked calmly, as his victim moaned in agony. Fear and searing pain had paralysed the landlord. His mouth was parched and he found himself unable to speak.

"What did he find?" Edmund repeated, moving the fire iron towards the remaining good eye, smiling.

"I ... don't ... know," the man whimpered.

"You defy me?" Edmund laughed. "Let it be known that I am not a man to be defied!" He moved the fire iron down towards the man's chest and pressed its tip against his clothing, quickly burning through to his skin. "Tell me now and this will stop," said Edmund slowly and quietly, his face now mere inches from the man's. He could smell the dread in his shallow breath.

"No ... I ... truly ... don't know," the man wailed.

Edmund pressed the iron forward and the landlord screamed. He smiled, and with both hands drove it hard into his chest until the screaming stopped.

Edmund felt exhilarated. The power that surged through him was intoxicating. Power over life and death. The man's blood had sullied Edmund's tunic. He could feel it leaching through to his skin as the life left the old man's body. He looked down upon the red stain, pleased. Its coppery odour reached Edmund's nostrils and he inhaled deeply. The landlord had partially slumped forward, but his body was held in place by the fire iron embedded in the chair. Edmund pushed the landlord roughly back and admired his handiwork. *Now I am a man, Father.*

As he stood over the corpse, he wondered fleetingly whether he could have extracted more information from the pathetic figure. *Perhaps.* But he'd been carried by the moment. He had the lodger's name, at least, so that would give the Brotherhood something to search for. He was also certain that word of his ruthlessness would reach his brethren.

They will respect me now. My Brotherhood of Amaury will be feared.

42

"Hello."

"Hi, is this Lisa Williams?"

"Who's calling please?"

"My name is Luke Shaw, I …"

"If you want to sell me something, don't bother. I'm not buying today," Lisa cut in quickly. She didn't sound aggressive, just weary.

"No, no. Please don't hang up. My name is Luke Shaw. Susan Colley is my mother."

A moment's silence.

"Aye?" A tentative, uncertain voice.

"I've just come back from New Zealand where I met her for the first time last week. She had an old letter from you. Gave me your name and told me you were in Castleford."

"Luke, did you say? How old are you?" Luke gave her his birth date. "Well, I'll be …"

"I'm sorry to call out of the blue like this. I only found out I was adopted a few weeks ago. It's been a … whirlwind."

"But you sound local. I remember when you were born. And adopted. In *New Zealand*. Do you live here in Yorkshire?"

"Leeds and Bradford. Since I was a lad."

There was a long silence as Lisa took it all in. "How is Sue? We kind of lost touch you know."

"I know. I think she blames herself for that. But she's good. She rang me yesterday."

"Oh, there's so much to catch up on. I should call her. Do you have her number? She's moved house a few times and I just haven't kept up."

"Yep, I do. She showed me a photo. Of me and her just after I was born. She said you took it for her."

"I remember that. It was a tough time. Our parents were beside themselves. Angry, disappointed, emotional, overbearing. All at once. Poor Susie was just devastated when they took you away."

"Could I come and meet you? Would that be all right? I could be there in about an hour and a half." Another brief pause, long enough that Luke wondered if she was going to say no.

"All right." She gave Luke her address.

By eleven o'clock, Luke arrived in Castleford. It was his first visit, and already he'd seen enough for it to feel familiarly depressing. After following the signs and making his way under the railway bridge, he emerged into an area filled with sad rows of brick terraces. There was no denying Madison was right about Harrogate. It had a different feel altogether from Bradford and Castleford. He navigated his way through the streets to find his aunt's little two-level terrace.

"Luke. Come in." Lisa Williams looked like his mother, although a few years younger. She looked tired but had laugh lines around her eyes. There was a young boy of about seven or eight standing behind her. "This is Jack. The girls are at school, but Jack says he has a sore throat. I was going to warn you he might be getting a cold, but I'm pretty sure he's just skiving off." Jack rolled his eyes.

Luke followed them into a small front room, and Lisa offered him a cup of tea. As she went off to make it, Jack followed her down the narrow hallway.

When Lisa returned with two steaming mugs, they sat down and Luke showed her the photo of himself and Susan on his phone.

It brought a wistful smile to Lisa's face. "She was so happy that day. Then they took you away that night and she just cried and cried for days."

Lisa told Luke about the heartache of her parents' decision to go back to Leeds when she'd just turned eighteen. Susan had never forgiven them and flatly refused to go. She said she wasn't leaving her son behind, and their father had said, 'He's not your son any more.' It was the final straw. So Lisa had reluctantly left her sister behind and moved across the world. They were a broken family. Like Susan, Lisa had married young and it hadn't lasted. She'd married again and had three children. Luke suddenly remembered something his mother had said.

"She doesn't know about Jack. She said you have two girls." Lisa shook her head in dismay. "Sorry, didn't mean to touch a nerve," Luke added.

"It's all right. I should have written. Or emailed, or something. Things weren't great, and ... well, I just didn't."

There was a loud crash in the next room. Lisa quickly went to look. It occurred to Luke that neither of them knew how to reconnect. Maybe he could help. He heard Lisa admonishing Jack before she returned.

"He can be a little shit sometimes, but I try not to be too hard on him. Boys need their fathers, and his isn't around nearly enough. Too busy with his new girlfriend."

"I think I know how he feels. Different reason, but same effect." Luke talked to Lisa a little about his childhood but soon found himself telling her about his renewed interest in history, one shared with Susan. He said how much he was enjoying working on some 'historical documents he'd just come across' although kept the details to himself. They chatted into the early afternoon, and Lisa made toasted sandwiches for them. He felt a warmth from her that was akin to the way he'd felt with Sue. It was something he hadn't felt since his mum died.

As they had their second cup of tea, Luke realised his trip back home to Bradford would have to be longer than planned. He'd left the documents in the kitchen drawer in Harrogate, and he still wanted to take them to Micky, as a kind of apology for the way their lunch ended yesterday.

"I'd better go," he said. "It's been brilliant to meet you and Jack. And thanks for feeding me!" Lisa texted him her email address so they could exchange photos and the like. They hugged each other goodbye, promised to stay in touch, and Luke headed back towards his train. It was a strange feeling, having new relatives close by. He'd never thought before of having cousins, and now he had three.

On the train back to Harrogate, he wrote an email for both Lisa and Susan. His way of helping to put the family back together. In his gut, he felt they both wanted to do it, but neither knew how to break the ice. Instead of pressing 'send', he decided to read it again later. It was too important to rush.

As soon as he reached the front door, Luke knew something was wrong. The door was closed, but the lock had obviously been tampered with. There were rough tool marks all around the keyhole, and it was difficult to open. He roughly pushed the door closed after he'd entered and bolted upstairs. The wall panelling was broken where it had been levered out, and the secret safe was open. Luke ran over to it and peered in. Empty! The ankh was gone!

43

Micky was still annoyed. It wasn't that Luke had a glamorous girlfriend. It wasn't even the dismissive way he'd introduced her. Madison had sized up Micky in the restaurant and had apparently decided she was no competition. But it wasn't that either. More than anything, Micky was annoyed with herself. She had run away. She'd got back to the shop and Mrs Sutherland could see she was upset. The look on her boss's face had said 'I knew that boy was no good'. *Why did I run away? Luke can have a girlfriend like that if he wants. So what?* She had turned it over in her mind dozens of times since yesterday. Lunch had been *fun*. She enjoyed talking about the map and the other documents. She enjoyed sharing her work, her translations, with Luke, and he was genuinely interested, she was sure of it.

Mrs Sutherland had assumed Luke was a boyfriend, and he'd just done something terrible, but she didn't understand. Luke had seemed like *a friend*. The kind of friend Micky found it hard to make. Kindred spirits almost. When he first brought the map in, he didn't want to know how much it was worth, he wanted to know what it was about. Just like her. He'd been so excited about finding the ankh carving. Just like her. The terrible murder had shocked them both, but the adventure, the promise of the map's secrets, had captivated them both. And even with the murder and Luke's police interrogation, lunch had still been fun.

But since the abrupt end of their conversation, other thoughts had plagued her consciousness. Why hadn't he trusted her with the originals? Why didn't he want to know more about Bernard de Péreille; surely it was *amazing* that she was related to someone from the very beginning of this 800-year journey? *Is he just using me? Am I a fool to be taken in by a charmer like him?* She pictured Madison asking Luke about his mousy little friend and him saying 'she's no one important'. Maybe that was unfair, but boys had done that to Micky since she was at primary school. Permeating all these thoughts was the map and the four pillars. She could feel herself being inexorably pulled into the story, the *quest*. Not only was she invested in the mystery, but it now had a hold over her. Since translating the documents, she'd had vivid dreams of Bernard's difficult journey, and of the four talismans. She could almost imagine the objects in their dusty medieval hiding places. The last one, the strange symbol near Barcelona, had not come into focus yet, but she'd envisioned the astrolabe and the lion's head somehow *within* stone walls.

She hadn't slept well, and it was beginning to unsettle her. And she knew that even if Luke was just taking advantage of her, she would keep going. She just couldn't let go now. The mystery had captured her. *I am a fool.*

"Fuck! They've got the ankh." Luke sprinted back downstairs and into the kitchen, ripping the drawer open. Nothing! Then he realised he was looking in the wrong drawer. *Stupid!* He pulled out the second drawer, and there they were, just where he'd left them. *Thank God.* Then he realised he hadn't checked the house for intruders. What if they were still there? He quickly closed the drawer and went through all the rooms, checking the back door as well, breathing a sigh of relief that he was alone. Nothing else had been disturbed, just the hidden safe. He could call the police, but what would he tell them? That thieves broke into the house, *with a safe-cracking expert*, to steal an old religious artefact? That maybe he's being pursued by an eight-century-old religious order? And yet he was in no way connected to the murder of the sexton of the eight-century-old church in Hessle? *That'd go well, I'm sure.*

Now it seemed blindingly obvious that the Brotherhood of Amaury *must* be real, and must be behind all this. His father was a guardian of the Collection, and they had hunted him down and killed him. And now he's the guardian. But they must surely have been responsible for attacking Luke in the house yet didn't kill him? Did that make sense? *Think man.*

The Brotherhood had tortured his father for information, which apparently he was courageous enough not to give. Then they'd killed him. They had searched the house, at least twice, and found nothing. So was Luke of more use alive? Were they waiting for him to lead them to the Collection? Had he led them to the Hessle sexton? And why was the sexton murdered? Had the poor man discovered something about the Brotherhood or their quest? Or was brutal murder simply the way they ended all their interrogations? But if Luke was some sort of lead to be followed, then *how?* And suddenly it dawned on him. *Oh God, I've been such a fucking idiot. Madison.* It seemed obvious now. *And I've led them to the ankh.*

He bundled the documents carefully into his backpack, tried to look as calm as he could and quickly left the house. All the way to the station he had to consciously stop himself from looking over his shoulder, and staring at every passer-by. He felt sick with anxiety, trying hard not to let it show. He cursed himself along the way. *How could I be so stupid?* But he knew exactly what his friends would say, if they ever found out. Taking a seat at the end of the carriage, he had his back against a wall and he could see everyone in it. For the first time in many years, he found himself wishing his father was there. He needed help. He needed *Micky's* help. *Shit, I've messed that up, too.* Micky had never replied to his text. She must have been seriously annoyed with him.

If he hurried, he could still make the shop before five o'clock. As he had that thought, he realised that she now might be in danger as well.

She was connected to him. Madison had met her. He almost took out his phone to call her, but there were people within earshot, and he calculated that he'd be there in half an hour anyway. Maybe they would have a safe or something similar at the shop for the documents. His mind was racing, and he realised he was sweating. He needed to calm down before he attracted attention to himself. He took out his phone again and tried to concentrate on the email he'd written for Lisa and Susan. But after a while he gave up and just pressed 'send'.

Ten minutes before closing, Luke rushed breathlessly through the shop door, ringing the bell. Mrs Sutherland was at the counter and peered over her glasses, giving Luke a scathing schoolmarm look.

"Hi, is Micky here?" he asked, undaunted.

"Michaela went home with a severe headache about an hour ago." *Leave her alone*, the tone implied.

Dammit. "Oh. Thank you. I'll call tomorrow." Mrs Sutherland merely nodded in response.

Luke left the shop feeling dejected. He texted Micky again.

Can we talk? It's important.

He pocketed his phone and walked briskly back to his flat. The documents in his backpack worried him; he had to find a suitable place to hide them. No response from Micky. He had no other means of contacting her, so all he could do was wait. Her phone might be switched off, he supposed, if it was a bad headache. As he reached the flat, a message pinged. He felt relieved, as he grabbed the phone.

I'm sorry but I have to go overseas for an unexpected urgent family matter. I think it's best we say goodbye for now, I don't know how long I'll be away. A kiss emoji.

Madison.

44

Edward Beaumont sat brooding in a wing chair, near the large stone fireplace in the library of Montford Hall. A portrait of Simon de Montfort, 6th Earl of Leicester and first Grand Master of the Brotherhood, hung on the opposite wall. The cold, unyielding face of Simon de Montfort gazed regally down upon Edward and his father, who was seated in the other wing chair. The Beaumonts' host had often repeated the story of his 13th-century ancestor, the man who had expelled the Jewish community from Leicester 'until the end of the world'. Montford was proud to say that he had done it 'for the good of his soul, and the souls of his heirs'. Edward was uncomfortably warm in the chair but had chosen it so he could look upon the object of his desires. Madison Temple sat opposite him, at one end of a brass-studded leather chesterfield.

Gerald Montford, seated at the other end of the chesterfield, assessed his two male guests. Sir Richard, obese and oily, with a prominent whisky-blossom nose, and his equally unpleasant son, the brutish and dull Edward. Neither man possessed the character or charisma, or the dignity, to lead the Brotherhood. The elder Beaumont had asked the Grand Master about Lucas Shaw, the sentinel's son.

Montford addressed the two men. "We will not be taking Shaw's son just yet. He is being watched and may still be of use to us. Do not question my strategy. I've been more successful than all my predecessors. *I found the Philosophy Talisman.*"

Gerald Montford could almost feel the power that he would soon inherit. The young Shaw may yet lead the Brotherhood to the other talismans. His strategy of using Madison to beguile the lad had been perfect. A servant entered the room holding a silver tray with several bottles. Gerald nodded his permission. The group sat in silence as the glasses were refilled, and Gerald's brandy was placed in the antique copper warmer. Montford looked across at Madison, and she smiled knowingly, subtly raising her glass in his direction.

Edward shifted in his seat. He knew Madison was Gerald's lover, and it made him angry. The man was twice her age. *When I am Grand Master, I will take her.*

"It's a great achievement, Gerald," Sir Richard said. "May we see it?"

Madison raised her eyebrows. Sir Richard was obviously feeling bold. She knew of her lover's disdain for the man, and she knew how brutal he could be. She stood as Gerald did, moving to warm herself by the fire. Edward's eyes hungrily followed her, and she enjoyed the effect she was having on him. Sir Richard watched as their host went to the desk, took a key from his pocket and opened a beautifully carved walnut box.

Gerald removed the ankh, holding his prize reverently to show the Beaumonts from across the low table. Sir Richard leaned forward and started to reach towards it, but the look Gerald gave stopped him in his tracks.

"And what of the other talismans, Gerald. Will Shaw lead us to them?" Sir Richard asked.

Gerald looked at Madison, his eyes inviting her to speak. "He led me to the sentinel's hidden safe, just as we'd planned, but he's not as rash and immature as we thought. I think he knows now that I wanted something from him, so I've ended it."

"Does he have the original map?" Sir Richard asked.

"I don't know," she replied tersely.

"We know it wasn't with the ankh," Gerald interjected. "*When* I deem it necessary, we will interrogate Shaw and others he's been talking to."

"What about Hessle?" Edward asked.

"Popa was careless. He entered the church to investigate the information we'd received, but the sexton was there. Don't worry, it's nothing more than collateral damage. He didn't know anything anyway." Montford waved his hand dismissively. "But enough of this detail. We're still watching the sentinel's son. Clearly *something* pointed him towards Hessle, yet there's nothing there on *our* map."

"Why not question him now?" Edward pressed. Montford considered putting him firmly back in his place but decided the young man might soon have some use. He would keep Shaw for Popa's attentions, but Edward might be just the right person to interrogate the woman Shaw had spoken with.

"I said we'll watch him for now. As I've told your father, we know Shaw and his son had not communicated for many years. There's been no indication that he knew anything – until Hessle. We'll watch and see what else he leads us to."

"But ..." Edward started, but a venomous look from Montford silenced him.

"Do not trouble yourself, Edward. Soon the power will be ours," Gerald said imperially. "Now, there's nothing further to discuss." He turned his back on the gathering to lock the carved box on the desk. Sir Richard and Edward took their cue and stood to leave. A butler entered to show them out. As Madison turned to follow them, Montford stopped her. "A moment, my dear."

"Yes, Gerald?" she asked sweetly as the other men left the room.

"You were careless. We would have got more from young Shaw if you'd been more careful." He wasn't pleased.

"He heard me in the study during the night. What would you have had me do?" She was firm, but respectful.

"You let your guard down." He shook his head. "Are you losing your edge, my dear?" The veiled threat was understood. If she was of no use to him, she knew far too much to be allowed to leave.

"Of course not. I got you the talisman, didn't I?" She put her glass down on the low table, signalling time to leave.

Gerald went over to her. "The night is still young." He grabbed her breast roughly as he put his other hand around her neck, wrenching her towards him. His kiss was forceful, hard and tasted of brandy. He pushed her onto the chesterfield as she yielded to his urgent desire. She pulled up her dress and could feel his belt buckle dig into the lingering bruises from their last encounter. As he moved heavily on top of her, she thought wistfully of Luke.

45

Dumped by text. Perfect. Luke thought he should feel hurt. Or sad. But he didn't. Their brief relationship had no substance to it. He hardly even knew her. It was just sex. *Or was it?* Was her text message confirmation that all she had wanted was the Collection? *And now she's probably got the ankh.* He consoled himself that at least the map and documents were safe. For the moment. Reading her message again, he wondered if he should respond. What would he say if he didn't think she was part of an evil fanatical cult? *'Thanks for the lovely text. Fuck you, too,'* crossed his mind. But no, that wouldn't do. *A sad face emoji?* That would be more like her. *Something flippant?* That would be more like him.

Oh! Good luck with your family emergency. Devastated of course. It's been fun. You know where to find me. L. He hovered over the send arrow for a second before pressing it. "Fuck it, that'll do," he muttered. He was still angry with himself for having been taken in so completely. Looking back now, it seemed so stupid. All those questions about his father; her pushing to see the Harrogate house, turning up out of the blue at the pub and then the café on Market Street. None of it coincidence.

He went to the kitchen bench to make a cup of tea. *That's odd*, he thought. *I don't remember leaving that out.* He'd left a letter from his work, his notice of final pay, sitting on the bench, but now there was a phone bill lying neatly on top. He was certain it had been in the kitchen drawer with the others. He never left phone bills out; he didn't even know why the phone company sent them. He paid them by direct debit. A realisation sent a chill down his spine. *Someone's been here looking around.*

He wished he had somewhere safer to store the Collection. What was left of it. Racking his brain for a clever hiding place didn't help. It was a small flat, with little enough storage and none of it lockable. Not that locks had provided much of a deterrent so far anyway. *Sock drawer might have to do tonight.* Not ideal, so he decided it would be best not to go out. A relaxing pint or two would have to wait; he didn't want to leave the documents in an empty flat, and he wasn't at all comfortable taking them with him.

Before putting it all away under a pile of socks and underwear, he spread the map out on the rickety coffee table. Staring at it again did not help; it remained impenetrable, and he wished he understood it the way Micky did. She had an insight that he did not possess. She'd pointed out a town near Lisbon, he remembered. Tomar. On closer inspection, it *did* look like it had been given extra attention by the map-maker. He couldn't make sense of the ornate details in the town, but the icon or talisman drawn near it looked clear. An astrolabe, she'd said.

Luke took out his phone and searched for 'astrolabe', getting a wide variety of images of scientific instruments, plus a New Zealand winemaker. Narrowing the search to '13th-century astrolabe' refined the selection of images further. A comparison of these to the illustration on the map seemed to remove any doubt. Somewhere in or near Tomar, Portugal must be the hiding place of the science talisman. At least, its initial location.

Further close scrutiny of the map yielded only a sore neck and the makings of a headache, so he hid it away under the socks and went to the fridge, hoping something nice for dinner had miraculously appeared. No luck. He had half a loaf of bread in the tiny freezer, so another toasted cheese sandwich it was.

While he ate, he checked his phone, silently wishing that Micky had texted him back and he'd somehow missed it. But no luck there either. In his inbox he had three new emails, though. The first was a long one from Lisa to Susan, reaching out with an apology, and a photo of Jack and the girls. The eldest, Sophie, looked a lot like Susan in the old photo. Luke was happy that he'd helped them make contact after years of drifting apart. His birth mother had seemed so lonely. Lisa's email also told Susan how wonderful it was to meet her new nephew, and once again Luke felt the warmth of his new family. His feelings were tumbling into each other; the realisation that Geoffrey Shaw was not the cold bastard Luke had always believed he was, that the woman he'd known as his mother, who had loved him and raised him, was not his mother after all. Then to find he'd been adopted, *abandoned*. And then meeting Susan and learning the truth, plus discovering he also had an aunt and three cousins. It was overwhelming. He started to feel emotional and didn't know quite how to deal with it.

The second email was a short one from Susan, just to Luke. It was still early morning in New Zealand, and she'd just seen his and Lisa's messages. She said she would write back to Lisa as soon as there was time later in the morning and was very grateful to him for breaking the ice. It was a brief but thoughtful note. The last email was from Lisa, also just to Luke. A thank you for finding her and writing the email to both of them. She said it meant a great deal to her, and signed it off with a 'please call me any time you want'.

All right then. He felt in need of human company, not to mention something to take his mind off today's turn of events. Why not give her a call now?

"Hi, Luke." Lisa's cheerful voice instantly made him feel better.

"Hi. I just wanted to say thanks again for meeting me today. And feeding me. It was great to talk, and meet my cousin."

"Aye, it was good to talk," Lisa said. "I'm so glad you contacted me. I've left it so long with Sue ... Thanks for sending that email."

"No prob. I'm sure she feels the same way." Luke said he hoped that one day there might be a family reunion, and that he'd also like to meet his other new cousins, Sophie and Lily. They chatted easily for another ten minutes, and Lisa caught Luke off-guard by asking about his girlfriend. He hadn't remembered talking about Madison at all. "Ahh ... Madison, well ..."

"Sorry, love, don't mind me. But didn't you say her name was Micky? The one you talked about this morning."

"Oh, it's a long story." He smiled to himself. *Did I really talk about Micky this morning?*

46

"Are you feeling better, dear?" Mrs Sutherland was a kind-hearted person, underneath the stern exterior. She looked genuinely worried as Micky put her bag under the counter.

"Yes, I am, thanks. I've not been sleeping as well as usual."

"That boy came in last night looking for you." *Is he upsetting you?* Mrs Sutherland didn't ask, but her tone implied it. "He said he would call today." She made it sound like a warning.

"Okay. It's all right, Mrs Sutherland. I'm fine, really. Just a bit tired." *Maybe I need a holiday.* She thought again of Bernard's journey northward through France and England. And of the journeys his brother monks must have made, depositing their talismans in their designated places of concealment. A slowly growing sense of foreboding was overtaking her, and she wished she knew where all this might lead. Since her lunch with Luke, she had worked out the likely location of the astrolabe more precisely and wanted to tell him, but at the same felt deflated that perhaps he was just using her. She sighed quietly.

"I'll put the jug on." A nice hot cuppa could fix most things, according to Mrs Sutherland. She had been worried about Micky for a few days now. The poor girl looked tired and drawn, and the last time she'd been that way was when she'd split up with her boyfriend last year. *And a good-*

for-nothing piece of work he was too. She's such a lovely girl, and beautiful with it. But she doesn't seem to know it.

The bell above the door announced a customer, and both women looked up to see Luke walk in. Mrs Sutherland gave him her best 'I'm watching you' expression, as he went over to Micky.

"Hi. Are you feeling better?" He looked genuinely concerned.

"Yes. Hi."

"I'm sorry about lunch the other day. I didn't ..." He didn't know what to say to her.

Mrs Sutherland looked wary but left them to talk.

"It's all right. I was so immersed in what we were talking about, it was just a surprise, that's all. I hope I wasn't rude to your girlfriend."

"Oh no, of course not ..." *How can I explain? She's just a friend? It was just sex? She's just dumped me? Shit.* "I'm really sorry. I was totally immersed in what we were talking about, too. I didn't want it to end like that," he said awkwardly.

"Your text said there was something important?" she asked, changing the subject.

"Yeah. My father's house was broken into yesterday and the ankh was stolen. It was the only thing they took, and they had to break into a safe to get it." Her eyes were wide with shock. "They knew it was there." He didn't want to explain *how* they knew. "At least they didn't find the map and the other documents. I think my flat was searched yesterday, too." He paused to let her take that in. She looked alarmed, and wary. "I brought the Collection back here, and a friend at my old work has put it in their strongroom for me." First thing this morning, Luke had texted Joseph and asked him for the favour, and he'd dropped his backpack in on the way to Sutherland's. "They'll be safe. He's a good lad."

"Anyway," Luke went on, "I tried going over the map again last night, but I just can't make sense of it. I wondered if you'd made any progress?"

So. He's here because he wants something. It wasn't a charitable thought, but it was the first one in her head. *Maybe Mrs Sutherland's instinct is right after all.*

Luke noticed her face change. Just before the closed expression, he thought he saw a vulnerability in her eyes. But it didn't linger.

"I'll call you if I do," she said, apparently wrapping up their conversation.

Mrs Sutherland returned to the counter. Perhaps she had been listening. Her look said 'get out of my shop'.

"I'm sorry about lunch," Luke said again, looking at Micky intently. Her amber eyes met his, and something passed between them. Something akin to 'you've let me down'.

Luke walked out into the street feeling glum. He *did* feel like he'd let her down. But he also thought it a bit unfair. It wasn't his fault Madison had turned up and had been so dismissive. Maybe he should have told Micky the full story, but he decided it would seem shallow. He *felt* shallow thinking about it. He'd been taken in, and he'd let Madison use him, but he'd used her, too. He'd been selfish. And now he'd messed up an emerging friendship with Micky. When Madison had walked into the café, he'd actually felt *disappointed*. He'd been thoroughly enjoying the conversation with Micky. The shock of the sexton's murder had all but dissipated as they talked through what she'd discovered. It had been *fun*, and he'd been looking forward to talking to Micky again.

And now she might be in danger. He may have led the Brotherhood to her. He *had* led Madison to her. He consoled himself that at least the copies of the document hadn't been out on the café table. And they hadn't been talking about them at the time either. Maybe his introducing Micky simply as 'a friend' was fortunate after all. Maybe he should tell her what actually happened with Madison, but would it sound like he was making excuses? Would it sound tacky? *It was tacky.* He shook his head. He felt awkward and dejected.

More than anything else, Luke needed a friend to talk to. He was tempted to call Susan, but it would be late at night in Wellington. If Valley Gardens was closer, he'd have gone there. Somewhere peaceful and quiet, to think. He just needed to do *something*! The bustling Bradford streets felt oppressive. *Maybe the Harrogate house?* He rationalised that he needed to sort through his father's papers anyway, and the house *had* already been searched. And then a thought dawned on him. He hadn't visited his father's grave. He hadn't even gone to the funeral, such was his anger at the time. But now he felt differently; he felt he owed Geoffrey something.

The walk from Harrogate Station was just over half an hour. He didn't know exactly where his father was buried, other than in which cemetery, but assumed there would be a map of some kind. In truth, he had no real idea what to expect. Trilby had never contacted him about funeral or burial arrangements, so Luke presumed his father must have prearranged it. Or, more precisely, he hadn't thought about it deeply at all. Until now. After entering through the gates, he found a sign directing him to the online gravesite search website, into which he put his father's details. It informed him that his father had been cremated and his ashes scattered in one of the gardens. No memorial, no plaque. He followed the map to the designated garden, finding a beautiful, lovingly cared-for area, shaded by a canopy of old oak trees. It conjured the same feeling he had sitting in Valley Gardens. A sense of solitude and peace.

"You should have talked to me, Geoffrey Shaw. You should have *said* the words you wrote in that letter fifteen years ago," Luke said softly. "I might have understood." He felt a lump in his throat. He wasn't sure he would have understood at the time, but it could have been a good step towards avoiding the years of cold distance that ensued. "You should have *trusted* me." He sat on a bench, remembering happier times. That holiday in Whitby, immortalised in the picture hiding the secret safe. The holiday that Geoffrey had evidently not forgotten, using it as the clue that led Luke to the Collection. "All these years could have been different." His eyes moistened, but tears did not come.

Two hours later Luke was back in Bradford and in need of some company. He'd texted the lads to find that Nick and Josh were already enjoying a drink after work. He found them standing outside the pub, around a small table, already on their second pint. Nick was regaling Josh and a passing waitress with a witty anecdote as Luke joined them. "Lads," he nodded.

"Ben'll be here in half an hour," Nick said, pushing the bar menu Luke's way. "Are you eating?"

"Yeah, why not. How's work?"

"Fairly shit. How's unemployment?" Nick asked.

"Living the dream."

"Living on the bones of your arse, more like," Nick shot back.

"Plenty of time for the blonde then," Josh observed. An inevitable taunt, and sooner than expected.

"She's had to go overseas." Luke wondered who would retort first.

"Sounds like code for 'she's moved on'." Josh got in ahead of Nick. "Was only a matter of time."

Luke's reply was a silent half-smile, as he wondered why he still drank with these guys.

47

With his head throbbing and mouth too dry to make normal human sounds, Luke forced an eye open. 6.30. He grunted and sat up slowly, wishing he'd had fewer drinks last night. As his dizziness settled, he dragged himself out of bed to get a glass of water and go to the toilet. He fell back into bed three minutes later, hoping to get another hour or two of sleep but to no avail. His body may have been sabotaged by the alcohol, but his mind was busy. He was still kicking himself for having offended or disappointed Micky. Or both. He wasn't completely sure. But he knew he needed her help, and without it his quest felt very lonely.

Forty-five minutes later, he got up to shower, feeling a little better for the glass of water. It seemed clearer to him that his drinking mates were shallow and not particularly good friends, although last night had been a good distraction and a few laughs. As he lay in bed, it had also occurred to him that sending Micky flowers might be a good way to show he was genuinely sorry about what had happened. She must think him one-dimensional, like Nick and the lads. He dressed and went out for his number-one guaranteed hangover cure – a traditional English fry-up breakfast – calling in at the florist on the way.

He spent the next ten minutes getting the shop assistant to

understand that 'no, I'm not trying to say I love her'. Nor was he saying sorry to a girlfriend for having done something unspeakable. The shop assistant was still showing him lovely bunches of roses.

"I'm just trying to say sorry to a friend for being an arse." In the end, he settled for a large bunch of lilacs, pink roses and some other flowers he could not identify. It had been those or a peace lily, and he didn't want to give Micky a plant that would require ongoing maintenance. A peace lily would be a liability in his own flat. Luke paid the girl, and she promised they would be delivered this morning.

After a hearty breakfast, Luke started to feel more human, and he ordered a second coffee to take away as he paid for his meal. A short walk later, he was sitting on the couch back at his flat, quietly willing Micky to contact him. While he waited, he picked up the book he'd borrowed from Susan, *The Four Pillars of Gnosis*. He remembered reading about the legacy of the Cathars towards the end of the book and went back to that section again. It was the chapter that referred to a potential treasure of the Cathars, and the legend that perhaps it had been spirited away from Montségur, literally just hours before the siege had ended in mass murder. The author hadn't elaborated further.

Next, Luke searched the web for references to the treasure. There he found a wide variety of speculation suggesting it was the Holy Grail (or something as important as that), it was of incalculable value not measured in monetary terms, or it was of great religious significance. All these sources unverifiable and spurious, as far as Luke was concerned, and very repetitive. He took away only two things from all the clutter. The treasure was sought after by many and often the seekers were zealots of one kind or another. And secondly, whatever it was, the church seemed to *fear* it. He put the book and his phone on the coffee table and lay his head on the cushion.

His phone rattled on the table as it vibrated and pinged with the arrival of Micky's text.

Thank you.

It was now nearly twelve; he must have dozed off.

I really am sorry. Can I come into the shop?

No response after a minute, so he followed it with another.

Please. tbh I'm afraid of Mrs Sutherland.

He waited. An interminable fifteen minutes passed.

Okay.

He texted Joseph immediately to say he would be in to pick up the backpack, and dashed out of the flat towards his old employer. He wanted to give Micky the originals to help earn her trust back. Fifteen minutes after that, he walked through the front door at Sutherland's, breathing hard. He saw the flowers sitting in a jug in the alcove behind the counter.

"Thank you. You didn't have to do that," Micky said, looking over at the bouquet.

"I wanted to. I was ... insensitive and inconsiderate. Your help has been, well, huge, but it's also made this ... *fun.*" It sounded foolish as he said it, but it was true. "Anyway, I wanted you to see these." He took the original documents out of his backpack and handed them to her.

"You don't know anything about storing priceless historical artefacts, do you." She gave him a brief smile.

"Nothing at all."

She picked them up and took them towards the back of the shop, soon returning with a robust cardboard box and some sheets of polyester film. Luke watched as she interleaved each document with a sheet of polyester and placed the whole Collection into the archive box. "I could store them in our strongroom, but to be honest, it's not that secure, and it might be an obvious target for thieves. And whoever took the ankh knows how to break into a safe." She leaned closer and spoke more quietly. "When Mrs Sutherland leaves, I'll put this box on the back shelves in amongst others just like it. It should be safer that way."

"That's a great idea. I thought you'd want to take a look at the original map, too. You know, the bit that isn't clear on the copy."

"I will. *After* Mrs Sutherland leaves. She said she has to go before five o'clock tonight," Micky explained.

Luke wanted to ask her if she'd made any further progress, but he now realised that perhaps she might have thought he was taking advantage of her. *Is that why she put the wall up yesterday?* "Are you okay?"

"Yes."

"I mean, after the Hessle murder, and the people who stole the ankh, and probably killed my father. It's pretty full on," he said.

"Yes. Well, no. I feel like it's pulling me in. I've had more dreams about it. I want to know what it all means."

"Same. I went over the map again last night, but I couldn't get anywhere. I was looking at the Portuguese location, trying to figure it out."

"It's the Convento de Cristo, in Tomar," Micky said matter-of-factly. "I worked it out yesterday. The only thing is, that's a huge convent and castle structure built over many centuries. It could take weeks to find something like a small talisman." She tilted her head. "Although only part of it was there in the twelve hundreds, built by the Templars, so that narrows it down, I suppose."

"Another Templar connection. The Cathars must have liked the idea of hiding their treasure right under their persecutors' noses. I want to go there," Luke finished boldly. "We could ..." The surprised look on her face stopped him. "I mean, *I* could search the old parts, like in Hessle, maybe with a bit of guidance from you ..." His boldness started to wane as quickly as it had emerged. Without Micky's help, he knew he didn't stand a chance. And there was no guarantee the talisman would still be there; tens of thousands of people must have been through that structure over the years. Not to mention archaeologists, historians, and who knew who. Was it feasible that *none* of them had found it? "I mean, would you ... want to come?" he added clumsily.

"Oh no, I couldn't. Mrs Sutherland needs me here. And how would your girlfriend feel about it?"

"She's not my ..." Luke hung his head, not knowing how to explain. "It's complicated." It was the best he could muster. "Well, anyway, I understand. No pressure."

They agreed they would both do some research on the building itself, to try and get a sense of the likely hiding places in the original structure of Bernard de Péreille's time, and Micky warned Luke this could be a lot more like the proverbial needle in a haystack. He could be wasting his time. Nevertheless, they both regained some of their earlier sense of excitement, and Luke felt he was starting to redeem himself.

"Be careful," he told her.

"I will. And thank you for the flowers. They're lovely."

Luke walked out into the street with a grin on his face.

48

"Tomás, my dear friend." Montford spoke with his usual air of imperiousness. "I have an important task for you. The heretic's son has led us to someone who may be of use to us. I want you to travel to Bradford tonight." Montford paused as he considered his words carefully, and Tomás waited in a respectful silence. "I have been disappointed that the map we seek was not in the heretic's possession, nor his son's, but it may be at this woman's place of work, a shop that deals in rare books and maps. It may be secured, perhaps in a safe, so you must equip yourself appropriately."

Tomás Popa had been trained by the best; Gerald had seen to it. Popa's function was not simply interrogation and eradication of the Brotherhood's enemies, but searching for their treasure. The big man had proven himself most useful on many occasions, and, in addition to his extraordinary skills, he possessed a quality that Gerald found deeply satisfying – blind obedience.

With a stern reminder of the noble and holy purpose of the Brotherhood's work, Gerald provided him the shop's name and address. A rudimentary check by a Brotherhood operative posing as a customer a few days earlier had confirmed for Montford that the shop only had a simple alarm system that was connected to a phone line. It would present no problem for the resourceful Popa.

"And the woman?" Popa asked.

"She will not be there after closing. We will continue to watch her and the heretic's son, but we will not alert them just yet. Their time will come." Then Montford remembered that Popa had encountered Lucas Shaw unexpectedly, and in the absence of any instructions, he had simply left him unconscious and taken off. "But if she sees you, find out what she knows, and then send her to God."

On a notepad, Micky started to flesh out her picture of the old convent as it might have been in the thirteenth century, basing it on several sources from the shop itself, as well as a few online sites. Satisfied, she put the drawing into her bag. Then she tried to remember her dreams – the stone walls she'd seen with her mind's eye – to attempt to draw them for Luke. *Maybe they'll be useful, or maybe they're just a figment of my overactive imagination.* While she mused, she absently doodled images of the talismans. After a few attempts, she was satisfied with her architectural drawings and popped them into her bag, too. She could send photos of them to Luke later.

While Mrs Sutherland was out for lunch, Micky risked taking the map out to have another look at the fifth Latin inscription, the one she'd been unable to fully translate. The map itself was slightly damaged, just like it appeared in the photo, but it seemed something had made a small hole in it, and tiny pieces of parchment had folded back on themselves when the damage had been done. Using a cotton bud she was able to gently coax some of the parchment back into place, getting a better view of what had once been present. Two words, including the all-important verb ending, became clearer. She was soon able to retranslate the phrase as 'the [talismans] will find their destiny through blood'. *Is that any more helpful?* She couldn't decide but noted it down anyway. Then, before her boss returned, she put the cache of documents carefully back into the archive box. After Mrs Sutherland left tonight, she might be able to get some serious work done on the next parchment if she stayed late. For the moment, she filed the box on a back shelf, between 'S' and 'V'. *'T' for Treasure seems like a good idea. Who would look there?*

Leeds Bradford Airport had no direct flights to Lisbon, so Luke would either have to fly from Manchester or take an indirect flight. Either way, the trip would be about two hours longer than he'd hoped. He would arrive in Tomar late at night or have to get a room in Lisbon, so he dismissed the idea of leaving that afternoon. Perhaps it was for the best; he could talk with Micky again tonight to compare notes and see if they could narrow the search down a bit. He'd looked online at the Convent of Christ in Tomar and, just as Micky had said, it was huge. A man could spend weeks, or *months*, searching it.

He booked a flight via Heathrow for the next morning, which meant an early start, but he should still be able to get to Tomar by late afternoon. A check of the map indicated that there were quite a few hotels with rooms available, mostly at the northern end of the town. They were all within reasonable walking distance of the convent and the railway station, so it all looked straightforward. No need to book ahead, he decided. With hours to fill, he took a jacket out of the wardrobe to go for a stroll and found his father's letter in the pocket. The one Trilby had given him, in which he learned about the Shaw family's centuries-old duty. He read it again.

Dear Lucas,

You will be reading this letter after my death. If we have not spoken of these matters before now, perhaps my death was untimely. In any event, I am sorry. I am sorry for adding to your burden. At the time of writing, you are barely a man, just eighteen years, and I must hope that the task I will pass on is one that you can accept and embrace. It is a task that has been with the Shaw family for many generations. The Collection has existed since the mid-thirteenth century, and it is our role to keep it safe.

We are its guardians. With this key you will find it.

As I write, I think of you in our younger days, and I am reminded of a happier time, gazing at the stars together, wondering what the future might hold. I have high hopes for you, my son, and now I am relying on your honour and judgement.

Affectionately,

Geoffrey Shaw

It seemed like a different letter. Or at least Luke was a different *reader*. The first time he'd read it, it had been so *unexpected*. And he'd been so angry. The last paragraph had included the veiled message that only Luke would be likely to decipher; the one that had led him to the Collection. But now he could better see the meaning of the first paragraph. First of all, there was 'perhaps my death was untimely'. Had Geoffrey Shaw foreseen his own murder? Then, 'I am sorry for adding to your burden'. He must have felt the weight of his task as guardian of the Collection. 'It is our role to keep it safe.' In other words, *keep doing what we've done for generations, while the Brotherhood keep getting closer and closer. Until they kill me.* It was still a mystery to Luke as to why his father had the ankh in his possession. Were the Shaws keepers of the map, or keepers of the talismans themselves? And why only one? To be guardians, should the Collection be *together*?

Luke felt now he was a part of this. A part of the ancient quest. *But what should I do? Complete the quest? Or stand by and hope the Brotherhood don't find the other talismans?* Too many questions.

His phone rang, startling him out of his confusion. It was after ten.

"Luke. There's been a break-in at the shop." Micky was clearly shaken. "Mrs Sutherland just called me. She said the alarm had been disabled, and the security storage had been broken into."

"Slow down. Are you okay?" Luke asked, as calmly as he could.

"Yes. I'm fine. She said nothing was taken as far as she can tell. The storage and staff areas were searched. They were looking for the

Collection, I'm sure of it."

"Do you know if ..."

"No, I don't. I'll have to go there and check," she replied quickly.

"Not tonight?" Luke was alarmed. He pictured the huge figure he'd glimpsed at the Harrogate house before he'd been struck down. Perhaps the man was still there, or watching close by. "If you do, can I come with you?"

"No, I'll go in the morning. And you'd better not come. Mrs Sutherland wanted to know your name and why you've been coming to the shop. She thinks you must be involved."

"What did you say?" he asked. At least Micky didn't think he was involved, or surely she wouldn't have called.

"That you had come in with some books you'd inherited and wanted to know more about them. I didn't know what else to say. I didn't want her to know about the map. I had to give her your name, sorry." She sounded sincere. And upset.

"It's all right. You had no choice. *Really*," Luke said gently.

"I told her I couldn't believe you were involved."

"Thank you. And I appreciate that you didn't tell her about the Collection. I hope it's still there."

"They didn't have long to search the shop. Mrs Sutherland said the alarm company saw a phone line fault appear, and before they'd sent someone, it fixed itself fifteen minutes later. When they got there to check, they found the front door unlocked. You can't lock it without the key." Her voice still sounded shaky.

"Are you sure you're all right?" A brief pause.

"No ... Now they know where I work. Maybe they know where I live, too. I'm worried."

"Do you want me to cancel my flight to Lisbon tomorrow? I don't know what I can do here, but I ... Well, it's my fault isn't it. I want to help."

"No, don't do that," she answered. "I want to know what this is about. I feel like I'm part of it."

"Well, you are part of it, Micky *de Péreille*." He mangled the French pronunciation and Micky laughed softly. Luke was pleased he'd made her feel better, even if just momentarily. "This morning I guess I got a bit overexcited when I asked if you wanted to come to Tomar with me. I'm sorry I put you on the spot. You're the only person I can trust with this stuff. You're the only person I can even *talk to* about this." He paused for breath, before plunging in. "With what's just happened, will you reconsider?"

Micky was happy that he'd remembered her story about Bernard. At the time, she wasn't sure he was listening. The break-in had shaken her and brought the dark side of this whole business right to her doorstep. Maybe it was a good idea to try and get to the bottom of it sooner. Before the Brotherhood got what they wanted. She bit her lip, and with some trepidation, she gave the answer he was hoping for. "Yes."

49

Nobody took any notice of the big man wearing a security company uniform and cap. After disconnecting the phone line into Geo. Sutherland Rare Books, Map and Antiquities he easily opened the front door using a locksmith's tool on his keyring. Inside the shop, he quickly looked around to satisfy himself no one else was in the building. After a scan of the shelves and counters, he disappeared from view out towards the back. His primary target was the large, secure storage cabinet, which presented no problem for a skilled lock picker like Tomás Popa. In less than a minute, he opened the doors and started to search its contents.

He checked his watch, having allowed himself a maximum of fifteen minutes to complete his search. The briefing he had been given included a drive-by roster for the real security firm, and although they were only scheduled to come by every hour, they were erratic enough that it could be as little as twenty minutes from the last time. He'd entered the shop just minutes after the last drive-by.

It took him almost ten minutes to check every item, every box, in the cabinet, and he was disappointed to find nothing of use. If not the map itself, he was keen to find *something* for the Grand Master. With just a few minutes left, he quickly searched the staff area and the shelves underneath the front counter, again finding nothing. In a moment of inspiration, or perhaps desperation, he emptied the rubbish bin onto the counter and looked through its contents. He found crumpled notepad pages with rough drawings of an old church or a castle, but the image that caught his eye was a carefully drawn representation of the ankh from the Brotherhood's map. On the same piece of paper were drawings of the other three artefacts stolen centuries ago. He was startled. It couldn't be a coincidence, surely? He'd never seen the original map, only the Brotherhood's portion, but he knew of the four pillars.

Tomás pocketed all the discarded notepad sheets, quickly scanned the shelves and benches again and left the shop. A minute later he had the telephone line reconnected. Relocking the cabinet and the front door had not been possible with his tools, but no matter, they would probably simply assume the last person to leave had forgotten to lock up properly. He had taken nothing other than rubbish.

Back in his car, a hundred metres away and out of sight of Market Street, he studied all the crumpled sheets, finding the words 'Convent of Christ' on one of the pages with drawings of stone walls. What would the heretics want with a Convent of Christ?

Disappointed with his efforts, he mentally prepared himself and called his master.

"Were you successful?" Gerald Montford asked, without preamble.

"The security was no problem, but I did not find the map." He thought he heard Gerald stifle a curse. "They know something. I found a drawing of the York talisman, the same as on the Brotherhood's map. And the words 'Convent of Christ'."

"Nothing else?" Montford demanded.

"Sketches of an old church or castle. Perhaps this convent?"

"Bring them to me." Montford ended the call. Montford Hall was almost an hour's drive away, but Popa did not mind.

In his library, Gerald considered the information Popa had obtained. There was now no doubt in his mind that the map the sentinels had protected for centuries was indeed the full four pillars map. The sentinel's son would lead him to another talisman and to the map that would soon be his guide to the remaining two. Earlier that evening, he had received word from the communications operative who was tracking Shaw's emails, and now also the Perrell girl's email. Shaw had booked a flight to Lisbon the next morning. It wasn't difficult to deduce that his destination must be the Convento de Cristo in Tomar. It appeared to be the only Convent of Christ in Portugal. Perhaps the girl's drawings would be useful, but Montford had already decided on the instructions he would give Popa. It would be easiest simply to let Shaw find the object, then kill him and take the map. Montford wasn't completely certain yet of how Perrell fit into the picture, but as soon as the Brotherhood had the map, it didn't much matter. If Shaw didn't have it, then she would have it, or know of its location. And Popa was expert at getting that sort of information. She would then be nothing more than a loose end for Popa to tidy up in the usual way.

Gerald Montford, Grand Master of the Brotherhood of Amaury, could almost taste success. He could *feel* it. The ancient power he so craved would soon be his.

50

Luke reached the Shipley Market Place bus stop right on time, his backpack slung over his shoulder and carrying another bag. It was the morning peak so there were people everywhere, but he spotted Micky standing in one of the shelters looking around anxiously. He almost didn't recognise her at first; her dark hair was swept back and loosely tied, instead of the usual tight braid. She wore blue jeans and charcoal trainers with white soles, and had a small overnight bag. Luke thought the look suited her well. "Hi. All set?" he asked.

"As much as I can be. Mrs Sutherland had a lot of questions this morning. I'm not sure if she's more worried about me, or about you. She gave me the rest of the week off, anyway," Micky said, trying to make light of it. "Here's our bus."

They quickly strode through the crowd and boarded the Yorkshire Tiger for Leeds Bradford Airport. There was enough standing room, but no empty seats. They took a space near the door and stood in silence until the bus pulled out.

"I'm happy you decided to come. I'd never have found that carving in the stone without your help." There were people all around them, so Luke was circumspect and spoke softly. At first he wasn't sure she'd heard him, but she looked up as she eventually replied.

"I'm glad I did, too. With the break-in, I'm nervous about going back to work." Her eyes were partly hidden behind the thick frames of her glasses, but he could see concern in them.

"I don't suppose you know if the Collection is still safe?"

"No. I couldn't go in to check and I couldn't ask Mrs Sutherland without her having a whole lot of questions. And if I had, she might be in danger too. Sorry."

"Never mind. We'll find out when we get back."

"I made a bit of progress with the location yesterday. I'll show you on the plane." The bus lurched around a corner, throwing them momentarily together. "Sorry," she said, holding the overhead rail tightly.

"Stop saying sorry. You don't need to apologise to me for anything." He gave her an encouraging smile.

"Sorr-" They both laughed. It seemed to Luke that it was just her way. She was an introvert with a naturally self-effacing personality, but of course that didn't mean she wasn't perfectly capable.

At a quarter past one they emerged from Lisbon Airport terminal, then found their way to the Aeroporto bus station. Micky had clearly done her homework, as she knew exactly where they were going and which bus stop to disembark at. Luke was happy to step back and follow her lead. It turned out to be an easy trip, at first along lovely tree-lined roads, but when they reached the busy Estação do Oriente railway station, he was glad Micky was their guide. She led him towards the platform for the train to Tomar, explaining as they walked that she'd already bought their tickets online. Luke marvelled at her innate ability with the Portuguese language. She asked a passing cleaner for directions, and her pronunciation of local names was so good the man responded to her in Portuguese first, before switching to English.

During the flight, Micky had shared her drawings and ideas with Luke, describing the dreams she'd had about the old buildings. She had no idea whether they were in any way prophetic, or just imaginings, though she described them so vividly Luke wanted to believe. They had so few clues that without some sort of guidance he couldn't see how they would succeed.

"I didn't book anywhere to stay," Luke told her, half expecting her to say she'd already done it online.

"It looked like there were plenty of reasonable hotels," she replied. "I didn't worry about it either. I'm sure we'll find something."

The train was a regional service, stopping at all stations on the way, but the ride was comfortable and there were plenty of seats. Luke and Micky lapsed into silence as they read the various tourist brochures for Tomar they'd picked up at the Oriente station. It looked like a great place to visit as a tourist. As long as there were no fanatical torturers and murderers on your trail. The tourist map confirmed for Luke just how much of a needle in a haystack this was looking like, but Micky was resolute and quietly sanguine.

The Convent of Christ was visible from Tomar railway station. In fact, it sat imposingly on a hill just west of the older part of the town and looked like it would be seen from almost anywhere. The weather was sunny, probably ten degrees warmer than Bradford. A gentle breeze cooled them as they made their way through alleys and streets of tired-looking buildings, to emerge onto the Praça da República, a town square with street cafés and tapas restaurants. While they walked, Micky slipped gently into teacher mode and tried to give Luke the basics of Portuguese. She told him that Lisbon, or Lisboa in Portuguese, was pronounced more like 'Leezh-boa'. Luke had expected the language to sound more like Spanish "*Boa tarde* is good afternoon, *boa noite* after dark, or of course simply *olá*. Thank you is *obrigado* for you and *obrigada* for me."

"Stop! I'm just a lad from Yorkshire. My brain might melt."

"Do you think we should find a hotel near here?" she asked, laughing.

"Okay. Sounds good."

They found a small hotel that looked adequate, and surprised the receptionist by requesting two rooms. It was off season, the man explained, so he could offer them a two-bedroom suite for the same price.

"That would be great," Luke said, looking at Micky for confirmation. She nodded. "Obrigado," he added, looking at her pointedly and grinning.

"Sleep well?" Luke asked, as Micky emerged from her bedroom into the main room, a compact combination of kitchen, dining and sitting space. It was 7.15, and Luke had already showered, having woken before the alarm.

"Yes, thanks. Much better than the night before. I'm glad I came." She wore the bathrobe supplied by the hotel over a T-shirt and pyjama pants, and her hair was loosely held in place by an elastic tie. "You?" she asked, opening the door to their tiny balcony.

"Like a baby. Until about 6.30. It's been good to have something to do, keeping my mind off..." *whoever is stalking us.* He didn't want to say it aloud. He looked at Micky, standing out on the balcony. There was an appealing wistfulness about her that perhaps belied her inner strength. *Is she thinking about happier times? A boyfriend?* "All right?"

"I'm fine. It's lovely here, isn't it. I was just thinking about the day ahead." She turned to face Luke. She'd taken her glasses off to rub her eyes. Without the thick, angular frames, or the tightly pulled-back hair, she was a different person. He didn't want to look away, but didn't want to stare. Then he wondered where these new, respectful thoughts had come from. *What has happened to the old brash Luke?*

The night before, they had worked through online pictures of the oldest parts of the convent, looking for likely prospects. From time to time Micky had stopped and stared into space, recalling the dreams she'd had. Without a laptop or printer, they had to work from their phones, which wasn't ideal. She took screenshots of the best candidate locations. After dark, they had ventured out into the square and found a restaurant. A relaxed and casual place that turned out to have outstanding food. Being a tourism-oriented town, English was no problem. The menu was in Portuguese, Spanish, French and English. Micky had ordered in Portuguese, earning the admiration of the young waiter. Luke asked her how many languages she spoke. 'Only two, really,' she'd said. 'English and French. But I'm a language geek.'

"The Convento opens at nine and it's about fifteen minutes' walk. I'd better get ready," Micky said, bringing Luke back to the present, as she headed back inside.

Luke peered down into the square and saw a big man wearing a black suit climbing out of a grey Opel Insignia. The man scanned the square, looking out of place. It was surely nothing, just a coincidence. Probably a tourist from somewhere north. He hadn't seen the face of the man who'd attacked him in Harrogate, and why, *or how*, would that man be *here*?

51

Micky led the way up a narrow set of stairs then along a path that emerged on the narrow road leading up to the Convento de Cristo. They saw only a few other tourists making their way along the tree-lined road. There were fewer than a dozen cars in the car park. Hopefully they would be able to simply blend in with the other tourists, while surreptitiously conducting their search. Both were wearing T-shirts, jeans and trainers, with Luke carrying his backpack.

After three hours of searching the oldest parts of the convent, Luke began to despair that it might be a fruitless trip. The place was simply too big. But Micky doggedly kept going.

"None of these walls have felt quite right. I know they're in more or less the right place, and they *do* look like my drawings, but I don't think we've found the right one yet," she said. "Maybe if we try to think like the man who brought the talisman here, eight hundred years ago." She tilted her head to one side as she tried to conjure an image.

"He lived in a time of superstition. Religious fervour was all around, and people were regularly murdered in its name. The Cathars were devout, too, but were a kinder and gentler people. Like the Gnostics before them, they revered knowledge; they rejected wealth and possessions. They were *spiritual*. They believed in a great cycle of life, a cycle that transcended death. The Gnostics saw reality as transcending humanity. The Cathars were anathema to the church because they believed people communed with God *without* the need for hierarchy; without the trappings of an immensely wealthy and power-hungry church." Luke watched, listening intently as Micky immersed herself in the words. "He would have regarded the talisman with a deep respect and probably *fear*. The warnings on the map are clear; these people were in awe of the four pillars."

She opened her eyes and looked at Luke. "But he wouldn't have *deified* it. Whatever he thought of it, it was still a material object and therefore impure." She was on a roll. Her eyes half closed again as she looked to the sky. "He wouldn't have seen it in the same way as the church sees, and glorifies, its religious relics and possessions. He would have wanted a resting place for it that was not sullied by the materialism of the church. Somewhere *ordinary*, but *safe*. Somewhere, also, where it could be found, when so ordained by destiny, many generations later." She looked at him again.

"So, probably a part of the structure that was neither fortification nor of religious significance. Maybe an internal foundation wall, one that was unlikely to be attacked, but important to the structure's integrity so unlikely to be modified or demolished. Not very ornate. And I think we're looking for a simple marker. Something that would not overtly offend the church, but isn't *of* the church."

"That was brilliant," Luke said honestly. "I wish I had your insight."

"*If* I'm right."

"If you're right, we've spent the past couple of hours looking at the wrong walls. Let's walk around these old sections again and try to find a wall that feels more right to you. One that's unlikely to have attracted the attention of archaeologists and historians, as well as all those brilliant things you just said." He winked at her.

After another unsuccessful hour, they stopped for lunch and found the café. It was a tourist trap with not much on offer, but all they wanted were sandwiches or filled rolls and something cold to drink, so it was adequate. The pastéis de nata were an unexpected delightful treat. As they left the café, Luke saw the man in the dark suit again. He appeared to be studying the direction signs. *Just another tourist.*

It was early afternoon when Micky stopped in her tracks and grabbed Luke's hand, pulling him back. "This is the one! In this light, it's right. It's the wall I saw. I know it was just a dream, but I feel sure."

"All right, let's have a close look."

It was a perfectly ordinary ancient stone wall adjacent to the original monks' cells. Its only distinguishing feature was the remains of an old trough, or ...

"Don't let it be down a bloody well," Luke muttered.

Up close, it was just an ordinary wall. Nothing about it seemed to stand out. It was around four metres tall and formed part of the inner wall of the complex and the early accommodation structure. While Micky studied the wall, Luke scanned the surroundings. An iron gate stood open allowing access to the dormitory. He walked along the passage past the dark, uninviting cells and was able to exit through another doorway into a gravelled courtyard that sat between the inner and outer walls. A few trees around its perimeter offered some shade. Twenty metres across the gravel was another iron gate that led out to the car park. He found what he thought was the other side of their wall.

"Micky," he called out.

"Hi." She was directly on the other side of the wall.

"Nothing on this side. I think I can climb up and see the top." Luke climbed a low branch of the nearest tree and managed to get just high enough to see the top of the wall. Nothing interesting there either. It was just flat stone, about a metre thick. He groaned inwardly as he realised that meant there was ample room to conceal almost anything deep inside the masonry. They were hardly going to demolish the wall. He pushed himself a little higher and saw Micky's head. "Over here." She waved and beckoned Luke to return. He jumped down and jogged back through the dark dormitory.

"What does this look like to you?" she asked, pointing at the decorative, semicircular bronze railing around the top of the old well. At first it looked nothing more than an old bronze curved bar. Somewhere to tie one's bucket, perhaps.

"It's not very well made," he said. "What are those lumps?" The railing had circular protrusions of various sizes, apparently in random locations.

"This could sound crazy, but I think this is a representation of the solar system. In the twelve hundreds, astronomers knew of seven celestial bodies. The sun, moon, and the five inner planets."

"There are eight of them."

"Yes. They often depicted Earth at the centre. Aren't the sizes more or less right?" Micky asked.

Luke looked more carefully, and it did seem to make sense. The sun, the moon, Mercury, Venus, Mars, Jupiter and Saturn, with Earth in the middle. "Out of proportion, but from an ancient night-sky observer's perspective, yes, you could be right!"

"I think this could be our marker," Micky said, as she leaned over to study the railing more closely. "It doesn't look inconsistent with the church's view of Earth at the centre, but, if I'm right, it represents astronomy. And the astrolabe was the astronomical instrument of the day."

A family walked by, looking at Luke and Micky, as if trying to work out what was so interesting about an old well. "We should probably act more like tourists," Micky suggested quietly.

"Yeah, you're right." Luke took his phone out and took several steps back. "Smile." He snapped a couple of photos and showed her.

"I don't like them," she said self-consciously.

"Could you take your glasses off?" he suggested.

She looked slightly bemused, but took them off.

He took another photo. "How's that?"

"Okay." She didn't sound convinced.

"Well, I like it," he said.

The family had moved on out of sight.

"I've been staring at this bronze for a while now, and its only other features are these ..." She pointed to a deeply etched inscription between Earth and Mars.

IX

XIX

"What does that mean?" he asked.

"It's two numbers. Nine and nineteen. They must signify something, but I don't know what."

"Maybe directions. You know, like a treasure map, or a safe combination."

"The monks' cells, maybe?" she offered.

"There are more than nineteen cells in there. I suppose it could be." They went inside and after a few minutes, so their eyes could adjust to the poor light, looked into each of the monks' tiny rooms. They studied the walls with their phone lights, stopping whenever another tourist came in, and emerged into the sunlight an hour later.

"We're getting nowhere," Luke said in frustration.

"What if it's simpler. Like a simple grid. The wall *is* a stone grid," Micky said, ignoring Luke's negativity. "Is this pointing out a particular *stone*?"

"Could be, I guess." Luke wasn't optimistic. He counted the rows of stone. "It's twenty rows high, and there are twenty-six blocks in each row."

"So, if it's a grid location, there are four possibilities. No, eight. It could be nine rows from the top or bottom, and nineteen blocks from the left or right. Or nineteen rows from the top or bottom and nine blocks from either side."

"I'd go with four options," Luke said, his enthusiasm returning. "Why would anyone count nineteen rows from the top or bottom, when there are only twenty rows. You would say 'one' surely?"

"That's logical," Micky said, as she started to count.

On the second attempt, Luke noticed that the mortar around the nineteenth block from the left looked slightly different from those around it. It actually looked powdery. He had to get closer and needed something to poke at it. *The iron gate.* There had been a bolt loosely attached near its padlock, so he went over, discreetly unscrewed the rusty nut and pocketed the bolt. *It'll do.* Even at nine blocks from the top, it was still two and a half metres from the ground, but if Luke stood on the edge of the well, he could reach it.

"Maybe you could take my photo? We've been here a while, and I'm worried people might have noticed," Luke said to Micky.

"Okay." She stepped back as Luke climbed onto the low stone wall around the well. As she took photos, he turned and pushed the old bolt into the ancient mortar. It went in easily. Within a minute, he had cleared mortar out from around the block, but he couldn't get his fingers in to move it. Micky signalled Luke to jump down as a young couple came towards them. They asked her to take their picture. She quickly obliged and the couple left through the monks' dormitory.

Luke climbed back up onto the edge of the well, pushed the bolt back into the gap under the stone and levered it downwards. The block slowly emerged about half a centimetre. He repeated the process, and this time it moved slightly further. The rusty bolt was starting to dig into his fingers, but he kept going, getting the stone block out nearly ten centimetres, while Micky scanned the area for anyone watching. Then, with one hand firmly on each side of the stone block, Luke pulled it all the way out and let it fall to the ground. "I hope there aren't any security cameras around here," he whispered, breathing hard.

He couldn't see all the way into the cavity he'd just created but plunged his hand in and felt something at the back. A piece of metal enveloped in dusty fragments that presumably once were its pouch or wrapping. He grasped it and turned to show Micky, instead seeing the large figure in the black suit now sprinting towards them, less than two hundred metres away.

"Run!" Luke yelled, jumping down and grabbing Micky's hand.

52

"Who *is that?*" Micky asked, shocked, as Luke pulled her through the dark dormitory and into the outer courtyard.

"Saw him this morning, in the square. I told myself he was just another tourist, but he looked out of place." Luke still held her hand firmly, running towards the iron gate to the car park. Micky turned to see if the man was following and almost tripped over. "Come on. He might be the killer," Luke said urgently. They ran into the car park, and saw a bus pulling out into the road back to town. Luke started to flag it down in a panic, as Micky looked back again to see the man in black emerge from the gate. He locked eyes with her and bolted towards them. The gap had closed by about twenty metres.

The bus driver slammed on the brakes and opened the door to shout something at them in Portuguese. They jumped aboard as Micky explained to Luke between gasps for breath that the driver thought they were part of his tour group. As the door closed and the bus started moving again, they saw the man in black run back towards the car park.

"How the hell are we going to get out of this?" Luke said, visibly shaken. "He'll easily catch us." As the bus rounded a tight bend and slowed down, Micky had an idea. She pulled Luke towards the driver, and in half Portuguese and half English, asked him to stop and let them out. She smiled at him and said she was very sorry, but they'd got on the wrong bus. The driver grudgingly stopped, chastised them and let them out with a stern shake of his head.

Micky pulled Luke's hand towards the low stone wall on the roadside. They leapt over it and ran behind the bushes. Passengers at the back of the bus stared at them as the bus disappeared out of sight. Safely in the cover of the trees, they watched as, less than a minute later, a grey Opel came down the road perilously quickly, their man at the wheel.

"That was genius," Luke said.

"If that bus is going to the station, we've got about ten minutes before he finds out we're not on it. There was a bit of luggage in the overhead racks, so if we're lucky it's on the way to Lisbon."

"Either way, let's get away from here!" Luke exclaimed, as he regained some of his confidence.

They climbed down to the road, crossed and quickly made their way down the path towards the square and back to the hotel. They watched the roads nervously for the grey sedan and, as they hastily checked out, realised that if they walked to the station with their luggage in tow, they would be an easy target if the man returned.

Luke checked his watch. "If that bus went to the station, or he's managed to stop it and get aboard, then he knows we're still here somewhere."

"I'm still wondering how he found us. It couldn't be coincidence, could it?" Micky looked through the hotel's front window into the square. She wasn't sure if it was safer to leave or stay inside.

"No, I don't think it could be. They must be tracking us somehow. Our online activity? Credit cards? Can they do that?"

"In the movies, all the time. In the real world, I have no idea," she replied.

"I booked my flight online."

"Same. And our train tickets," Micky said. "So let's assume they knew we were coming, and they knew *how*."

Luke thought for a moment. "There's a cash machine two doors down.

I'll get some euros and we can get a taxi back to the airport."

Micky looked surprised, but before she could say it's too far, Luke went outside, leaving her with their bags.

He returned a few minutes later. "There were a couple of taxis in the street. They'll love the fare, I bet. Come on," he encouraged, grabbing his backpack and overnighter.

Micky followed him out, still feeling nervous, but it didn't sound completely unreasonable. Luke spoke to the driver of the first taxi and he agreed to take them, but wanted 120 euros up front. They were both relieved, and Luke happily handed over the cash.

It seemed a very long hour and twenty minutes, as they kept their eyes on the traffic, looking for the grey Opel. They were booked on different flights because Luke's was full but decided not to risk either. It was too dangerous. The Brotherhood had obviously tracked them to Tomar. They consoled themselves that the man would have been delayed by their tactic with the bus, and if he'd been aware of their flight details, he might simply be following the bus to the airport, ready to catch them when they arrived. If that were the case, they could have as much as a half-hour head start. Micky suggested they change their flights at the airport, rather than online, so there was a chance the Brotherhood wouldn't pick it up. Then they would get airside as fast as possible. It wasn't much of a strategy, but it was better than staying where they were.

After switching to a direct flight to Manchester, they made their way through the mercifully short queues and paid for lounge access, hoping that would keep them out of sight of their pursuer. They sat in a booth at the back, watching other passengers come and go.

"We can't go home," Luke said, redundantly. He still had the astrolabe talisman in his backpack, where he'd quickly shoved it when they boarded the bus. They hadn't even taken it out for a closer look. They both knew the Brotherhood wouldn't give up until they took it.

"No. Can't go home," Micky echoed. "They know where to find us."

"What next?" Luke asked, although he knew she had no more of an idea than he did.

"I've got a friend in Manchester," Micky suggested.

"Shouldn't we stay in a hotel or something. I already feel partly responsible for that guy in Hessle being murdered."

"It's not your fault," Micky said. "Anyway, my friend in Manchester is actually away on a dig at the moment. Somewhere in Malta. I could ask her if I could borrow her flat for a couple of nights. I don't think she'd mind."

"Okay." Luke quickly warmed to the notion. "It would be good to have somewhere private to work out what to do next." *And examine that astrolabe.*

"I'll call her. I don't want to text." Micky went into one of the cubicles kept for private phone calls. Luke wished they had the map with them. He was keen to try and work out the location of the next talisman and stay ahead of the Brotherhood. It seemed the only way out of their predicament.

Micky returned looking less anxious. "Amanda says it's fine. Her neighbour has the key. She feeds Amanda's cat," Micky explained. "I didn't tell you before, but I have the copies of the map in my bag. That's another reason I was so afraid of being caught. We could work on it tonight."

"You're good at this."

53

"Hi, Jess? Amanda said she texted you earlier. I'm Michaela. This is Luke." Amanda's neighbour seemed surprised that Micky wasn't alone but didn't say anything.

"Hi. Yes, she did. Nice to meet you. I'll grab the key." Jess returned in a moment and told Micky that if she wasn't home when she returned the key, just drop it into her mailbox. Inside Amanda's flat, Luke and Micky sat on the couch together, exhausted but still hungry and more than a little wired. They looked at each other. *Now what?*

Luke went into Amanda's kitchen and found a pizza delivery flyer on the fridge. "What do you think?"

"All right. Why not?" Micky replied.

They ordered their meal, then Micky opened her small suitcase and retrieved the documents. She spread the map out on the coffee table, lining up the two A3 pages. They started looking at the location in Italy as a likely next contender when Micky tilted her head to one side in thought. "You know, I still can't work out how they knew to search the shop. Do you think they were actually following you?"

Luke hung his head. "In a manner of speaking, yes. I said it was my fault, but I didn't tell you why." He looked into her eyes. "It was Madison. She wasn't my girlfriend. She was using me to find the ankh and the map.

She's with them, and I stupidly fell for it. I'm sorry."

"Oh."

Micky didn't know what to say. Luke was embarrassed. A loud knock on the door broke the moment. He went to the door and paid for the pizza while Micky cleared some space on the table. They each took a slice and ate it directly out of the box. "She's very attractive," Micky said, between bites.

"I didn't want to tell you. Apart from feeling stupid, I thought you would think me shallow, or something."

"I didn't like her much," she said, disregarding his last comment.

"You know, as I look back on the last couple of weeks, I didn't like her much, either. Oh God, that makes me sound worse."

"It doesn't matter."

Luke could see in her face that she meant what she said. It was kind of her to say it. *But it does matter. I led the Brotherhood to you.* "You might be safer if you stay here. I can go to Italy alone."

"No, I want to see this through. I want to solve it before the Brotherhood does. It's like I'm *bound* to this whole thing. The four pillars. I feel like I don't have a choice."

"Are you sure?" He was pleased to hear it but wanted to give her every chance to step out if she was uncomfortable.

"I'm *sure.* And we were a good team today," she said.

"Yeah, we were. Okay, Italy it is."

"We probably should have stayed in Europe," Micky said. "It's not possible to travel anonymously if you're flying." They finished the pizza and went back to the map on the coffee table. "Now, we need to get here. The town that's drawn in good detail is Poggibonsi. It's roughly a thousand years old, so there are a lot of old buildings, but the one on the map is, *I think,* the Castello della Magione. It's at the south end of Poggibonsi, and it's a lot smaller than the convent in Tomar, which should help. The only thing is, it's currently closed for renovations. We might have to sneak in after dark."

"That could work. As long as it's not locked up and guarded."

"Hmm. There might be another catch, too. About forty years ago it was gifted to the Militia Templi, the Order of the Poor Knights of Christ. It might be a long shot, but it sounds to me like something the Brotherhood could be connected to."

"Shit. I don't like the sound of that."

"It's just a guess. They're probably a perfectly benign organisation. They have a nice website."

"Okay," he said, sounding uncertain. "No way to know without going there, I guess. Looks like we fly to Florence and then what? Train again? I don't suppose you drive?"

"No. I've never needed to. I can't afford a decent car anyway."

"Same. We could get a taxi again," he ventured.

"All right."

Luke offered to pay for their flights, and the taxis, but Micky refused. She said it was her quest, too.

"I *want* to. Just this time?" he persisted. "My father left me a lot of money along with this guardian's legacy. And I led the Brotherhood to you. Please. To make amends. Just this time?"

Eventually she relented. "All right. But just this time."

"Thanks. I feel it's the least I can do," Luke said, smiling. "Let's buy our tickets at the airport tomorrow; that way they won't be able to find out where we're going until we actually leave."

They sat on the couch looking through photos of the Castello della Magione, trying to find clues to the hiding place of the art talisman. From the illustration on the map, it was a circular object depicting a man sketching or painting a lion's head and mane. The image looked as though it once had bold colours, though these had faded and yellowed. They were looking for some sort of artistic clue, but there was nothing that appeared promising in any of the photos they found.

"We don't even know how big it might be, or what it's made of," Luke said.

"The astrolabe! Let's have a look at that!" Micky exclaimed.

In all the excitement and drama of the afternoon, they had both almost forgotten about it. Luke fetched it from his backpack, sat down again next to Micky and handed it to her. "Bronze?" he asked.

"Yes, I think so. It's beautifully made, isn't it?"

Yes it is, Luke thought. "Very detailed and precise. Only thing is, I don't know what an astrolabe is supposed to look like," Luke said.

"There's something not quite right about it. It's supposed to be at least a thousand years old. In fact, if we believe the map, all the talismans were already 'as old as time itself' in the twelve hundreds! From a 'lost golden age'. They should have a considerable patina. Centuries of ageing should have made them blacker and probably with a good deal of verdigris."

Luke looked at her blankly.

"Verdigris is the green tarnishing old copper acquires," she explained. "Bronze is mostly copper."

"The ankh was like this too. Barely tarnished at all."

"It's as if there's something *protecting* these talismans."

54

Tomás was still hurting from the scornful censure he received from his mentor. Gerald Montford had been apoplectic that Shaw and the girl had got away with a talisman. *His* talisman. 'How could you lose them?' he'd snapped into the phone. 'One of our sacred objects in the hands of heretics!' Tomás was despondent. He felt a burning need to make amends. And now the Grand Master was phoning again.

"I am sorry. I will make up for it," he started.

"Yes, yes. You will go to Italy. The heretics have just boarded a flight from Manchester to Florence." Gerald had been advised that their passports had been scanned into the immigration system an hour earlier. It still amazed him just how far a good computer hacker could get, usually undetected. "We don't know exactly where they're headed, but our people are watching carefully."

"I will go to Florence immediately," Popa said, in his soft, almost childlike voice. He could sense the fervour in his Grand Master's voice.

Taxis were abundant outside Florence Airport. It was mid-afternoon, and after a long trip, with a stopover in Frankfurt, they were glad to be outdoors. Luke was right that the taxi driver would be happy to take 150 euros cash in advance for the drive to Poggibonsi. With the money in his hand, he said he was honoured to take the *bella coppia* in his car.

Micky was feeling happier than she had yesterday, hopeful that the Brotherhood couldn't have tracked them to Italy, since they'd bought their tickets at the airport. Of course, they'd had to provide identification and Luke used his credit card, but the worst case seemed to be that the man in black might get to Florence long after they'd travelled further south. She'd also had a reasonably good night's sleep, Luke having insisted that she take the bedroom while he slept on the couch.

The drive from the airport took them down a lovely wide, tree-lined road, which narrowed as they approached the inner city. Micky was slightly worried about where the driver might be taking them, but soon she saw signs for the autostrade and Siena. Fifteen minutes later, they were on the motorway.

An hour later, they drove into the town of Poggibonsi, and the driver asked where they needed to go.

"Do you know any hotels near the Fortezza Medicea di Poggio Imperiale?" Micky asked, jumping in ahead of Luke.

The driver gave her a wide smile. 'Of course, *bellissima*."

Ten minutes later they checked in at a hotel which was a ten-minute walk from the fortress. Luke wasn't happy that the hotel receptionist took copies of their passport identity pages. A guest registration document for police was apparently a requirement in Italy. After they'd thanked their driver, Micky explained to Luke that the fortress was just east of the castle. That was why she chose it. "In fact," she said, "our castle is about three hundred metres from here, I think."

After depositing their bags in their rooms, Luke went back into the lobby to find Micky already waiting.

She was scrolling on her phone. "I've found another site with some good pictures of the castle. Do you want to see?"

"Sure. Can you send me the link?" Luke's phone pinged a few seconds later.

"Oh, damn. Do you think I should have done that?" Micky asked.

"What?"

"Messaged you. Can they track it?"

"Shit, I didn't think of that. I don't know. Best we get this done then and get out of here. Sorry."

"All right, shall we?" Micky led the way out of the hotel following directions on her phone and trying not to dwell on whether or not the message to Luke's phone was 'safe'. They followed the streets around to the Via della Magione, a quiet country lane.

"I've seen so many beautiful places in the last few days I need a bit of ugly, cold, damp and bleak concrete to remind me of home," Luke joked.

Micky laughed, and it made him reflect that she was a delightful travel companion. They'd become very comfortable together, and she'd been right when she said they were a good team. Even with the worry of being tracked, and the ever-present Brotherhood threat, she could maintain her calm.

They crossed the railway line and a bridge over a stream and found the castle. Its gardens were directly opposite an incongruous industrial site of some sort. The castle was a fraction of the size of the Convento de Cristo, but all its doors and gates were locked. They were able to walk around most of the perimeter, and it seemed there was no one in the area. Looking through the heavy iron gate at the front entrance, they could see where tradespeople had been working on the masonry, presumably doing some restoration work.

"That could be earthquake repairs or strengthening; this area is known for quakes," Micky told Luke.

"Have a look at that garden by the well," Luke said quietly, pointing out a part of the outer courtyard. "The stone wall around the cypress pine is about a metre high. The wall above it is maybe another 1.2 metres, and then the outer wall behind that another metre again. From there, you're pretty much on the roof."

"I see what you mean," Micky replied.

"Do you think you could climb that?"

"Yes. Then what?" she asked.

He looked through the gate again. "There's a staircase over at the back that leads up to the second level, just by the outer wall. I think we could get down that way. Then all we have to do is figure out how to get back out again, obviously after brilliantly finding the talisman." He winked at her, and she started to check her phone.

"All right. There's a near full moon tonight and it's supposed to be a clear sky, so that should be enough light. Can you see any sign of alarms or cameras?"

"You're getting into this, aren't you? This breaking-and-entering lark."

"You started it," she fired back, grinning.

There it was again, that cheeky spark he'd seen in the café near Sutherland's days ago.

"No cameras or alarms I can see, but there's a security company sign on the wall. Maybe they do patrols at night."

They finished a casual dinner in the hotel restaurant and after Luke retrieved his backpack went outside, ostensibly as a couple going for an after-dinner stroll. Ten minutes later they were back at the Castello della Magione, having encountered nobody along the way. It was a quiet and peaceful moonlit night. Their eyes had adjusted to the dim light, and they sat on the low wall by the well, listening for any sign of human activity inside. There was none.

"Ready?" Luke asked.

Micky nodded.

He climbed up onto the wall, steadied himself and turned to extend his hand to her. By the time he turned, she was already standing next to him. "Oh, right," he whispered. I forgot you're experienced at this B&E thing." He followed her up onto the terracotta roof. It required some care to traverse as it was slippery with moss in places, although luckily it had a shallow pitch. They made their way along the roof to the back and were able to climb down to the outer wall then jump about a metre onto the second-level stairs.

Over dinner, Micky had suggested that maybe the Cathars who cast the talismans 'to the four winds' all had specific instructions that would make the future retrieval of their artefacts possible. A planned modus operandi or pattern to follow. It sounded logical to Luke. They searched online and found where the original monks' dormitory would have been in the days of the Knights Templar and decided to start there.

"In Tomar," Micky said, "I think the Cathar emissary must have hidden his talisman and then had the bronze railing with its inbuilt clues added afterwards." Luke asked her about Hessle, and she said, "Hessle was different. There's evidence it wasn't the original location. Even so, it still had the Templar connection and an inscribed clue."

"Okay. That makes sense," Luke said.

As they looked around in the pale moonlight, Micky beckoned him. "I like this wall. It feels familiar."

"Did you dream about this place, too?"

"I don't know. I just saw stone walls. This looks like one of them."

"Right then. I'm trusting your instinct." He took a step back and scanned the wall intently.

At the top, there was a worn, sculpted protrusion. He pulled a wheelbarrow over from nearby masonry work and placed it against the wall. Standing in it, he was half a metre closer to the carving. "It's a lion's head!"

"Shh!" Micky said, as Luke was getting a little excited. "Can I see?"

Luke stepped down, and she climbed into the wheelbarrow. "Not only is it a lion's head, but its front paws might be telling us something. One has four claws, the other has five!"

"Does it look *original*, or has someone messed with it recently, do you think?" he asked.

"It looks untouched to me."

"Okay. Four and five. A grid reference again?" Luke started counting out the stone blocks, just like in Tomar. He pinpointed the fifth stone in the fourth row from the top. It was just out of reach, even with the barrow. "Dammit." He jumped down and ran over to what appeared to be the masons' storage area, just inside an alcove out of Micky's sight. Moments later he returned with a small stepladder, a stone chisel and a grin on his face.

Two minutes later he was chiselling out some of the soft mortar as a car drove past.

"Hurry!" Micky whispered urgently. "I think it's turning, or stopping."

"Hopefully it's for the industrial place over the road," he whispered back, as he levered the stone block out of the wall. It hit the ladder with a loud crash. He reached into the empty space and found what he was looking for. A cold, dark circular metal object.

"Hey!" a man yelled, as torchlight shone through the gate. A bundle of keys jangled. "Hey! What're you doing here?" the man yelled in Italian.

Luke didn't understand him, but in a single fluid move, he pocketed the talisman, jumped down off the ladder and pulled Micky towards him.

"Let's let him think we're here for something that's not illegal," he whispered urgently into her ear. She understood, and he was surprised at how quickly she acquiesced, falling against him. *Any other time ...*

"What're you doing here?" the man shouted again.

"*Scusi, scusi,*" Micky said. "Sorry." She pulled Luke's hand towards the open gate, and they ran out as the man waved his arms at them. Out of the corner of his eye, Luke saw the man stare at the ladder and the hole in the stone wall, and he started to run after them.

"Run!" he said to Micky, but she needed no encouragement.

55

"*Arresto! Arresto! Profanazione!*" the man yelled, keys jangling as he ran after them. Luke's backpack bounced around as he ran, slowing him down slightly, but the caretaker was losing ground, although still yelling at them. They sprinted along the Via della Magione and lost the man when they turned into Via Senese. Micky thought about running past their hotel, not wanting the man to see where they were staying, but when she looked back, he was nowhere in sight. He must have given up.

"Oh my God, that was too close," Micky said, breathlessly, after they entered the hotel lobby. They took the stairs up to the first floor and went into Micky's room. "Can I see it?" She could still feel the adrenalin coursing through her.

"What was that guy yelling at us?" Luke asked. "He didn't look like police or a security guard." He pulled the talisman out of his pocket and handed it to her.

"*Arresto* means stop. He must have seen what we'd done because he was shouting about desecration. That's probably a major crime here in Italy!" She ran her fingers around the artefact. "It's beautiful." Her eyes shone as she touched it reverently. "Bronze, like the others, and somehow preserved from tarnishing, too."

They both stared at the ancient object in her hand. It was a depiction of an artisan sculpting or painting a lion's head and mane. The lion had been enamelled in a dark-yellow ochre, all still intact, although crazed.

It is beautiful, Luke thought. "The art talisman."

"Yes. Now we have art and science. The ankh is philosophy, or life, so that leaves mysticism. I still don't know what the illustration on the map represents," Micky said, holding the talisman. "And we haven't yet worked out exactly where it is. Barcelona's a big city."

"Do you want to look at the map again?" Luke said, withdrawing the documents from his backpack. He lay them on the table, the written parchment copies sitting on top of the A3 map sheets.

"I haven't translated that one yet, either." Micky pointed at the single page filled with text, its Latin script written in a shaky hand. "My ancestor, Bernard de Péreille, wrote it."

Luke could see her excitement beginning to wane. "Come on, I think we could risk a small celebration of tonight's efforts," he said, smiling at her. "Let's have a drink at one of those nice little places we ran past." Micky didn't seem certain at all. "What harm? That caretaker couldn't have been with the Brotherhood. And how could he know what we found?"

"All right. I guess it shouldn't do any harm," she replied, returning his smile. "And it is lovely here."

Luke was pleased. "If we do run into the caretaker again, we can just pretend to be two innocent young lovers." He winked at her conspiratorially and put the documents and the talisman into his backpack.

Micky picked up her handbag and they went downstairs.

Across the street, fifty metres from their hotel, was a quaint trattoria taverna with tables outside. "This looks nice," Micky said.

They sat, and Luke pushed the backpack carefully under his chair, acutely aware of its precious contents. A few minutes later a waiter came over. They ordered a bottle of Prosecco to celebrate their lucky find.

"I suppose we should go to Spain tomorrow. On the way, I'll try to work out the actual location."

"How? If we fly, they can track us." He searched on his phone. "It's over a thousand kilometres, and about eighteen hours if we don't fly. I don't think we have much choice."

"Maybe we could fly to somewhere near Barcelona and then get a taxi, just using cash again?" Micky suggested.

"Okay. Maybe Girona? Less than a hundred kilometres from Barcelona."

"All right. Shall we buy our tickets at the airport again? Then we should be able to get out of Girona before they can get there. Hopefully." The waiter returned with a bottle and two glasses, carefully filling them.

"Cheers," Luke said.

"*Saluti.* On the way tomorrow, I'll try to finish translating Bernard's parchment. Then all that's left to do is figure out where the last talisman is hidden."

"And maybe what it looks like. That could help us find it," Luke said. He finished his drink and stood. "Back in a minute, just need the bathroom." He pushed the backpack out of sight under his chair. Micky sipped the last of her Prosecco thoughtfully. Luke disappeared inside the taverna and she refilled their glasses.

She glanced across the street to their hotel and suddenly caught her breath as she saw a familiar figure in a black suit walk out the door. She gasped in horror and quickly picked up the menu to shield her face from his view, but it was too late. His eyes locked on her and he sprinted towards the taverna. She jumped out of her seat, knocking the flimsy wooden chair over and drawing the attention of the other couple sitting outside. The man was almost upon her as she started to run. "Luke!" she screamed.

She ran up the road in a blind panic, covering less than ten metres before she felt the vice-like grip of the big man around her upper arm. He spun her around like a doll, jarring her neck. She lashed out at him with her free hand, but it was like hitting a brick wall. His facial expression startled her. She'd expected hate, or evil, or a malevolence of some kind, but instead she saw desperation. He dragged her across the street towards a parked SUV.

"Luke!" she screamed again.

The man struck her hard across her face, and her glasses flew off onto the road.

56

As her attacker fumbled with his car keys, Micky tried again to free herself. He tightened his steely grip. She knew that if he got her into the SUV, she was very likely going to die. *Horribly*. The image from her nightmare, the unyielding grip, the red-hot fire poker flashed before her eyes and her scream turned into a terrified whimper.

He got the car door open and shoved her roughly inside, pushing her across to the passenger seat, all the while gripping her arm so tightly she was sure he'd cut off circulation. As he reached out to slam the door, she glimpsed Luke and another man sprinting towards the car. She heard the other man shout *'Carabinieri'* to his girlfriend as he ran. Micky lashed out, trying to shove the giant of a man at least part way out, blocking the car door. She was petrified that if he got the door closed, Luke wouldn't be able to help her.

Luke glimpsed her face in the car, her eyes wide in panic, as he dived on the massive figure in black. The man from the next table at the taverna was right beside him, having seen Micky's obvious distress as she was pulled away. The two men grabbed her attacker's arm and tried to pull him out of the car. He struck Luke on the side of his head, momentarily stunning him. He seemed to have superhuman strength. As the two men tried to pull him out of the car, Micky struggled in vain to wrestle herself free, earning a ferocious growl from her captor. The stalemate continued for a few minutes, as the big man was unable to fend off the two men outside the car with only one hand. The look of determined desperation on his face was beginning to give way to anger.

Luke saw blue flashing lights approaching from some four hundred metres down the street and with his free hand waved wildly at the police car. The man in the black suit saw it, too, and released his grip on Micky so he could fight off the pair outside. Micky opened the passenger door and threw herself out, falling onto the pavement. The big man landed a heavy blow to the stranger's head and shoved Luke away violently. The police car slammed its brakes on to avoid hitting Luke as he staggered backwards.

Two police officers leapt out and into the fracas, just as the man in black pulled his door shut and slammed the SUV into reverse. He quickly turned the vehicle, almost running Micky over, and took off towards the south. The Carabinieri officers jumped back into their car and gave chase, shouting something in Italian at Luke and his companion.

"*Grazie, grazie,*" Luke said to the stranger as he ran to Micky. She was just getting back on her feet, ashen-faced and eyes still wide. "Are you all right?"

"I think so," she stammered, shaking.

The stranger approached them and said something in Italian.

"The police want us to wait here," Micky translated.

Luke didn't know what to say, he was still shocked and running on adrenalin for the second time in as many hours. He retrieved her glasses from the road. Both lenses were smashed. He flicked the last bit of broken glass out and put the frames in his pocket.

"My bag," she said. "I dropped it." She looked around and saw the girl from the taverna pick it up from the pavement and bring it over. She thanked the couple in broken Italian, and the girl switched to English.

"Are you okay?" she asked. "It was ... a shock," she said, searching for the right word. "Do you know him? That man?"

"No," Micky and Luke both said in unison.

"It was lucky the Carabinieri were close," the girl said.

Micky just nodded in reply. *It was very lucky indeed.*

The couple walked back towards the taverna, expecting Luke and Micky to follow.

"We can't talk to the police," Luke said. "They could be back any minute. Let's get back inside the hotel."

Micky shuddered and shook her head. "That man came *out* of the hotel. He *knew* we were staying there."

"Shit. We can't stay here." He took her hand and led her across the street towards the taverna. "I'll get my backpack, and we need to get out of here." He pulled some euros out of his wallet and left them on the table then shouldered his backpack.

They thanked the couple again and ran northwards towards the main part of the town, as the couple watched in quiet disbelief.

Fifteen minutes later, and a kilometre further on, they stopped outside a small B&B.

"This might do," Luke suggested, breathless. "We can't get our bags, but at least we've got the documents. And our passports?" It was a question. Micky patted her handbag, nodding.

"That man must have found us because of the police registration form. I can't think of any other way. We can't register ourselves here," Micky said.

"We can tell them we were robbed and our passports and luggage were taken. I have plenty of euros left."

"They'll fill in one of those forms, though. We need to give different names," Micky suggested. They quickly decided on names and went inside. The establishment had one room available so they took it, registering as Amanda and Nick from Leeds. The woman who took their details was sympathetic, noticing their obvious distress. She finished the forms quickly and escorted them upstairs.

The room was on the first floor and beautifully furnished. There was a television on the cabinet that looked out of place with its cheerfully bright screen advertising the sights of Poggibonsi in silence. The room didn't have its own bathroom, but there was one just next door which the woman said was theirs to use. As soon as their host left them and closed the door, Micky started to cry. Luke went over and held her close.

"It's just the shock," she said. "I've never been so afraid in my life."

"Me neither."

"I'm sorry."

"Don't be. It's okay." Luke held her until the tears subsided.

"Thank you," she said, as she sat on the edge of the bed.

"No. Don't. I just did what anyone would've done. And I got you into this." He tried a smile and got a half-hearted one in return.

He put the backpack on the cabinet next to the television and the screen flickered. A patch of green slowly invaded the picture on the screen near where the backpack sat.

"Odd." Luke took the two talismans out of the backpack and moved them away. The screen returned to normal. "I didn't think bronze was magnetic," he said, confused.

"I don't think it is," Micky answered. "That *is* a bit odd."

Luke returned the talismans to the backpack and put it on the floor then turned off the television, shrugging his shoulders.

Micky's adrenaline rush had been replaced with an overpowering exhaustion. She stifled a yawn. "I wish I had my things," she lamented. "Even just a toothbrush."

Luke handed her a basket from the top of the cabinet. It had some basic supplies in it. She took it into the bathroom and returned a few minutes later, handing him the basket. "Thanks."

He took his turn and came back into the room to look for a spare blanket. "I'll sleep on the floor," he said.

"It's okay. It's a king-sized bed. After what we've been through today, you don't have to do that." She took off her shoes and socks and climbed into bed in her clothes. Luke did the same and turned off the bedside lamp. The radio alarm clock said it was just before one thirty.

"Goodnight," Luke said.

"You know, I had an odd recollection earlier. Before that man ... When I was a girl, I remember my great uncle Roger telling me a story. I remember him saying it was an old family legend, but at the time I thought it was just a story. He told me that one day a Perrell would inherit a great treasure. In fact, I'm sure he said a *de Péreille* descendant."

"Spooky," Luke said, and Micky punched his arm. "No, I really mean it. That *is* spooky."

"Hmm. Goodnight."

57

Tomás Popa had abandoned his rental car the previous night. With
a sufficient head start, he'd lost the Carabinieri quickly then driven
into the rear car park of a commercial business. He wiped the car clean
of fingerprints, changed his clothes and walked away carrying his small
bag. He had then broken into a church, as he'd so often done in the past,
and found a quiet, carpeted place to sleep after making his peace with
God. Making his peace with Gerald Montford had been a more difficult
matter. Having provided Tomás with the location of Shaw and the girl,
courtesy of Brotherhood informants in the Caribinieri, his mentor had
been expecting a call confirming that the talisman and map had been
obtained and the pair were dead.

Upon hearing what had happened, the Grand Master had coldly
reminded Tomás that his duty was to God, and he had allowed the
heretics to defeat him. His very soul was now endangered by his
incompetence. Tomás had wept for his failure and his weakness. A sure
sign that the devil was upon him.

This morning he had been tempted to wait in the church for the
priest to arrive so he could make confession, even though Gerald
Montford had cautioned him many times about the dangers of
confessing to a potentially corrupt priest, one in league with the heretics.

Montford himself had heard Tomás's confession on several occasions, in his capacity as Grand Master of the Brotherhood of Amaury, an order established and blessed by a Pope.

Tomás's thoughts were interrupted by a phone call. "Yes, Grand Master," Tomás said respectfully, bracing himself for another tirade.

"We are advised that last night, before you *failed* us in dealing with the heretics, they had *desecrated* a holy place." Montford chose his words carefully, as ever. "The Castello della Magione was their target. In their search, they damaged a stone wall, revealing something of interest to us." Montford went on to explain about the lion's head marker, the cavity in the wall and the caretaker's interest in it as a medieval curiosity that could draw in more tourists. "The man has already suggested exploiting it, though thankfully the man he spoke with in the Vatican is a friend of ours. I want him silenced now, and the castello *discreetly* investigated. We cannot allow the heretics to learn anything of our lost inheritance. We cannot allow the devil to get his vile hands upon it. You must redeem yourself, Tomás."

The caretaker of the Castello della Magione sat in his kitchen talking with his wife. Out of the window he saw a dark-grey Fiat sedan drive slowly past but took little notice. Consisting of mostly three-storey residential buildings, the street was usually busy. It was late morning, and the caretaker had just finished his breakfast after an eventful night. His wife had just come indoors from their garden with a handful of tomatoes and some fresh herbs for the evening meal. The man continued regaling his wife with his story of the break-in and his disappointing late-night call to his masters.

"I don't know why they're not interested," he lamented. "It's a great opportunity for us to put the castello firmly on the map. It was amazing. In all the years I've worked here, I've never noticed the strange lion carving with its different paws." The caretaker's wife listened quietly while heating an old stovetop espresso pot. "And then those people last night! They must have known it was there. Imagine, an ancient mystery hidden in our walls during the time of the Templars. We could bring in thousands of tourists and pay for the renovations in half the time. They should have listened!"

A noise at the side door startled the couple. The caretaker went out to look. A big man stood in the hallway. "Can I help you?" the caretaker asked.

"Oh yes," said the giant, in an uncannily childlike voice. He strode towards the caretaker, striking him across the face and pushing him back into the kitchen. The man's wife dropped the espresso pot onto the stone floor, crying out as the hot liquid burnt her legs.

"*Vos scitis a veritate. Oportet te mori,*" the giant said.

The couple just stared at him. Neither spoke Latin, but the man knew the words 'truth' and 'die'. They were similar to the Italian words. "Greed is a sin," the big man added, in accented Italian. He struck the man again, and he fell back into a chair, as his wife screamed. Tomás withdrew a length of rusty steel from inside his jacket. Unable to take his weapons of choice on the flight to Florence, he had improvised, finding the small piece of building reinforcement steel near the commercial site where he'd abandoned the SUV.

"Tell me what you want!" the man implored. "Take anything!"

But the giant did not listen. In a move so quick the caretaker could barely let out a scream, Popa drove the steel bar into the woman's chest. She fell to the floor with a stunned look of terror. The giant watched dispassionately as her life ebbed away. The caretaker sobbed in his chair as urine dripped onto the floor, his face now alabaster.

"*Vos scitis a veritate,*" Tomás Popa repeated calmly, as he tore the rusty steel out of the woman's body, leaving jagged, bloody flesh exposed. Blood spurted upwards from the wound briefly, until her heart stopped beating. He pressed his makeshift weapon against the caretaker's heart, soiling his shirt with his dead wife's blood. "Keys." The man whimpered as he nodded towards the sideboard, upon which sat a large set of keys.

"Please!" the caretaker begged. "Take anything!"

"Greed is a sin," Popa said softly. "*Oportet te mori.*" With inexorable force, he drove the rusty steel into the man's chest and through his left lung, pushing the chair over. The man's eyes bulged as he made a gurgling sound. Popa withdrew the steel bar and stepped back distastefully as the man coughed, choking on his own blood. The last thing the stricken man saw before his life seeped away was his killer making the sign of the cross and uttering something that sounded like a prayer, in an unfamiliar European language. As the caretaker gave his last choking breath, Popa smiled. The Grand Master would be pleased.

The old kitchen stove had a small fire burning in it. He took a passport, a credit card and some papers out of his pocket and threw them into the fire. After the incident with the Carabinieri last night he would be unable to use that identity again. He sat and watched as the paper burned away to nothing, avoiding stepping in the pools of blood from his handiwork. Then he stood and crossed himself one last time before pulling out the remains of the passport and credit card using the steel bar. Helpfully, the molten plastic stuck to the steel. Finally, he put the keys into his pocket, took the kitchen towel and wiped down the door handle as he closed the back door. After burying the blackened plastic remains in the garden and covering the area with leaves, he wrapped the bar in the towel and put it back in his jacket. The steel had served him very well, so he kept it for his next task.

The stonemasons and other tradespeople would leave the castle at four o'clock, so he decided to fill in the next few hours driving through the town in the hope that he might run into the Shaw heretic and the woman again. The Grand Master said they would be long gone after he'd showed his hand and then let them slip from his grasp, but maybe he would be lucky. Then he would be able to give the Grand Master the excellent news he craved. Tomás Popa would truly have made amends for yesterday's failure.

58

Micky awoke early, as the morning sun streamed through the curtains. She quietly climbed out of bed and went to the bathroom next door, wishing she had her toiletries and clean clothes to wear after her shower.

"Good morning," Luke said as she returned.

"Hi. Does that hurt?" she asked, looking at his black eye.

He got out of bed, dishevelled in yesterday's clothing, and looked in the mirror. "I'm okay. Looks worse than it feels. Fist like a brick, that guy." Luke went off to take a shower, muttering as he left. "Need clothes." In the bathroom light he could see his black eye was going to attract attention. Maybe sunglasses would help. If only he had a pair.

When he got back, Micky was sitting on the bed with a paper and pen and one of the documents, trying to make sense of it. "I can't do this without my glasses," she said, shaking her head. "It's worse than the others. I think Bernard de Péreille must have written this when he was old or sick. It's a very shaky hand."

"Can I help?" Luke asked.

She handed him the document and waited as he stared at it. "I guess not. I can barely make out any letters at all in this script."

"You have to get used to it. It takes time," she said, resignedly. "Do you think it would be safe to go out?"

He considered for a moment. "My guess is yes. Wouldn't he have assumed that we got the hell out of here, after that lucky escape last night?"

"I thought that, too, but then thought perhaps I was just being hopeful. I want to get some clean clothes."

"Maybe we could go back to the other hotel now," Luke ventured.

"No. I won't go there. He knows we were staying there. Who knows what arrangements he's made. It could even have been the hotel that tipped off the Brotherhood, not the police or their registration system."

"True."

They decided to risk going out briefly after something to eat. The food at their pensione was excellent, and after a good breakfast and coffee they ventured into the street. Within an hour they had managed to find enough clothing and other basics for a few days, as well as new overnight bags. On the way back, they walked past a pharmacy.

"You might get glasses in there," Luke said.

Micky was about to explain the complexities of her eyesight prescription but realised he might be right. Generic glasses wouldn't be perfect, but maybe they would help. "All right." She went inside, Luke following.

After watching the couple looking at glasses for a few minutes, the woman behind the counter came over to assist, looking at Luke's black eye. "*Buongiorno. Inglese?*"

"*Si.*" Micky explained what she was looking for and showed the woman the pair she'd chosen, a very similar style to the broken pair.

"No," the woman said. She put the pair back on the stand. She framed Micky's face with her hands. "*Bellissima.*" She explained the importance of style and face shape to both of them, half in English and half in Italian, then she took two pairs from the next stand, with the same corrected lenses as the ones Micky had picked out, and told her to try them on. Luke watched as Micky did so. She seemed very uncertain.

"Those look great on you," Luke said, indicating the darker of the two pairs. "Really. I think they suit your hair colour, too."

"*Si, si,*" the woman said, nodding.

Micky looked very uncertain as she checked them in the mirror, but Luke encouraged her.

"They're also a *different* look for you," he said, hoping she would take the hint.

"All right. I'll take them." Being harder to recognise seemed like a good idea.

"*Buono,*" the woman said, looking at Luke's eye again.

"Sunglasses?" he asked.

The woman first went to find him a small eye-patch ice pack then helped him choose sunglasses. He glanced at Micky for her approval, and she nodded.

Back in their room, Micky put her new glasses on and tried the document again. It was a distinct improvement. She picked up the pen and paper to start work.

"They *do* look good on you," Luke said. The glasses suited her face much better than her old pair, he thought. They accentuated her lovely amber eyes, rather than hiding them. With her hair up rather loosely, a few wisps dangling, it occurred to him that she was no longer the bookish girl he'd first seen behind the counter in Sutherland's.

"Thank you." She looked up at him for a moment then went back to her work.

"Do you think we should plan our travel to Spain?"

"I don't know yet. There might be another clue in here." She went back to the document. Her look said 'let me do this'.

Luke lay on the bed, searching on his phone for options to get to Barcelona. It was the most likely location for the last talisman, as far as he could tell. If they were going to avoid flying, it would be a full day's travel. A full day and night almost. If they left soon, they might be able to get halfway, say to Marseille, by this evening. There would be plenty of time on buses or trains to work on the translation. He wanted to suggest it, but Micky seemed determined to at least get a sense of this last document before deciding, and her instincts had been right every time so far. He bit his tongue and took out the A3 maps to see if he could make any sense of the final location. The document remained as impenetrable as ever, but he didn't have to wait long.

"This document is about the last talisman!" she declared animatedly. "I've been trying to work out why Bernard wrote about somebody else's journey into Catalonia, and I think I've done it. This was a Cathar brother's journey *with the talisman*." Her enthusiasm lifted Luke's spirits. "I think this is part of the Collection because it's telling us the last location changed."

"To where?"

"I don't know yet. Give me another ten minutes."

"Okay. Tea?"

"Yes, please."

Luke made the tea quietly, and let her get on with it. While she studied the text and made her notes, he realised this document was likely the only evidence that had ever existed for the hiding place of the last talisman. If they could get there, wherever it was, without presenting their passports or using credit cards, maybe the Brotherhood would have no way of following them this time. *Maybe we should turn our phones off, too.*

"It doesn't say," Micky announced, cutting through his thoughts.

"Doesn't say what?"

"The new location. He talks about the fighting between the Catholics and the Muslims in southern Spain, and a change of plans." She looked at Luke. "Ironically, in the 13th century, the Moors were far more enlightened than the Christians. Education was encouraged, tolerance was very often the norm. Anyway, he doesn't say," she said, shaking her head.

"Shit. Now what?"

"Bernard hints that the new location might be 'the origin' of the talisman." She made quote marks in the air. "There are handwritten notes on the parchment that could have been written by your ancestor,

Robert Schaw, suggesting that 'the origin' could mean the Middle East."

"And there are no other clues?"

"Nothing. Unless I've missed something in the documents." She rubbed her eyes. "I'm going to need something for a headache soon. These glasses are definitely better than nothing, but they're not quite right."

"I'll go and get something at the pharmacy," Luke offered.

"No. Don't go yet. I can wait until we leave." She took the glasses off and rubbed her eyes. A moment later, she tilted her head. "Let's think about what we have." Luke waited for her to collect her thoughts and continue. "This is probably the only document that gives the new location of the talisman. Bernard would have known that, of course. In his mind, he'd have wanted to protect the talismans from the forces of evil, as he saw them. But he would also have wanted to ensure that a future, enlightened generation would be able to find them."

"Is there something in the other documents that might give us another clue?" Luke asked.

"This happened in Bernard's time, so apart from the journal of his own trip through France and England, there's only this document."

"And the map."

"True. But we've been through the map. I've translated those passages, and I'm reasonably sure of them. Anyway, this document of Bernard's was written after the map was finish-" Micky stopped mid-sentence. "Oh. Can you pass the map?" She put her glasses back on.

Luke handed her the two A3 copies, and she picked up the western half first. "What are we looking for?" he asked, leaning in close.

"Something that was changed *after* the map was made. I wish we had the original with us."

For ten minutes they scrutinised the map in silence, until Micky sighed. "I can't see anything that's been modified, except the York flower."

Luke had an idea and picked up the eastern half. "What if something was added, not changed?"

"How would we know?" she asked.

"Hmm." He studied the map carefully, testing his idea. Although he couldn't read any of it, he eventually saw there was indeed something subtly different, in exactly the right area. "Have a look at the Latin inscriptions. They all look like the same calligraphy, at least to a lay person like me, but would you say the inks are identical?"

She looked at each one, and a smile started to appear on her face. "Oh my God. You're right." She squeezed his arm enthusiastically. "The Montségur one is slightly browner. That ink has aged differently from the others!"

"I'm not entirely sure what it means, though," Luke said.

"How does this sound: Bernard receives word of a change of plan by his fellow Cathar emissary. He needs to record it somehow for others to follow in a more enlightened time. But he has to do it *safely*. He would have known that the Church believed the talismans were ancient and powerful relics from a golden age. For the church, such relics *all* came from the Middle East. Am I making sense so far?"

"Yes. Go on."

"So a hint at 'origin' suggests Israel – or that part of the world – to the Church, if they find his clues. Remember the Templars had taken control of the Temple Mount in Jerusalem just a hundred years earlier. There are a lot of stories of them digging under it and finding treasure." Her eyes were shining with excitement. "Bernard needed to leave a clue for the *enlightened*. All the inscriptions on the map are warnings, *except* for the one near Montségur. It says 'the talismans are as old as time. They belong to a lost golden age'. It's about their *origin!*"

59

Sitting in the Fiat Tipo, parked under a large tree on the town side of the railway tracks, Tomás sat patiently waiting for four o'clock. He was disappointed that his search through the town of Poggibonsi had not been successful, though Montford had said it would be fruitless. He was also worried that people might notice him. His height and pale skin made him stand out in Italy. Nonetheless, he'd hoped God would again be on his side, leading him to the heretics. If he'd been lucky, he knew what he would have done. Subdue the girl and quickly take her, then the man would follow. Tomás had recognised in the heretic's face last night that he cared about the girl.

As he'd driven south from Florence, he'd seen an abandoned farmhouse a few kilometres outside of town and had slowed to take a closer look. An ancient stone ruin with a large chimney should serve his purposes well. It was isolated enough that no one would hear the screams.

A utility vehicle with two men inside passed by on the Via della Magione, coming from the castello. It was soon followed by a motorbike then another small truck. No one took any notice of the man waiting in his car under the tree. The last of the workers passed by on foot, one carrying a beaten leather bag. Tomás waited another fifteen minutes then climbed out of his vehicle, caretaker's keys jangling as they hung from his belt.

It took him several attempts to find the right key for the padlock on the iron gate at the entrance. After almost half an hour searching inside, he realised the masons must already have repaired the damage the heretics had done. He scoured the old walls for the irregular lion's head sculpture, eventually finding it. As soon as he did, he could see the wet mortar surrounding the stone block that had been removed the previous night. Using the masons' tools and stepladder, Popa levered out the stone once again and peered inside. In the low afternoon sun, it was clear there had been a cavity carved out behind the stone. No doubt an ancient hiding place built into the structure during the 13th century. It was remarkable. But it was even more remarkable that the pair had been able to find it. They had only pulled one stone out, and it had been the right one. *How could they have known?*

He inspected the stone block, and there was no obvious marking upon it. A random choice, four rows from the top. *How?* He climbed higher and examined the lion sculpture. The feet. Four claws on one and five on the other. *That must be it!* Sure enough, it was the fifth stone in the row. But such a tenuous clue! How did they know which wall? How could they know that the lion's paws were the clue? It was the same in Tomar. They'd gone straight to the correct stone. *Do they have detailed directions? Is the devil guiding them?*

In Tomar, after he realised he'd lost them when the tourist bus pulled into the station, he had returned to the convent to search for the sign that must have guided them. He remembered the unusual bronze sculpted railing with its inscription. IX XIX. He'd not known what that could mean at the time. He took out his phone and found the picture he'd taken of the wall. Ninth row from the top, nineteenth stone across! But again, how could they have known which wall, or how to interpret such an obscure clue. *The devil must be their guide.*

Now Tomás understood the pattern, all he needed was the last location and the heretics would be of no further use to the Brotherhood.

The sooner the devil's agents are exterminated, the better for this deeply troubled world.

"Yes." Gerald Montford had been waiting impatiently for the latest news from his people. He had wanted to know everything about the girl who had eluded his inquisitor, Popa. And, more than anything else, he wanted to find the final location. He could imagine himself holding the four pillars, the power coursing through him.

"Your Lordship," the caller said nervously, "we've picked them up travelling to Toulouse. Their flight will land in about half an hour." *Excellent*, Gerald thought. *They must have worked out where the fourth talisman is hidden.* The man continued, unnerved by Montford's silence. "And the girl. She's a historian and a linguist. Honours student. Smart girl."

"So," Gerald said majestically. "I was right. There is more to her than we first suspected." *She's worked out more in the last week than the Brotherhood has in the last five centuries. She will be useful.* "Those two must have put together information that has not been connected since the days of the creation of our order." Montford's sense of urgency intensified as he realised the young pair might actually find the last artefact and would then have three of the four pillars. *Would that be enough to feel the power?* The Brotherhood needed to find them now. *We are close!* He could feel the ancient power almost within his grasp.

"Sir?" The man awaited instructions.

"Track them. I need their final destination." Montford hung up and reflected on his next step for a brief moment. Then he made another call.

Tomás answered with some trepidation.

"You will go to Toulouse. Do not kill the girl. She will be useful. She has information we want. Kill the sentinel's son, take their map, but keep the girl alive."

"I have information, Grand Master."

"What did you find at the castello?" Montford ignored the question.

Popa explained his find, and that he had dealt with the caretaker and his wife. He also started to explain about having changed identities, but Montford was not interested. "What information?" he cut in.

Tomás described the clues in the lion sculpture and the bronze at Tomar. "As soon as we know the final location, I could eliminate the heretics," he ventured boldly.

"You will not kill the girl," Montford repeated, raising his voice. "I want you to extract all the information she has before she dies, and *I* will decide when that is."

Micky and Luke landed at Toulouse-Blagnac, having travelled by train to Rome first. There was no way to avoid presenting their passports for identification when they bought the air tickets, so they had decided to risk it and get out of Toulouse as fast as possible. Luke had withdrawn a large amount of cash at the airport, and they would use that to pay for taxis, trains or whatever they needed.

Micky bought two maps in Rome, one of the Mediterranean and another of southern France. She was uncomfortable using their phones, not knowing whether it was possible for the Brotherhood to track them that way, but also because they'd lost their chargers in Poggibonsi and hadn't yet replaced them.

She put her new glasses on and unfolded the map. "I think we should get a train to Foix. We can do that completely anonymously. If we get a cab from here to the station, the driver won't know our destination," Micky said. "I don't know if I'm being overcautious or not."

"Let's do it anyway. I don't think it will delay us much. And I'll feel happier, too," Luke replied.

On their way out of the airport they bought phone chargers. Twenty minutes later they paid off their taxi driver in cash and entered Toulouse Matabiau station. Luke handed Micky some euros and she bought their tickets, speaking in rapid, fluent French. Luke once again marvelled at her innate ability with languages.

"A year in Montreal was handy," she explained.

"It's another thing about you that's amazing," Luke said, embarrassing her a little.

"We arrive in Foix in an hour and forty minutes," she said, leading the way to the platform.

They boarded the SNCF train and plugged in their mobiles. Luke did not notice his phone come back to life, switching itself back on as he connected the charger cable.

60

"I don't know how we're going to find the last talisman," Micky said in a hushed tone. "It has to be at Château Montségur, but that's been in ruins for centuries. It could be buried, or could have been found and taken during any number of repairs or modifications over all those years," she lamented. "We've just been *lucky* so far."

"We have to hope," Luke answered. "And I don't think it was just dumb luck. We figured out the last two places, actually all *three* if I include Hessle, because of a combination of the map and documents – *your* translations, your intuition and your dreams. It's more than luck."

"I guess so."

"We know the Cathars' method of concealment and how to decipher the ancient clues, too. Let's look at the map again. Every time we've searched it, we've figured out another little clue." He pulled his backpack out from under the seat, being careful of the phone cable attached to the charger. "Fuck." He stared at his phone in dismay. "My phone. It must have switched back on when I plugged it in." He quickly turned it off.

Micky checked hers to find it still safely off.

"I didn't use it for anything. Let's hope it's okay." Luke tried to push the worry from his mind and took the western half of the map out of his backpack. He unrolled it as Micky put her glasses on again.

They studied Montségur closely but couldn't find anything that might have been a subtle clue, or a modification or addition of any kind.

Micky stopped looking and closed her eyes for a moment. "You know, thinking about what you said before, about intuition, I do *feel* strongly that it's still in Montségur. I just wish that feeling came with *directions!*"

Luke started to fold the map, and she stopped him.

"That drawing of the last talisman. Do you see anything in it?"

He stared at the strange circular illustration she was pointing at. "Maybe a triangle? Could it be?" he suggested.

"Yes, I think so." She adjusted her glasses and leaned closer. "Isn't there a masonic symbol with a triangle?"

"That's more my father's thing, but the all-seeing eye sits inside a triangle, I think," Luke said. "I don't see an eye anywhere."

"Hmm. There are two triangles, maybe. One upside down, overlaid on the other."

"Are you sure?" Luke was struggling to see anything more in it.

A magnifying glass might have helped, but they didn't have one.

"I think so. I think it could be a hexagram."

"Like a Star of David? A *Jewish* symbol? But ..." He didn't know what to say.

"Yes, like that, but it's not just a Jewish symbol. I think it's the Seal of Solomon." Luke looked bewildered. "That's an ancient symbol linked to all three of the major monotheistic religions, not just Judaism. It's an old Middle Eastern legend. The seal itself signifies mysticism. It would be perfect!"

"Yeah, okay, I can see a hexagram in it now." Luke found her enthusiasm infectious once again.

"The seal reputedly gave Solomon the power to command demons and jinns, or genies."

"Then, like you said, it seems a perfect fit for the mysticism talisman. *All we have to do is find it.*" Luke put the map away, and they sat together in contemplative silence until they pulled into Foix station, ready to disembark.

Walking along the bank of the Ariège River, they could see the imposing Château de Foix on their right, overlooking the entire town. They crossed the river at the first bridge they came to and found a small hotel opposite a café with al fresco tables.

"What do you think?" Luke asked.

"It looks fine. Should we give them our false names? We can say we've been robbed again."

"Good idea." They entered, prepared to go through the story they'd used in Italy, but the whole check-in process was over in minutes. Luke hadn't understood much of the conversation, but the man at reception didn't seem to care about identification. He asked for a credit card, and Micky replied that they were happy to pay cash in advance. They went upstairs to leave their bags in the room, Luke noticing the large king-sized bed.

Micky caught his look. "The man didn't believe it when I said a 'twin room'. But in the end I think he got it and said he'd send someone to take care of it," she explained. "I'm starved. Let's get something to eat."

"Okay, great. Me too. It's been a long day."

They had been travelling for almost eight hours. Even though they felt confident their pursuer would not be able to find them, they decided to eat at the hotel rather than risk being out on the street. Luke also wanted to keep the backpack close by. They were comforted by the fact that stopping in Foix was an almost random choice, and they had not used any identification, or their phones, though Luke's phone had been on for a while on the train.

Micky still felt apprehensive and on edge, not yet knowing how they might find the last artefact. She wished they could look online for pictures of the château to see if anything looked 'right', just like Tomar and Poggibonsi, but they couldn't risk it. "Maybe there'll be brochures with photos for the Château Montségur back in our room," she suggested.

They were keen to get back, craving more information, and as a result, dinner was somewhat lacklustre. The food was good, but they were tired and not entirely sure of the next steps, other than taxiing to Montségur early the next morning.

Upon returning to their room, they found that someone had separated the bed into two singles, made up separately, but still pushed together.

"Well, this *is* France," Luke joked. "I guess they don't understand the concept of two people *not* sleeping together." Micky laughed.

They took turns in the bathroom, and by the time Luke emerged, Micky was already in her bed. She had made a small gap between the two.

Luke stripped down to his T-shirt and underwear and climbed into his. "Good night."

"You've been a good travelling companion," she said. "It's not exactly the sort of trip I'd *choose*, but I wouldn't want to be here with anyone else."

"Thanks," he said, not quite sure what to make of that.

"Good night, Luke."

A strange smell hung in the air. A dank and fetid odour. Water dripped slowly in the distance, and it was as black as pitch. *What* **is** *that smell?* Taking a tentative step forward, she felt a rough, hard wall of rock ahead. She reached out to the side with both hands and felt the same cold, rough stone. She strained her eyes as best she could in the oppressive darkness, and thought she could glimpse a sliver of light ahead, just slightly to the right. She bit back her fear and, reaching out, found the narrow gap. She squeezed herself through it, entering another chamber that was marginally larger than the first. The dampness in the air seemed more overbearing, and the odour assaulted her nostrils.

The dripping had become louder and the air colder. She gasped as she sensed movement behind her. She turned suddenly and saw a huge figure in black reaching for her. She leapt backwards and ran into another figure. An arm fell around her neck and shoulder, an arm draped in rags, with exposed bones and rotting flesh. She screamed as the figure in black put his ice-cold hand on her throat.

"Micky!" A voice from the distance. From outside this awful dark place. "Micky!" A soothing voice, closer now. The arm on her shoulder moved, shaking her gently. "Micky!"

She opened her eyes, frightened and breathing hard. A light shone in her eyes.

Luke had switched on the bedside lamp. He was sitting on the edge of her bed, gently stroking her head, face full of concern. "It's a dream. You're all right," he said softly.

She sat up slowly. Luke sat with her, in silence, as her breathing returned to normal. It was a quarter past three. As he sat quietly next to her, he thought he could hear an almost inaudible hum coming from the corner of the room.

"Are you okay?" he asked.

"I think so. I'm glad you're here."

"I wouldn't want to be here with anyone else," he replied, putting his finger to his lips. He listened again. "Do you hear that sound?"

She sat still and listened, still holding his arm. "Yes. A faint hum?"

"Yeah. Coming from that corner." Luke stood and picked up the backpack. The sound emanated from it. *Not the phone again!* But the phone was off. He took the art talisman out of the backpack and the sound diminished. "What the ...?" He looked at Micky, and she just stared at the talisman.

"Put them together again," she said eventually.

Luke withdrew the astrolabe and sat them together. The soft hum returned. It seemed to be coming from all around, not the objects themselves. It was very subtle, but unmistakable. He separated them again and repeated the effect. "That is seriously spooky," he said.

"The song of the mystics," Micky replied. "That's in the map. A little side note I assumed was just some religious waffle. Is this the song of the mystics?"

"We didn't hear it in Poggibonsi," Luke said.

She pondered for a moment. "In Poggibonsi we weren't close to the last talisman." It was a guess, but it felt right to her. Luke raised his eyebrows, in silent, surprised agreement. She watched as he put the two talismans back into his backpack, and suddenly realised the significance of her nightmare.

"I think I know where the last talisman is hidden."

61

The technician had not been happy about calling the Grand Master, but he'd found information that he was sure His Lordship would want, albeit still incomplete. And therein lay the problem. Montford wanted answers. All the answers. And he was not a patient man.

"Yes?"

"Sir, I've located them. Well, I found them briefly. Shaw must have switched his phone on and then off again."

"Get to the point, man. Where, exactly?"

The technician swallowed nervously. "South of Toulouse, near a small town called Foix. They were moving, so probably on the road. Or a train."

"Keep tracking them." Gerald hung up.

That had been hours ago, and there had been no further update. *No matter*, Gerald thought. He supposed he could call the man back and demand more, but the pair's destination seemed obvious.

Now sitting in his favourite room, Gerald eyed his guest, the young Beaumont, his would-be successor. The boy looked ungainly, sipping the whisky Beaumont senior preferred. He had chosen it for show.

Montford's usual brandy sat in the warmer.

"So, Shaw and the girl have two talismans now. Why haven't you killed them?" Beaumont demanded boldly.

"You are young and impetuous, Edward. Even your father would know better," Montford replied derisively.

Edward pressed further. "They have half the power you seek. Do you not care?"

"As I said, Edward, these matters are beyond you." Gerald calmly stepped over to the brandy warmer and picked up his glass, sniffing the intoxicating bouquet.

Beaumont rose to the bait and approached Gerald. "You have entrusted our treasure to a zealot who has lost his edge. Are you losing yours, Montford?"

Gerald Montford's calm facial expression did not change as he grabbed the copper brandy warmer and flung it in Edward Beaumont's face. The molten wax of the tea light sprayed Beaumont's cheeks and eyes, burning his soft skin. Edward's next mistake was to angrily fight back. In his fury, he attempted to strike Gerald Montford, but before he could land a single blow, Montford had produced a gilt-edged dagger from inside his jacket and had the tip of it pressed against the young man's Adam's apple.

Montford's other hand was pushing the back of Edward's neck forward in a painfully firm grip. A drop of blood ran down the blade and onto Montford's hand. He smiled. "Where is *your* edge, Edward?" he asked coolly.

A side door to the library opened and Madison Temple entered, dressed seductively in a low-cut, tight black dress. Gerald released Beaumont and the young man ogled Madison hungrily while dabbing the blood on his neck and pulling pieces of hot, solidifying wax from his face.

"Ooh, did I miss the fun?" she asked sweetly as she walked over to Montford and kissed him. Edward's burnt face reddened further.

"Madison, my dear, I was just explaining to Edward that I make the decisions. I think he may have misheard." Madison laughed.

A servant quietly entered the room and on a nod from Montford righted the warmer and replaced the candle. Gerald smirked and sipped his brandy as he watched. "Sir Richard is in London on business. If he were here, I'm sure he would be able to help young Beaumont appreciate matters of the world more clearly."

Edward stood by the fireplace, feeling impotent and quietly fuming. *Montford will get what's coming one day. And so will I,* he thought, looking at Madison.

"Now, my dear, we have news," Gerald continued. "I believe we have the final talisman within our grasp. Your Mr Shaw and his girlfriend," he said the words pointedly to provoke her, "are in the Languedoc. We've tracked them close to Foix. We have often heard the legend that the treasure had returned to the region where our quest started, and many Grand Masters have dismissed it. It now seems it may be true, at least in part. I believe their final destination will be the Château Montségur." Gerald Montford's eyes glowed with lust for the power that was rightfully his. Madison looked ardently at him. His triumph would be her triumph, too.

"It's almost poetic, don't you think, Edward?" Montford asked. He glared at Edward, waiting for his grudging assent before continuing, addressing Madison. "We will let the pair do our work for us, and then, for them, the journey will tragically end. Popa can have them. Or you could have the girl, Edward," Montford said, as if throwing scraps to a dog.

Madison poured herself a brandy from the silver tray and clinked glasses with Gerald, smiling.

"Leave us," Montford said dismissively to Edward. The young man strode out, shutting the door heavily.

Madison laughed. "He's a fool."

"He's a fool *for you,* my dear. Perhaps when I tire of you, he can have you," Montford said, in a mocking tone.

Madison looked at him with distaste. "He's a pathetic thug. He'll be like his father, but with even less intelligence and charm. I'll kill him first."

"You may have to," Montford observed dispassionately.

62

Neither Luke nor Micky slept well. Knowing they were so close to the last talisman had created in both of them a nervous energy that would not rest. Micky's fitful sleep was also troubled by her nightmare. The image of the dead man had rooted itself in her mind. For Luke, after Micky's nightmare and then the discovery of the two talismans' subtle 'song of the mystics', he'd only managed to doze, off and on, until dawn. And there was Micky's declaration that she knew where the last talisman was hidden. She'd said the meaning of the nightmare must be that the talisman is concealed in a cave or catacomb, under the château, not in the ruined walls that might be teeming with tourists. Helpful, but she had no idea where to start looking. Luke had tried, unsuccessfully, not to dwell on those things.

After a half-hearted breakfast, they decided not to check out just yet. Whether or not they were successful today, they would need somewhere to stay. Leaving all but the backpack at the hotel, they found a taxi. The ride to Montségur was only about thirty kilometres and apparently a regular trip for local taxis. Their journey took them through beautiful lush green countryside, consisting mostly of farmland and the occasional village. After turning off towards Montségur, the terrain became more mountainous, the hillsides steeper, and the roads shaded by the forest canopy. Tall pine trees blocked out the sun. Then the countryside opened up again into farms as they approached the village of Montferrier. Ten minutes later, through more forest and a gentle hilly climb, they rounded a bend to see the imposing sight of the ruins of the Château Montségur looming over the valley from a steep rocky outcrop.

Less than half an hour after leaving their hotel, the driver pulled into a small roadside car park and announced their arrival. As they climbed out, Micky and the driver had a brief exchange in rapid-fire French that Luke could not pick up.

"He says there are tracks and some steps leading up to the château. It's less than an hour's walk. He also said there are always taxis waiting here in the afternoon, so a ride back shouldn't be a problem."

"Okay. Let's check that out," Luke said, pointing to the information sign at the base of the track. There were only a few cars there. They scanned the tourist information, which wasn't particularly helpful but warned them a payment was required at the booth partway up.

Keen to commence the search, Micky started up the track, and Luke fell in step with her. The sky was clear, though the breeze had picked up since they arrived. They soon entered a more heavily wooded area where they found the ticket booth. Micky again spoke in rapid French to the cashier.

"She said it's apparently a quiet time of year, and today is even quieter than usual," Micky explained.

"That might be helpful."

They carried on climbing, seeing no other tourists on the narrow path. "Might have been handy to pack a water bottle. I didn't think of it."

"Maybe there's something at the top. Or in the Montségur village," Micky responded.

As they climbed, she noticed there was the occasional overgrown side pathway that seemed to lead nowhere. Perhaps old routes up to the ruins? An idea occurred to her.

"Let's stop for a moment. I want to see if the talismans have anything to tell us." They both strained to listen, but the noise of the strengthening wind made it impossible. "Do you mind?" she asked, ready to unzip Luke's backpack.

"No, go on." Luke nodded, intrigued. She reached in and he could see from her face that something was happening.

"They're *vibrating!*" The excitement shone on her face. "It's subtle, but I'm certain of it." She looked back down the track then, with no one in sight, handed them to Luke. He felt it too.

"*Fuck me!* Sorry. That's astonishing." He put them back quickly as voices approached from below. "We must be getting closer. That couldn't mean anything else, could it?"

"I don't think so."

They continued climbing, the ruins within sight most of the time as they rounded the bends of the track. Eventually it brought them to the walls of the ruined fortress where they saw a handful of people exploring and taking photos of the monument and the sweeping views all around. *It's truly a majestic place*, Micky thought. *But not the place from my dream.* They walked all around the walls, finding a plaque which explained that the ruins around them were actually from a later period than the Cathar massacre, although similar to the original structure.

"Can I check them again?" she asked, nodding at the backpack.

Luke stopped, took it off and held it for her.

She unzipped it again and reached in. "I don't feel anything." She tried to listen to them without taking them out, but the wind was now brisk, perhaps due to the higher elevation. The sky was more overcast, too.

"Maybe we were closer to our target before," Luke ventured.

"Maybe." Micky didn't know, but it sounded logical. "Let's have another look around for pathways that might lead to a catacomb or something like that."

Luke shouldered the backpack, and they searched again, looking at the descriptive plaques for anything that might yield a clue. He was tempted to switch on his phone to start searching for more information but realised that not only was it not worth the risk, but mobile phone coverage at a place as lonely and isolated as this may be poor or non-existent anyway.

From one of the vantage points, they could see back down to the lower portion of the track, and as they both gazed down, Luke thought he caught a glimpse of a familiar figure. "Shit," he exclaimed.

"What is it?"

The woman disappeared from view into the forested area. She appeared to be part of a small group.

"I just saw a blonde woman who looked like Madison."

Micky opened her mouth but didn't speak.

"I could be wrong. She seemed to be with a couple of others. Maybe just a group of tourists." *At least, I hope so.*

63

"We should hurry. Let's get back to where we first felt the vibration, before that group get there. Just in case," Micky said firmly.

"We'll just run into them sooner."

"We can get off the track, onto one of those old side paths. I think that's where we need to be anyway." Micky was resolute and started to head back down the hill.

Luke fell into step once again, having no other suggestions. *She's been right every time, so far.* His mind was filled with thoughts of what they could do if they ran into the man who had almost seized Micky; the man who had almost certainly killed his father, and the church sexton in Hessle. In Tomar and Poggibonsi they had been lucky. *Very lucky.* And last time, he'd had a desperate look. Luke comforted himself that he hadn't seen the big man on the track; only a woman who looked like Madison.

Luke watched after Micky, a step behind her on the narrow path, as she marched determinedly ahead, seemingly unafraid. It didn't seem to bother her that she could be walking directly into the arms of the Brotherhood. Luke was afraid *for* her. Her last nightmare had been shocking. He'd woken to hear her fast, irregular breathing and knew something was wrong – it had become more of a frightened whimper. He'd jumped out of his bed to make sure she was all right and sat next to her for three or four minutes, stroking her head, gently trying to wake her. It seemed to take an eternity for her to come back to him. It had upset him almost as much as her, although he hadn't told her so. Since Tomar, it had been *her* intuition and instinct they were following, yet he felt responsible for leading her into danger and couldn't shake the notion.

As they strode down the path, he turned over thoughts of trying to bargain with the Brotherhood using the talismans. But no, why wouldn't they simply kill them and take what they wanted? *Maybe if we hid them now ...* No, he thought, as he remembered Harry telling him about Geoffrey Shaw's brutal murder. The Brotherhood's methods for extracting information made him shudder. A cold wind blew down from the rocky peak as if to amplify the effect.

"Here. I think this is where we stopped earlier," Micky said.

Luke took off the backpack and opened it. The two talismans were faintly but steadily vibrating.

Micky reached in and held them, too. "Same as before. It must mean we're closer." She looked at the narrow, overgrown track snaking off down the hill to the right. "Let's try this way."

Luke quickly closed the backpack and put it on again. The sooner they were out of sight of the main path, the more comfortable he would feel. The sky had now darkened with low cloud cover overhead as the wind stiffened. They walked into the forest, but just five or six metres in, the track petered out. "Now what?" Luke asked.

"Over there, I think," Micky said, pointing to an opening beyond the bushes in front of them.

They pushed through the undergrowth and rounded a large tree, and Luke could see the old narrow path again. It was heavily overgrown and barely navigable, but with care they could follow it. He scanned around and could not see the main track at all. Micky continued through the brush until she reached a fork in the track, stopping so suddenly that

Luke ran into her.

"Sorry." He looked at the paths ahead. "The one on the right?"

It seemed to circle around nearer to the stone wall far above them. He glanced up, seeing occasional droplets of rain penetrating the forest canopy. "The weather's packing in. It was sunny just an hour ago, and now there's a storm brewing." A cold gust emphasised his point.

"Let me get the talismans out. Maybe if I hold them they'll guide us." She looked less confident than she sounded.

"Okay. It can't hurt." Luke opened the backpack and took them out. The vibration was unmistakable, and he thought he could hear the faint humming, but with the wind it was impossible to be sure. He handed them to Micky, and she took the right-hand path, with Luke following. They continued for another twenty metres as the path wended its way around the rocky crag until Micky stopped suddenly again.

"This isn't right." She handed the talismans to Luke with a questioning look.

They might have been vibrating less, but he couldn't be sure.

"Your instincts have been right every time, so let's try the other path."

They turned and walked back towards the fork. The wind felt five degrees colder and it had started to rain, although the forest canopy gave them some protection. As they reached the fork, Luke could hear muffled voices from the main track, carried by the wind. He touched Micky's shoulder and mouthed a silent 'shh'. She nodded and turned back to take the lower path, brushing past the shrubs, then disappeared around a tree. Luke quickly followed her. The path appeared to be going in the wrong direction, down the hill and away from the fortress. Luke was about to suggest turning back when Micky turned to face him with a triumphant look.

"Look at these," she whispered animatedly. "They must be centuries old."

Luke followed her eyes to a heavily worn set of stone steps cut into the rock a few metres ahead. She pressed the talismans into his hands, and this time the vibration was unquestionably stronger. Through the trees, they could see black clouds now directly overhead, and the wind carried her voice away as she turned her head. "Come on!"

If Micky was feeling anxious about the Brotherhood being close, she didn't show it. For Luke, it was a knotted feeling in the pit of his stomach. Somehow the Brotherhood had been able to find them, only hours behind at most, at every talisman location. And they had left a trail of beaten, tortured dead bodies. If it had been Madison on the track earlier, today the Brotherhood were just minutes behind. A flash of lightning brightly lit the rock face ahead, and just a second later the clap of thunder startled them both.

"That's too close. Should we find some shelter somewhere?" Luke suggested urgently.

"We're nearly there. I can *feel* it," Micky replied. She went up to the rocks, peering around the closest trees and shrubs. As Luke watched her, she suddenly disappeared.

"Micky!" he called in alarm, then checked himself, not wanting to alert anyone who might be following. He ran to where she'd disappeared from view and heard her calling him. The rain was now steady, and water dripped down his face and neck.

"Luke! Luke! Behind the tree." The urgency in her voice scared him.

He followed the sound and saw a dark split in the rock face. The opening had been completely obscured by the tree in front of it. It didn't look like anything other than a narrow hollow in the rocks, but Micky's voice came from within. He walked into it, and into the dark, as it turned a sharp corner just inside. A dank odour reached his nostrils. He took another step and bumped his head. "Micky?" He jumped back in surprise when a warm hand took his own.

Micky led him through the narrow entrance. Just slightly to the right ahead was a narrower gap with a faint sliver of light on the other side.

He followed her through the gap into a chamber. Water dripped slowly down the walls, and the light seemed to be coming from a tiny crack in the rocks overhead. Slowly his eyes started to adjust to the darkness.

"It's just like the dream I had last night. The mysticism talisman *must* be here ..." She jumped as a booming crack of thunder shook some debris loose from the rock above their heads.

64

"Switch it to flight mode!" Micky said urgently. Luke had just powered up his phone to use the torch.

"Good idea." He quickly complied as Micky took her phone out and did the same thing. By the light of the phones, they found themselves in a cave roughly the size of a small bathroom – or a large cupboard – whose walls had no obvious markings or features. They spent the next fifteen minutes carefully examining them.

"This just looks like a natural hollow in the rock, except for the far wall," Micky said.

Luke moved closer and saw that the end wall looked more like a pile of debris than a solid rock wall. "A collapse, maybe?"

"Do you think we should try and dig through?" Micky asked.

"I could go back outside and try to find some branches or something to use as a tool, if you think we need to."

Micky paused to think for a moment. "Do you hear water dripping?"

"Yes. The rain was just picking up when you found this."

"No, *inside*. It's just like in my dream. It must mean something," Micky said.

"It's dry in here," Luke observed. "All the walls are dry." He started looking around the floor, and Micky followed suit.

Light flashed near the entrance, followed by another dramatic crash of thunder that shook the walls.

Micky squeezed Luke's hand as the rumbling continued for a few seconds. "Sorry," she said. "I don't like dark, closed-in spaces."

Luke wasn't keen either but didn't say so. The rumbling subsided, and they continued their search.

"Look at this." Micky pointed to a small hollow low on the wall adjacent to the old rockfall. They both shone their phones into it, and it didn't seem to end. She got down on her hands and knees and shone the light as far inside as she could reach. "It's another chamber. Bigger than this one, I think." She looked at Luke nervously. "I could probably fit through."

Luke could see she wasn't at all comfortable with the idea. "It's my turn to go first," he said, with a feigned lightness. He handed her the backpack and pushed his phone through as far as he could. A moment later he disappeared from view, leaving Micky feeling very alone. Until she heard him whistle. "You should see this!"

Micky steeled herself and slowly crawled through the hole, holding her breath all the way. As she emerged into the second chamber, she looked all around. It was three times the size of the outer cavity, but its most striking feature was the stone wall directly ahead. This chamber, or at least part of it, had been *constructed*. Luke took her hand and helped her up. She brushed off the dirt and took out her phone again.

To her immediate left, she could see where the ancient rockfall had separated the two cavities and perhaps enclosed the original entrance. They were standing in part of an old refuge or storage area of some kind. Perhaps part of a catacomb or crypt, although she couldn't see any coffins. The sound of dripping water came from the other side, still in darkness. In medieval times, this could have served as storage for siege provisions, or a hideaway from marauders. Maybe it was part of the original château fortress from Bernard de Péreille's day.

"I wonder if this once connected to the château above. Hidden rooms and tunnels were common in medieval times," she told Luke.

"The Cathars could have collapsed the entrance deliberately, before or during the siege," he said.

"Or collapsed it *after* returning the mysticism talisman, hiding it from the Crusaders and the Church."

"But why hasn't anyone found it before?"

"Well, it wasn't easy for us to find. If we didn't have the other two talismans, or I hadn't had that dream, I doubt we'd have found it," she countered. "That fissure we came in through could have opened up recently. They do have earthquakes here, although usually mild ones." She started shining her phone light around the walls. "Let's see if we can find it."

They started to navigate around the walls, circling in opposite directions from the old rockfall. Luke's side seemed to be nothing more than a rough-hewn rockface, chiselled out centuries earlier. "Nothing interesting over h-"

Micky's scream cut him short. He ran over to her, almost tripping on some loose rocks on the floor.

"I'm all right," she said breathlessly. "Just got a fright." Directly in front of her was a human skeleton draped in the rotted remains of a thick robe. Its awful, bony grin mocked them as they both stepped back, aghast.

"So, I guess we're in a crypt," Luke said.

"Maybe not. I don't see any other remains, or any coffins or sarcophagi. Maybe this man *died* here." She shivered at the thought.

They continued searching the walls and floor for any sign of the talisman or any other clues. A dramatic clap of thunder shook the walls, releasing some debris from above. Dirt and small pieces of rock rained down upon them. Luke thought Micky had gone a shade paler, but she said nothing. "Let's hurry," he said, speaking her mind for her.

But they searched for another quarter of an hour, covering every part of each wall without success.

"It must be close," Micky said, more in hope than certainty. "The talismans led us here, after all."

Luke had started to feel they were wasting their time; the artefact could have been buried under metres of rock and still be 'close'.

"There's one thing we haven't searched yet," Micky said.

Luke raised his eyebrows, waiting for her to explain. He followed her gaze to the ancient skeleton.

"Oh ..."

They both went over to it, Luke tentatively prodding the chest, wincing. The rotted robe turned to dust where he touched it, and fell away. They both poked at it and soon saw there was something around the neck. Something dark, round and metallic.

Micky took a closer look. "It's Solomon's Seal. I'm sure of it! It's the talisman!" She grasped it and lifted it towards her, but it wouldn't pull free. Its leather cord had not fully rotted through.

Luke took one side of it and pulled it harder, causing the skull to tilt forward and roll off the shoulders towards Micky. She shrieked and leapt backwards, tripping up as the hideously grinning skull landed on her leg. Luke kicked it away in shock. He helped her up and her breathing returned to normal as they looked upon the mysticism talisman; a relic last touched by a living soul – its grim protector – eight hundred years earlier.

"Let's get out of here," Luke said.

Micky didn't need any further encouragement. With talisman in hand, she crawled through the narrow gap to the outer chamber. Luke pocketed his phone ready to follow. "Could you shine your torch through here?" he called, struggling to see the opening. Other than the sound of the growing storm outside, there was no answer. He was going to call her again, but another crack of thunder was followed by a deep rumbling, drowning out any possible reply. He got down on his knees again and started to crawl through. The rumbling seemed to grow louder and shook dirt from the rocks above him, liberally dusting his head and shoulders.

He pulled himself through the aperture. "That storm's getting worse."

Micky didn't say anything. He looked up in the faint light and thought he could see someone standing behind Micky. A heavy boot pushed the back of his head sharply until his face hit the dirt floor.

"Mr Shaw. So glad you could join us," said a cultured English voice. The foot released him, and he slowly stood to see the familiar large figure holding Micky, hand over her mouth. Next to them stood an older, well-dressed man holding Solomon's Seal and smiling. Luke saw his backpack against the wall near the man's feet. A younger thug, the owner of the heavy boot, trained a pistol on Luke's chest.

"Thank you for my talisman," said the older man politely.

65

"The song," Micky started, alarmed. A rough squeeze of her neck from the giant silenced her, but Luke knew what she meant. The hum they'd heard before was now clearly audible above the storm. There was a vibration, a resonance, in the air all around them. It reverberated through the cavern walls. Another person entered the cave. Luke recognised the blonde hair and trim figure before he could see her face clearly.

"Madison, so good of you to join us," said the older man sarcastically. She shook her hair gently, and water droplets fell around her. "Your friends are already here." The man held out his hand, and Madison retrieved an object from her handbag to give to him. *The ankh.*

"Gerald." She acknowledged the man and looked at him oddly; a curious mix of scorn, desire and subservience. It seemed completely out of character to Luke, who had only ever seen a very confident visage. The young thug stared at Madison lustfully, distracted, and Luke briefly wondered whether that would give him some opportunity to try and take the gun. But the big man still had Micky in his grip, so Luke dare not try anything yet.

"Mr Shaw, I assume my two remaining artefacts are with you. I'll take them now, thank you," Gerald Montford said calmly.

Luke did not respond immediately, and Popa put his arm across Micky's throat.

"In the backpack. I'll get them," Luke said quickly, stepping forward until Montford put his hand up.

"No. Stand still, Mr Shaw. Madison, if you please."

Madison picked up Luke's backpack and reached inside to retrieve the science and art talismans. She threw the backpack on the floor as she withdrew the two ancient artefacts. "It would appear that both of you are now surplus to our requirements," Montford said, with a feigned look of sadness. "No matter. Perhaps in another 800 years someone will find you in here."

Madison and Montford each held two of the artefacts. As Madison took a step closer to her master, the hum intensified. The sky had darkened further outside, and a flash of lightning lit the cave brightly, followed almost immediately by a rumbling crash of thunder. The cave seemed to be at the epicentre of a violent storm. The walls of the chamber vibrated, shaking debris loose from the ceiling.

Montford had contempt in his cold eyes as he addressed Luke. "Your father was a fool, as were the others before him. You cannot deny destiny. And this is *my* destiny." He was enjoying his moment. "Before you die, you can bear witness to a great event. Today, history will change." Montford extended his hand towards Madison, reaching for the two talismans she held.

"Gerald, wait," Madison said abruptly. The raging elements continued to fight their way into the cavern, as if choreographed by the four pillars. "What about the ancient warnings?"

"You misunderstand, my dear," he said dismissively, never taking his eyes off the talismans. There was greed, or lust, dominating his gaze. Madison, too, had a hunger in her eyes that made Luke wonder whether she was worried for Montford or if she wanted the talismans for herself. "Yes, yes, I know, 'No man may look upon the talismans else his life will be forfeit'," Gerald recited, waving his hand for effect. "And yet, here we are, still alive. The texts were written in superstitious times. They were written to protect *our* destiny."

"What if there is a trick, or a *ritual* for you to follow to receive your destiny? We don't have all the texts." Madison held the two talismans tightly, and her lust shone in her eyes. Luke still could not discern whether it was for Gerald Montford or the objects. Whatever it was for, it was an ugly, covetous look that marred a face Luke once thought beautiful.

"It is written that the instruments will seek their destiny through blood. *My* blood. Montford blood!" Montford said firmly.

As Micky heard Montford's interpretation of the phrase she had translated, she wondered whether the Brotherhood had a different information source. Something other than the map. *What if he's right?* She looked across at Luke, but he hadn't noticed. All she could see on his face was concern.

"Then *she* can be your guinea pig. If it's a trick, let *her* die," Madison said, pointing at Micky, but Montford did not seemed convinced. He was, as ever, supremely confident in himself. "It's *your* destiny, so you have nothing to lose. She's a *shop assistant*, for God's sake," Madison railed, as she tore her gaze away from the talismans to look at Montford. Luke decided it must be lust for *him*. Or perhaps the power he would soon have. Another lightning flash and violent thunderbolt emphasised her words, the lightning catching the young thug's malevolent stare as he watched Madison imploring Montford.

"Let me do it!" Luke yelled. "You don't have to kill her!" He stepped forward towards Montford. Micky saw fear in his eyes.

"Aww, isn't that cute?" Madison said to Montford. "I think he loves her." They both laughed.

"Tomás, if Mr Shaw moves again, kill the girl," Montford directed nonchalantly. Popa nodded obediently. The young thug smiled as he turned the gun back to Luke. "Very well, Madison, you can have your wish. It might be amusing to see my power destroy the unworthy wretch."

66

Montford was curious. He knew the power of the talismans was *his* destiny, and his alone, as the last of his bloodline. He was certain it would kill an unworthy subject who dared to touch all four pillars. *But how will she die?* It might be illuminating to watch. He nodded to Madison, who then placed the lion and the astrolabe talismans on the ground in front of Micky.

Luke looked at Popa, then at Beaumont. Both were watching Madison. *Could this be an opportunity to ... do what?* He glanced at Micky, who was gazing at the two bronze artefacts. Unbelievably, she appeared to be calm. It didn't make any sense. He willed her to look his way, but she wouldn't. *How can I stop this madness?* Luke was desperate but felt powerless; he would have given anything to make it stop; to get Micky safely away from these people. *But how can she be calm? Did I misjudge her too?* He banished the thought from his mind as Montford handed Madison the ankh and the seal talismans.

Madison placed the second pair of artefacts next to the first, a mere twenty centimetres apart. The ground seemed to shake with another violent thunderclap, although this time Luke didn't see any lightning.

The humming was now so loud Montford had to raise his voice. "Pick them up," he ordered, and Popa released Micky. Beaumont took his cue and pointed his gun menacingly at her. "Pick them up, *now*," Montford repeated.

Micky took a step forward and reached out her hand. Luke threw himself at the talismans, trying to get to them before they killed her. Edward Beaumont whirled to the right to shoot, but Popa got there first, striking a vicious blow to the side of Luke's head. A shot rang out but harmlessly hit the dirt half a metre from Luke. He struck the floor hard and momentarily blacked out.

"We're still waiting," Montford said, his impatience now showing. "Pick them up," he added testily.

Micky reached down and picked up the astrolabe and the lion; science and art. Then she swallowed and reached for the ankh and Seal of Solomon, picking them up in her other hand. Montford, Madison and Popa watched Micky. And waited. Beaumont watched Madison.

Luke opened his eyes without moving, just as another lightning flash lit up the chamber. He could see Micky's amber eyes in the flash, mesmerised by the four artefacts. He couldn't bear it, but he couldn't look away. She didn't seem afraid.

Nothing happened. Montford and Madison looked disappointed, while Popa just stared in awe. Micky still had her eyes on the talismans in her hands as she brought her hands together. "No," Luke groaned inaudibly. He expected something apocalyptic. Something biblical.

Slowly, the hum and vibration enveloped Micky. She closed her eyes and started to shake. Then suddenly, she gasped, and the breath seemed to leave her body as she dropped to the floor, breaking her glasses.

With all the strength he could muster, Luke launched himself towards her as she lay still on the cave floor. He held her face in his hands, tears streaming down his dusty cheeks. "No!" he wailed.

Montford laughed. "Unworthy!"

Madison stared at Montford as he reached down to pick up the artefacts. He held them aloft and placed his hands together just as Micky had done. Popa crossed himself and closed his eyes in a fervent prayer.

Luke's heart leapt when suddenly Micky opened her eyes and

urgently pulled him closer. "Hold me, and close your eyes. Tight!" she whispered into his ear.

The raging storm fought its way into the cave. Luke could feel the wind as he held on to Micky. The look in her eyes had somehow calmed him, and he no longer felt afraid. In a single look, a single moment, he realised how much Micky meant to him, and her eyes had told him she was going to be all right. Now he kept his eyes shut as she'd implored and felt debris falling on him. He covered Micky's head and face to protect her. Thunder roared in his ears as the ground shook under his body.

Edward Beaumont watched the turmoil around him, increasingly fearful. The wind was now swirling inside the cave and the walls shaking. Montford and Madison stood still, together, staring at the talismans. The skies must have darkened further, as there was no longer any light coming through the cracks in the ceiling, yet strangely Edward could still see. The talismans themselves emitted an eerie luminescence that had started to envelope Montford and Madison. She had pressed her beautiful body against Montford, her face glowing in ecstasy. Beaumont was incensed but mesmerised. He stared as both their faces glowed. The radiance appeared to consume them. Montford's expression slowly changed to one of surprise, and then to unexpected horror. As he realised something was wrong, Montford tried to release the objects, but they had become one with his hands. The glow bound them to him. And to Madison. Her beautiful face, too, now registered an abject terror that aged her at least ten years.

Beaumont wanted to look away, but he could not. He felt the ghostly glimmering drawing him in, a vortex from which he could not escape, an insect in a spider's web. He now felt the fear he'd seen on Montford's and Madison's faces. He lifted the gun and fired shots into the shimmering maelstrom, aiming at the talismans. The bullets travelled *through* them, and through Montford and Madison harmlessly, as though they had become unworldly. He screamed, but there was no sound. It was as though his very soul was being ripped from his body. Before his eyes, he could see flashes of his own wickedness, of the sins he had committed. He saw brief images of people burned or put to the sword by the Brotherhood over centuries. He opened his eyes to see Madison's face just centimetres away. He had become part of the swirling, glowing energy. And then he was no more.

Tomás Popa prayed ardently for God to show the way. The forces of hell were all around them. He beseeched his God to shine a light before the devil took them all. The talismans were supposed to be that light. They were supposed to invest in the Brotherhood a divine power that would be the troubled world's salvation. The Grand Master had always taught him that. But the Grand Master had revealed himself today. He had shown greed. He had shown lust. He had shown pride, and he had shown wrath. When he picked up the talismans, there had been no revelation. No enlightenment. The devil's forces around them had grown *stronger*. Demons had surrounded Montford and Madison, and had lured the young Beaumont into their evil clutches.

Tomás prayed for their souls and then for his own. As the raging tumult had enveloped his mentor, a desperate fear had enveloped Tomás. He had received a terrible gift of enlightenment. He realised, with sudden vehemence, that he had given his life to a false idol. A false calling. He forced his eyes open, ready to throw himself into the maelstrom and die for his sins, but he knew that, too, would be a sin. As he opened his eyes, he saw a lingering flash of lightning. It seemed to enter the cavern, its fiery tendrils caressing the terrible spectre of Montford, Madison and Beaumont, all now a single presence, pulling them inexorably outside. Then, without warning, the light withdrew as fast as it had entered, leaving the lifeless bodies of his Brotherhood family to fall to the ground.

67

In his confused and disoriented state, Tomás gazed down at Luke and Micky, both lying prone on the floor. Luke's hands still covered her head, protecting her as best he could. She raised her head just a little, and Tomás saw her eyes, serene and knowing. In Micky's eyes he saw the peace he desperately craved. The revelation he'd had as he prayed for salvation had cut deeply through his heart. Instinctively, he reached out to help her up. Luke recoiled as he, too, raised his head and saw the big man reaching for Micky.

"It's all right," she reassured Luke. Her calmness was jarring. Their captors lay dead in an awful repose, and the resonating vibration continued as the violent storm raged on. Luke wondered if the talismans had somehow affected her. Somehow damaged her mind. He searched her face for a sign but was interrupted by another crash of thunder.

This time, the rumbling did not stop. The floor of the cave shook under their feet, and debris, now larger and heavier, fell from the ceiling. Micky tried to stand but the shaking made her unsteady on her feet. Or perhaps it was the effect the talismans had on her. The rock wall above the narrow crawl space shook violently, and Luke watched in alarm as the hole filled with rubble, completely closing in. Water dripped onto his head, and he glanced upwards to see the crack in the ceiling widening, allowing a sliver of the strange, storm-wracked, morning half-light to pierce through. Coarse, gritty fragments fell upon his eyes and face. An intense fear suddenly gripped him. *We are going to be buried alive!*

The shaking intensified. *It can't be the storm.* "Earthquake!" he shouted hoarsely, but nobody heard him. Micky was still unsteady on her feet. Suddenly, Popa stepped towards them, picked her up and carried her outside through the crevice they'd first entered. Luke panicked and pushed himself fully upright, just as a large rock fell from the loosening ceiling and struck his forehead. As dizziness enveloped him, he could hear Micky crying out to get him out, too. He fell to his knees and slumped forward, consciousness ebbing away quickly. His last awful thought before blackness was that he would be buried alive under tonnes of rock, while Micky was outside in the clutches of a murderer.

Micky half sat, half lay on the ground, trying to stand. She watched as the rock face above the cave began to slowly, inexorably slip downwards. A tree disappeared from view as it sank into the cavity that had opened up beneath it. "Luke!" she screamed. He would be crushed alive. The big man fearlessly ran back and squeezed his huge frame through the fissure and back into the chaos. The ground shook sharply, knocking Micky back down. The heavy rain pelted her, washing off the last of the cave's dirt. She had a fleeting thought that the sunny morning on which they had started this day's adventure had been replaced by a version of Dante's hell. A brief glimpse of souls being buffeted by unrelenting winds.

A large section of the rock face collapsed in front of her. The fissure through which they entered the cave started to close up, piled with stones and rocks, as the rumbling deepened. "Luke!" she screamed again, watching in horror. The rockfall rushed down the slope towards her, as her tears flowed, indistinguishable from the rain that soaked her. *Is this how it ends?*

She managed to get to her feet finally, staring in horror as the cave was buried forever. *But no, this is not how it ends.* Her vision, when she'd held the four pillars, was not one of death. A pale and bloodied arm appeared from the rock fissure. Then another. Then a strange sight, as a man seemed to float out through the crack. *Luke!* Being half pushed and half lifted out by the big man.

Popa thrust Luke out of the collapsing chamber, and then, using all of his immense strength, hauled himself out. He picked Luke up like a toy and carried him across to Micky. His eyes were open. *He's dead,* she thought, as fear gripped her once again. And then he blinked and coughed out some dirt.

Tomás laid Luke down on the ground, away from the falling rubble, and helped Micky over to him. Then the big man sat. Micky could see he was weeping. Luke lay on the rocky ground, while Micky and Tomás sat next to him for a few minutes without speaking. The beating rain cleansed their skin and clothing.

The lightning had become less frequent as the storm began to abate. The wind chilled them, but it, too, started to ease. Luke slowly lifted his head, then sat up. He looked at Micky, searching her face to know that she was all right. He took comfort from the calmness in her eyes.

"Why was I spared?" A soft, childlike voice, incongruent with the imposing figure of Tomás Popa. "I do not deserve to live."

"You saved us," Micky said gently.

"I have served the devil." He shook his head hopelessly.

"You were beguiled by a devil." Micky regarded the big man compassionately.

"I have done terrible things in the name of a false God." Popa's tears flowed down his cheeks. "I saw it, all of it, as I prayed inside the cave."

"You saved us," Micky repeated. "It is never too late to seek forgiveness." Micky was not an expert in any religion, but she was confident that all Christian religions taught tolerance, repentance and forgiveness, even if the Brotherhood did not. She hoped her words would penetrate his pain and remorse. And his evident shame.

The three figures turned as the rock face gave one final convulsion, rubble covering the place where the cavern used to be. The rain flowed down the rocky surface, cleaning away the dirt and leaves, washing away the memory of the talisman's hiding place. In a final biblical act, the raging elements entombed the remains of Montford, Madison and Beaumont.

Luke could not remember seeing the four talismans with the bodies inside. Perhaps the objects were consumed by the eerie glow that enveloped the Brotherhood leader and his disciples. Either way, the resting place of whatever was left inside was now obliterated, invisible, as if erased from history. But the image of the unseeing, blackened eyes of the corpses inside would be with him for a long time.

"I killed your father," Tomás Popa said to Luke, contrition in his eyes as he knelt.

"I know," Luke said.

"Can you forgive me?" It was a simplistic and childlike notion, accompanied by a childlike action of kneeling to beg for absolution. Micky looked at Luke, waiting for him to answer the man's plea. For Luke, a range of emotions circled in his mind. He had hated his father. Or at least he had thought he hated his father. But that had changed. He had hated and feared this huge, troubled man who knelt in front of him. In his mind, the Brotherhood had grown to be a powerful and hidden force, but it had turned out to be just a man powered by greed and lust for power, with only a handful of followers. This man, this tormented killer kneeling before him, had been its instrument, but also its victim.

"I forgive you," Luke said.

Micky looked at Luke, pleased for him, and pleased for the big man.

"What is your name?" Micky asked him.

"I am Tomás," he said. "I do not know my last name. They call me Popa. It means 'priest' in Romanian."

68

The rain eased to a steady drizzle, and the wind had died down considerably. It was time to leave this place behind. Micky stood, extending her hand to Luke to help him up. Popa put his hand under Luke's arm and lifted him effortlessly. His head injury had already swollen and started to darken.

"Can you walk?" Micky asked.

"Yeah. I'll be okay. Got a hard head." He grinned half-heartedly. "How's your nose?" Her glasses had cut the side of her nose as they broke when she fell.

"I'm fine."

They trudged back along the overgrown path to the main track, where they met a slow but steady stream of tourists making their way down, having presumably sheltered among the ruins above. Most of them looked just as bedraggled as Luke, Micky and Tomás. There were also small groups walking up, most talking about the freak storm that had now thankfully passed. Some stared at Luke's head wound. 'Slipped and fell' was his oft-repeated response on the way to the car park. In the quiet moments, when there was no one coming up the hill, Micky started to explain.

"As soon as I held the four pillars together, I could see what would happen. It was like a flash, a gift of knowledge that just flooded in all at once. It's hard to put into words." She paused to collect her thoughts for a moment. "It's like an intuitive, instinctual thing, not on the same level as logical thought. It's just *knowing*. *Gnosis*. The treasure of the Gnostics' never was about power in the way that people like the Brotherhood think about it. For the Gnostics, knowledge and enlightenment was everything." Luke turned to her, and he saw peace and serenity in her eyes.

"I also saw something ancient and unfamiliar. Something lost to us, sadly. A society living in complete harmony. A society without greed, without hostility. I could feel a true sense of happiness and belonging. I can't explain it. It's so foreign to us. The long-lost golden age in the texts. Imagine, a society that didn't need money, didn't need to wage war or even defend itself. A place where everyone *belonged* and was cared for. A utopian dream. If I told anyone else, I'd be laughed at," she said wistfully.

Luke remembered her calm expression before she picked up the talismans. How could she have known? "You knew it would be okay to pick those things up, didn't you?"

"I guessed. I *hoped*. I worked out that the inscription saying the objects would 'find their destiny through blood' must have meant finding their destiny in the bloodline of the true Gnostics. Or in this case, those who carried on their traditions, the Cathars. In other words, Bernard and Raymond de Péreille's bloodline. *My* ancestors."

Popa spoke solemnly. "For eight centuries your ancestors, and yours, too, Lucas, have protected this sacred knowledge from the Brotherhood and the Inquisition. From *my* Church." He had tears in his eyes again.

"Not your Church, Tomás. Just some evil and powerful men. And women. Those who have corrupted others. The four pillars represent a deep spiritual knowledge that powerful people have feared for centuries. You shouldn't blame your whole Church. It does a lot of good work. Most religions do good work, I think." Micky smiled at him. "And let's not forget that two hundred years after the Cathars, the Church had started to embrace the arts and philosophy, and even science to a small extent. The Church leaders of the day knew it as '*Rinascimento*'. We call it the Renaissance. It started to bring the four pillars back together."

Tomás fell into a contemplative silence as he considered her words. Luke felt slightly awed that Micky was the one who was 'worthy'; the one who could receive the ancient knowledge of the Gnostics. She also saved his life. Back in the cave, she told him to close his eyes and hold her tight. That must have protected him.

"How did you know to tell me to close my eyes?"

"I only knew that to look upon all four talismans with anything other than a pure heart wouldn't be good." She averted her eyes, embarrassed. She had noticed the way Luke had looked at her these past few days, and she knew he had feelings for her. She'd put them to use. *But how do I tell him that?* "While I held them I could see your ... concern. Your caring. I said 'hold me' so that ..." She didn't quite know how to finish without embarrassing him.

"I think I get it. You don't have to explain." There wasn't any doubt that he had a crush on her, and it must have been written all over his face. He squeezed her hand. "You saved my life." Luke gazed at her in admiration, as the three of them walked past the ticket booth and out into the open towards the car park.

She had a new air of understated gracefulness about her. An aura that radiated around her. It was as if the knowledge of the four pillars had released her from the shackles of a childhood in which she was never good enough. In which all bad things she experienced were *her* fault. It was uplifting. It was beautiful. She seemed to read his thoughts, in more than her usual insightful way, as if to make the point that Luke had just been thinking about.

"You're finding your peace, too, Luke Shaw. You're not the same man who started this journey. I can see it." Once again, the sun shone on them, warming them and drying the last of the rain from their clothing.

Luke knew she was right, perhaps even in a deeper sense than she might have realised. He had inherited the Collection from a man he thought he hated. And he'd been so angry about the way he learned he was adopted that it had taken him months to learn of his special inheritance. He'd foolishly been drawn into a shallow, meaningless dalliance that could have cost him, and Micky, their lives, and he'd realised that he had more or less squandered years of his life, consumed by the ill feelings he had held on to. It was no way to live. Visiting his father's grave had been more than a revelation. Having the threat of the Brotherhood, along with the weight of the task his father had bequeathed him as *the sentinel*, lifted, he could look ahead to finding his way with his new family. Life held new promise, for the first time in years.

He looked at Tomás Popa, silently walking next to them; a man who had just had the mother of all revelations, yet seemed to be able to function. He, too, appeared calm, the desperation Luke had seen in his face in Poggibonsi now absent.

"None of us are the same as when we started this journey," Luke observed.

Epilogue

Mrs Sutherland came over to the counter with a hot cup of tea for Micky. "Penny for your thoughts?" She could see Micky had something on her mind.

"Oh, thanks, Mrs Sutherland, that's just what I need." Micky had her phone out on the counter. "Do you remember Luke? The one you didn't like?"

"Of course, dear." Her eyebrows went up.

"I just got an email from him, in New Zealand."

"It wasn't that I didn't like him, I was just worried for you. He seemed … *troubled*, and I remember how much he upset you." Mrs Sutherland remembered all too well how distressed Micky had been after 'that boy' had taken her out for lunch. She was so fragile then, although now, since they came back from Europe, Micky had been happier and more confident. She looked so much better, too. It wasn't just that she had nice new glasses that better suited, in fact accentuated, her beautiful face, nor that she wore her hair differently, not pulled back so severely, it was that Micky just seemed to be somehow radiant *in herself*. It was a remarkable transformation, Mrs Sutherland thought.

To Micky, Mrs Sutherland was a genuinely good person. Just like a nice old aunty who kept an eye out for her. It was one of the reasons she had stayed on at Sutherland's these past four months, after Montségur. She had restarted her studies, this time taking philosophy, keen to gain an evidential and analytical basis for the intuitive understanding she received from the four pillars. But working at the bookshop wasn't simply to make enough to pay her rent, nor was it just because she liked Mrs Sutherland; it was because she still loved the place. The ancient books and maps fascinated her, just as they always had. She still loved the ambience and the smell of the place.

"I know. And I appreciate it, but it wasn't like you thought it was. We're friends. He's a good person. Just 'finding himself', as people say." Micky smiled, remembering their trip home from the Languedoc. She had told him that he had a journey to finish, a journey of the soul, not the body. That he needed to go and *become* part of his new family. He'd been a little disappointed, but she knew that deep inside he'd known it was true. She read his email again.

Hi M,

You were right. I needed to do this. It's been brilliant getting to know my mum better. I'm coming back to sort out Dad's stuff in a few weeks, and Mum's going to come with me. My aunty Lisa is really looking forward to it, and so am I. Looking forward to seeing you, too. There's no one else I can talk to about, well, you know what. Who'd believe us anyway?

I've had a lot of time to think about things, and I understand now why my father hadn't ever talked to me about the family legacy. He'd taken plenty of precautions for an early death, and it must have weighed very heavily on him. I don't think he wanted me to have that weight, at least not until there was no other choice.

I don't believe I ever told you about the old letter. The one he wrote just after my adoptive mother died. Her death nearly broke him, and he'd never let on. He withdrew and hid his emotions. Anyway, I've made my peace with him and forgiven him. To be honest, it's a weight off.

Talk soon, L.

Coffee in a couple of weeks?

She felt happy for him. He *sounded* happy.

Micky had settled back into a more or less normal life, a *new* normal, but normal enough, and she knew he would, too, but first he had some baggage to offload and some new bridges to build. In some ways, she envied him; his birth mother sounded lovely, and their relationship was going well. Micky wished she could say the same thing about her relationship with her mother. She, too, had time to think and try to deal with her 'inheritance'. Some days it was challenging. Her insights sometimes came unexpectedly. She just *knew* how things would work out, almost subconsciously, and it was spooky. Not just for her. When put on the spot and asked 'how did you know that?' she couldn't answer. That was one of the reasons for studying philosophy. If not a better understanding, it would at least give her better answers.

The bell interrupted her thoughts, as a man pushed open the creaky old door and came over to the counter.

"Hi, can I help?" she asked cheerfully. He looked to be in his mid-thirties and had an earnest but kind face.

"Yes, hi, I'm not sure really. I've been trying to make sense of something I've recently acquired." The man's accent placed him from somewhere near West London. He started to speak then held up a finger, implying 'wait a moment'. After briefly fumbling in his pocket for a pair of tortoiseshell-rimmed glasses, he opened his old leather satchel and withdrew an ancient tome. "Let me show you," he said cheerily.

It was a handwritten codex, several centimetres thick with hardwood front and back covers, bound in light-brown leather. It smelled of damp and had patches of black mould on the leather. "I found it wrapped in oilskins in a stone sepulchre on my uncle's estate. In Brittany. Maybe you can help me out."

Micky grinned. An unrestrained and unguarded smile that took the man by surprise.

He smiled back, his face uncertain. "Yes?" he said tentatively.

"Oh, I'm sorry. I love books like this. It made me think of something else that someone brought in recently. It's a long story," she said, looking back to the book. "Did you say it's been in your family for a while?"

Author's Note

First of all, I wish to thank my family for their patience, support and encouragement. Louise Kendall for encouragement and linguistics advice. And by no means least, Adrienne Charlton at AM Publishing for frank feedback, insightful advice and her sharp eye.

There are many others who have listened, advised and contributed in important ways, including Gina Tesmann, Conor Occleshaw and Marie Occleshaw.

Any residual mistakes are, of course, all mine.

Gnostic Tradition and the 'Four Pillars'

There are a variety of sources of information on the Gnostics and their traditions. Most are unverified, although across these there are considerable consistencies, including the 'four pillars' as a basis. These are commonly described as philosophy, science, art and mysticism (or religion). The symbols I chose to represent these are simply an invention of convenience. While it served a purpose in the story, it is unlikely that the Egyptian ankh would have been used to symbolise philosophy; its meaning typically is 'life'.

Massacre at Béziers, July 1209

Immediately before the Massacre at Béziers, Abbot Arnaud Amaury (also known as Arnaud Amalric) was reputedly asked, 'What shall we do, for we cannot distinguish between the faithful and the heretics?'. The abbot is reported to have answered callously, *'Caedite eos. Novit enim Dominus qui sunt eius'*. Kill them all, for the Lord knoweth them that are His. There are also contradicting reports, although it seems to be generally agreed that almost all inhabitants of Béziers, a Cathar stronghold with up to 20,000 men, women and children, were slaughtered on 22 July 1209 in the first major military engagement of the Albigensian Crusade. His role in this tragic event was my basis for naming the fictitious Brotherhood of Amaury.

Siege at Montségur, May 1243 - March 1244

The siege progressed for many months, leading up to the final breach and subsequent massacre on 16 March 1244. Reports indicate that up to 10,000 men were amassed by the French royal forces, working under the guiding hand of Pope Innocent III and his Crusaders, and these were held at bay by a few hundred defenders ensconced in the Château Montségur. Stories indicate that a traitor betrayed the weakness at a fortified gate, and the army broke through in early March 1244. People in the château were allowed to leave, except those who refused to denounce their Cathar faith and embrace the Catholic Church. On 16 March, about 210 Cathar Perfecti and unrepentant credentes were incinerated in a terrible bonfire.

A decade earlier, in 1233, Raymond de Péreille, Seigneur de Montségur (Lord of Montségur), had agreed to allow the Cathars to make the château their stronghold. They survived the siege for nine months by keeping supply lines ope, with the help of sympathetic local people.

Bernard de Péreille is a fictitious character. Likewise, while there is much speculation about a treasure of the Cathars, to my knowledge there is no evidence it exists.

The Albigensian Crusade

The Cathar Crusade, or Albigensian Crusade, waged in southern France from 1209 to 1229, is reasonably widely viewed by historians as genocide. As one of its early fanatics, Arnaud Amaury (mentioned above), Papal Legate for Pope Innocent III, seemed a good figurehead for my fictitious Brotherhood of Amaury. I am not aware of any such (or similar) brotherhood or organisation in existence.

Simon de Montfort, 6th Earl of Leicester, 1208-1265

Simon de Montfort was a key figure in thirteenth century English nobility. He was a fervent Christian and crusader, including having a role in the Albigensian Crusade. The Brotherhood of Amaury is fictitious, so obviously de Montfort was not its Grand Master.

William Schaw, 1550-1602

In 1583, King James VI appointed thirty-three-year-old William Schaw Master of Works to the Scottish Crown for life. His responsibilities included overseeing stonemasonry for all royal castles and palaces. Schaw established the first and second 'Schaw Statutes' for all stonemasons and was purported to be instrumental in the inception of the Scottish Freemasons. There is no evidence I've found which suggests Schaw was involved with any treasure of the Cathars (if any exists). William Schaw's fictitious elder brother Robert is my invention for this story.

Bubonic Plague in Medieval York

I referred to a Black Death event in York in the year 1583. As far as I know, this is the product of my imagination, although sources indicate that Yorkshire did suffer at least four bubonic plague epidemics between 1550 and 1645.

All Saints Church, Hessle, Yorkshire

The Parish Church of All Saints is, by all accounts I've read, a delightful and important historic building. It is not as I've described in this story. The features I've depicted inside the building, and the people Luke and his medieval predecessors encountered, are all products of my imagination. The ancient crypt and the Templar coffin are also my inventions. More information can be found at allsaintshessle.karoo.net. A special thank you to Eve Johansson, All Saints' Church Assistant Churchwarden, for providing very helpful information and answering my questions.

Militia Templi, the Order of the Poor Knights of Christ

I've referred briefly to this religious order, simply because I chose the Castello della Magione as a location for one of the four talismans. In Chapter 53, Michaela hints that they might be connected to my imaginary Brotherhood. That is pure fiction, of course. I make no suggestion that this order does anything other than good work.

A strange relic is found deep under the Antarctic ice, but before it can be analysed it is lost in a mysterious plane crash on a remote island.

Anthropologist Peter Hennessy investigates the relic and its implications, while within days of the crash people on the island begin to die from an unknown illness.

Biological samples are brought from the island to Australia for analysis, and a rogue diplomat seizes his opportunity. Police are soon investigating murders.

As he explores further, Hennessy discovers medieval maps that depict Antarctica in impossible detail, and the mystery deepens ...

A former colleague of Hennessy, Dr Nicole Palmer, is working on the seemingly unstoppable plague, and the pair soon find themselves in a race against time to prevent a deadly pandemic and piece together how the relic is connected.

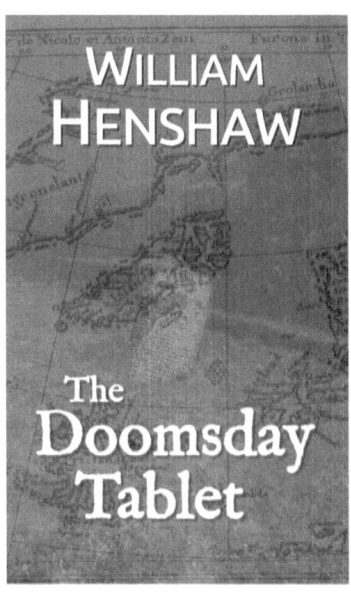

WILLIAM HENSHAW

The
Doomsday Tablet

An ancient stone tablet is dredged up from the Mid-Atlantic. Generations later, archaeologist John Foxton begins to decipher the tablet's dark and mysterious omen.

Daniel Reade, historian, discovers notes his great-grandfather Foxton had concealed before his murder during World War II. Foxton believed the tablet was more than a doomsday prophecy. Something far more dangerous.

Archaeologist Elisa Mansfield is drawn into the mystery and soon unearths another tablet. The pair are thrown into a dangerous adventure involving an ancient civilisation destroyed by its own hand, a secret organisation born during the Nazi era, and a cataclysmic weapon based on the lost technology.

A fourteenth-century map and lost manuscript seem to hold the key to the destroyed civilisation, but how is this possible?

The stakes are high as Daniel and Elisa race to stay ahead of the organisation, and to understand what happened thousands of years earlier.

www.williamhenshaw.com